Robert G. Barrett was raised in ⬚⬚⬚⬚⬚ worked mainly as a butcher. After thirty years he moved to Terrigal on the Central Coast of New South Wales. Robert has appeared in a number of films and TV commercials but prefers to concentrate on a career as a writer. He is the author of twenty books, including *So What Do You Reckon?*, a collection of his columns for *People* magazine, *Mud Crab Boogie, Goodoo Goodoo, The Wind and the Monkey, Leaving Bondi, The Ultimate Aphrodisiac,* and *Mystery Bay Blues.*

To find out more about Bob and his books visit
these websites:
www.robertgbarrett.com.au
or
www.harpercollins.com.au/robertgbarrett

Also by Robert G. Barrett and
published by HarperCollins:

So What Do You Reckon?

Mud Crab Boogie

Goodoo Goodoo

The Wind and the Monkey

Leaving Bondi

The Ultimate Aphrodisiac

Mystery Bay Blues

ROSA-MARIE'S BABY

ROBERT G. BARRETT

HarperCollins*Publishers*

The quote on pages 24–25 is from *Occult Visions of Rosaleen Norton* by Keith Richmond. Reprinted with thanks.

HarperCollins*Publishers*

First published in Australia in 2003
by HarperCollins*Publishers* Pty Limited
ABN 36 009 913 517
A member of the HarperCollins*Publishers* (Australia) Pty Limited Group
www.harpercollins.com.au

HarperCollins*Publishers*
25 Ryde Road, Pymble, Sydney, NSW 2073, Australia
31 View Road, Glenfield, Auckland 10, New Zealand
77–85 Fulham Palace Road, London, W6 8JB, United Kingdom
2 Bloor Street East, 20th floor, Toronto, Ontario M4W 1A8, Canada
10 East 53rd Street, New York NY 10022, USA

National Library of Australia Cataloguing-in-Publication data:

Barrett, Robert G.
　　Rosa-Marie's Baby.
　　ISBN 0 7322 7817 1.
　　1. Norton, Les (Fictitious character) – Fiction I. Title.
A823.3

Cover painting: *The Goddess* by Rosaleen Norton (1917–79), circa 1955, private gallery, copyright Walter Glover
Cover design by Darian Causby, Highway 51 Design Works
Typeset by HarperCollins in 12/20 Minion
Printed in Australia by Griffin Press Pty Ltd on 80gsm Bulky Book Ivory

5 4 3 2 1　　　03　04　05　06

DEDICATION

To the Bali victims. Ours and theirs. I'll leave it at that.

As usual, a percentage of the royalties from this book
is being donated to:

The Wombat Rescue and Research Project
Lot 4, Will-O-Wynn Valley
Murrays Run NSW 2325

and Avoca Surf Club.

AUTHOR'S NOTE

Firstly I have to thank everyone who came along to the *Mystery Bay Blues* book signing. Especially the people in Merimbula and Newcastle. They made me feel like visiting royalty. When I get down on my knees in front of the queue and say, 'I'm not worthy, I'm not worthy,' I mean it. And an apology to the woman in the bookshop at Narooma for causing her cash register to seize up. She sold more books in the short time I was there than she would in a month. Luckily my publicist was quick-witted enough to throw a bucket of cold water in the till and we got it going again.

To all those nice people writing to me, I'm doing my best to write back. You haven't been ignored. There's just a lot of letters, that's all. And to all the mad people who write to me — yes, you know who you are. It doesn't worry me if you're on medication and counselling. But could you please settle back, take another pill or whatever and try to write a little more clearly. I don't mind deciphering gibberish and the ravings of people who are a strawberry or two short of a punnet. But if I can't read it, it's impossible. Fair dinkum. At times I believe the government's Subsidised Prescription Drug Program has got a lot to answer for amongst some of my readers.

Also, to my many readers enjoying a vacation care of Her Majesty and wanting books for their libraries, plus the people from Words On Wheels: I'm doing my best. But crime appears to be a growth industry at present, and there's a lot of punters bunged up in various nicks all over Australia. I can only get so many books. Write to Bryce Courtney and ask him for some. He's always waffling on about how good reading is. On second thoughts, don't bother. The puzzle's hard enough as it is, without clubbing yourself in the head with one of Bryce's wheel-chocks. Ask your librarian to order in some books by Charles Bukowski. Charles tells it like it is.

About this book: some of those churches around Lorne and Apollo Bay are real and some aren't, I just changed the names around. But that radio station, 607.5 FM PBS, is for real. When I heard those dirty ditties I had to put them in the book somehow. But what a good radio station. Between the ditties and the Tibetan monks chanting mantras, they play some great music. If you live around Melbourne give it a listen and become a subscriber. If I lived down that way I would.

Rosa-Marie Norton is a fictitious character, but Rosaleen Norton was a real person and an absolutely fascinating character, as well as a great artist who bordered on genius and gave the establishment of the day a well-deserved finger. The cover of this book is actually one of her paintings, *The Goddess*.

2

If you want to read a book about a totally outrageous woman who was years before her time, Keith Richmond, co-owner of the Basilisk Bookshop in Brunswick Street, Fitzroy in Melbourne, is the authority on Rosaleen Norton. He should have a comprehensive biography on Rosaleen Norton, the Witch of Kings Cross, finished by the end of the year. After spending some time with Keith, I'm certain it will be a fascinating and interesting book, and I can't wait for it to come out.

People have been writing in to the publishers telling me it's about time I got my finger out and updated my website. They're right, too. I'm getting a bit slack. So I'm going to attack it shortly and you'll see photos from my trip to the Norfolk Island Writers' Festival, where I wowed them and Dr Colleen McCullough baked me a chicken dinner at her house. She fair dinkum did. And when I got back I addressed the troops of the DFSU at Randwick Barracks. The Deployed Forces Support Unit. What a great team of men and women and what a great day I had. These people make me so proud to be an Australian. Even when they got me and my publicist and shoved us into gas masks, Kevlar vests and helmets. We looked like Darth Vader and Mickey Mouse standing next to each other. The website is also the place to check out what's going on with the Team Norton T-shirts and caps. Please note, the address is: Psycho Possum Productions, PO Box 382, Terrigal, NSW 2260. We're cutting down on some of the T-shirts, so when you order, include a second preference along with your phone number so we can get back to you. Also, remember to put your name and address on the back of the envelope. It makes it easier for us. Ta.

What more can I say? I hope you like the latest Les Norton. I had a lot of fun hanging out in Melbourne and travelling along the Great Ocean Road doing my research. It's a beautiful part of Australia down there. Plus I think I rose to a new low in filth and sunk to new heights of violence to keep everybody happy. And Les managed to leave everybody happy in the end. Except him. I'll do my best again next year. See you then, and thank you for reading my books.

Robert G. Barrett

Summer was officially over and it was a typical autumn afternoon in Sydney towards the end of March. A light north-westerly was blowing, taking the edge from any heat and humidity still lingering around, while it pushed the air pollution out to sea along with whatever clouds were drifting across the clear, blue sky above the city. After training earlier in the day with Billy Dunne, and lunch at the Diggers, Les was seated comfortably on a banana-chair in the backyard of Chez Norton wearing a pair of blue shorts and a white T-shirt, casually tossing grapes to a pair of water dragons that had decided to make his backyard, with its small fountain, their home. On his lap was a copy of *Nexus* magazine and an article he'd been reading about water-fuelled cars, while on the stereo inside, the Alabama 3 were growling out country, acid-house rock off their CD *Exile on Coldharbour Lane*. Les finished the article, smiled and shut his eyes as the CD cut out in the lounge room. It was Tuesday afternoon and he didn't have to be at work till Thursday.

On Monday there'd been a fire and explosion in the German restaurant next-door to the club. Water from the fire-hoses had poured into the club, mixed with decades of putrid Kings Cross grunge from when the pipes burst in the old building that housed the restaurant. Price cursed the fire brigade and the owners of the restaurant to the heavens, threatening all sorts of diabolical retribution. But there wasn't much he could do, except recarpet the club, get the smell out, then open up again on Thursday night before claiming five times the cost of repairs on insurance.

Not that work worried Les. If anything, the job seemed to get easier all the time and Les often enjoyed sitting in the new front foyer talking to Billy and the punters. Price still had to grease the odd palm here and there, but by paying taxes on his substantial rake-off from the card games and easing up on the hits and limb dislocations, Price had the Kelly Club humming along that close to legal, Les and the others were starting to think they were solid citizens. Besides an amiable work environment, Les also had other reasons to smile.

He was cashed up and fit as a fiddle. He still heard from Roxy, the friendly, good-looking blonde from Victor Harbor, who was now somewhere in Arnhem Land still working on her book. He'd been back to Narooma to see Grace and had a great time again down the south coast. He got on good with Grace's daughter Ellie, and shouted them a week in Sydney at the Swiss Grand. With Grace wearing one of her T-shirts tucked into a pair of tight hipsters, Les took her up to the club one night where she wowed everybody with her figure when he introduced her around, then wowed everybody again when she won several thousand dollars playing manilla. Now Grace was in California, taking Ellie to see Disneyland. She rang Les on Sunday night to say they were both having a good time except the queues were a bit punishing and driving around LA on the wrong side of the road was like a fun ride on its own.

So life was good. Les was happy, Grace was happy, Roxy was happy and, despite the frozen looks on their faces, Les was convinced the two water dragons munching grapes in his backyard were happy. The only person not happy at the moment was Price. However, two of his horses had got up on the weekend, so he'd probably be happy when the club reopened on Thursday night. Yes, smiled Norton as he soaked up the last of the afternoon sun on his banana-chair, life's good and everybody in the garden is rosy. Nevertheless, there was one person whose well-being gave rise to Norton's concern. The boarder. Norton didn't know if he was using the correct medical terminology, but he was firmly convinced Warren was an extrovoid schizophrenic.

They'd both been watching *Nero Wolfe* on the ABC. Warren taped it for Les while he was at work and Les liked the TV show about the fat, pompous private detective, set in New York during the forties. Warren, however, had become besotted.

Especially with Nero Wolfe's dapper assistant, Archie Goodwin. Now the boarder was Warren Edwards, advertising executive by day, but when he went out at night he was Archie Goodwin, private eye. Right down to Archie's double-breasted suits, art-deco ties and two-tone shoes. Warren had even effected Archie Goodwin's mannerisms. His jaunty, shoulder rolling, chin up, elbows by his side walk — with added jaunt — and the way he spoke in clipped tones out of one side of his mouth. Les wasn't sure what had sent Warren into the darkened nightmare world of schizophrenia. Work? Flashbacks from the magic mushrooms down at Narooma? The super-strong pot he was cunningly growing in the backyard concealed amongst a bed of mint? Les glanced across at the tiny heads ripening in the sun alongside the back shed. Certainly Warren wasn't doing any harm, and he did resemble Timothy Hutton, the actor who played Archie Goodwin. And Clover didn't appear to mind Warren's dressing up like a 1940s private eye. Les also had to reluctantly admit Warren did look sharp when he and Clover stepped out at night, they'd even managed to get their photos in the social columns and 'Sydney Confidential'. But Warren's condition could become a worry. It wasn't that long ago he was getting around in a *Star Trek* uniform with a tri-corder, convinced he was Croden, a humanoid fugitive from Rhakar in the Gamma Quadrant. What if Warren developed multiple personalities? What if he went drag? What if he decided to become Dolly Parton or Kylie Minogue? Les felt he'd better keep a close eye on Warren, AKA Archie Goodwin.

And talking about Warren. Archie would be home soon to get changed. He was taking Clover to the opening of some new night spot at North Sydney. Les glanced at his watch as the sun disappeared behind a bank of clouds. It wasn't getting any earlier and his stomach was starting to rumble like a pre-dawn artillery barrage. He folded his magazine and went inside.

Les had a shave then walked out to the kitchen and opened a large bottle of Grolsch from the two cases Warren had brought home from the advertising agency. He took a mouthful and peered into the fridge. Dinner for one shouldn't be too difficult. Frozen vegetables in the microwave and a juicy big T-bone in the George Foreman griller. Les soon got that together, ate it and was glancing through *Nexus* again and dunking arrowroot biscuits into a cup of Russian Caravan tea when he heard the front door open and Warren walked into the kitchen with Clover. Warren's dark-haired girlfriend was carrying a small overnight bag and looked neat in a green top cut low in the front and a pair of green slacks. Warren was wearing designer jeans with a horizontal-striped blue shirt hanging out over the top. He was holding a letter in one hand and had an odd smile on his face as he caught Norton's eye.

'Hello Woz,' nodded Les. 'Hello Clover.'

'How are you, sexy?' replied Clover.

Les dunked another biscuit in his tea. 'I'm good. Especially when I see you, gorgeous.'

Warren continued to stare at Les. 'So,' he said. 'The truth's finally out. You are an old drag queen.'

'I'm a what?' retorted Les.

'You've finally come out the closet, Les,' smiled Clover.

'Yeah, all right,' said Les indifferently. 'I used to be a cross-dresser. But I stopped, because every time I wore women's clothes I couldn't parallel park. What are you pair on about? I'm trying to enjoy a cup of tea and a biscuit in peace. Do you mind?'

'So what made you pick Rosa-Marie for a drag name?' said Warren.

Les screwed up his face. 'What?'

'Here Rosa.' He handed Les the envelope. 'I've just been down the post office, and this came for you.'

Les took a long manilla envelope from Warren. It was a little brown around the edges and addressed in neat, sloping handwriting to *Rosa-Marie Norton, Post Restante, Kings Cross, Sydney, NSW*. Under that someone had stamped a finger pointing and roughly printed on it, TRY POST OFFICE BONDI. Les turned the letter over. In the same neat handwriting on the back it said, *From Emile Decorice, C/o PO, Te Aroha, New Zealand*. Les examined the front of the envelope again then knitted his eyebrows at something.

'Oh, I get the picture,' he nodded to Warren. 'It's some sort of gee-up. You've gone into Archie Goodwin mode again and we're playing back to the forties. You definitely need help, Warren.'

'What?' said Warren.

Les handed the letter back to Warren. 'Where'd you get the old threepenny stamp?'

Warren looked in the corner of the envelope. Beneath the

circular blur where it had been stamped by the post office, was a green stamp with a crown on it that said *Australia, 3d.* 'Shit! It is too. I never even noticed. Hey, have a look, Clover.'

Clover stared at the envelope. 'Well, I'll be,' she said, genuinely surprised. 'It is too.'

'So just what are you trying to pull, kiddies?' said Les, returning to his *Nexus*. 'Though I will give you ten points for authenticity. The old stamp's a ripper.'

'We're not trying to pull anything,' said Warren. 'This letter was in the box with two others for me.'

Les took the letter and looked at it again. He used to get the odd letter addressed to him care of the post office at Kings Cross. So he told the post office to redirect any letters for Norton to the mail box at Bondi. However, he'd never received anything like this.

'Rosa-Marie Norton?' Les shook his head. 'Never bloody heard of her.'

'It might be one of your inbred relatives in Queensland,' said Warren.

'Why don't you open it?' said Clover.

'You can't go opening other people's mail, Clover,' answered Les.

'Why not?' said Clover. 'It's probably been lost in the dead-letter office or something.'

'Dead-letter office?' said Les.

'Yeah,' said Warren. 'These things happen. People often get letters and postcards sent as far back as the First World War. They get lost in the system.'

11

'Going by the stamp and the envelope, that has to be years old,' said Clover. 'Go on Les. Open it up.' She turned to Warren. 'Ooh! This could be exciting.'

Les stared at the envelope for a moment. 'Okay,' he shrugged. 'Why not?'

Les reached over to the kitchen drawer and got a knife. He carefully slit the envelope open and removed the contents as the others took a chair each on either side of him. It was a neatly written four-page letter.

Dear Rosa

Well, dreadful witch of Kings Cross, I hope this letter finds you as well as circumstances can prevail. I sent it care of the post office rather than your flat because I don't know how long you'll be in Melbourne. And you never know with the police always snooping about. I'll make this as brief as I can, but you know me. I am a poet who likes to express himself, so if I start to ramble I'm sure you won't mind.

They let me out of Callan Park just after you left for Melbourne. Those nervous disorders and headaches turned out to be a brain tumour. So I decided to make a quick exit out of Sydney. I sold everything and I'll be on the Wanganella back to New Zealand tomorrow. If anything should happen, I'd like to be with my family in Te Aroha. But what a time I had with you. We certainly showed them a thing or two in Australia. God, I wonder if this country, with its figleaf mentality, will ever change? Bugger them anyway.

In the meantime, you've certainly got your share of problems with the stupid bloody police and customs department, now opening an exhibition in Melbourne and having to have another abortion at the same time. I think it is a better idea you having it down there. Apart from the money, getting one in Sydney is disgusting and I would dread to see you finish with blood poisoning again. God, you were half dead in the awful flat behind St Luke's and the police still wanted to arrest you. It's hard to believe what the police have done to you at times. And me. Especially that fat, loathsome pig of a thing McBride. And for what? But, Rosa my treasure. I have some great news for you. I managed to put one over on the bastards. I saved three of your paintings before they could burn them. When they released me, I managed to find out where they were. So I simply put on a pair of white overalls, walked in like I owned the place, then wrapped them up in a blanket and just walked out again. They'd taken them out of the frames so it was easy. I even caught the tram back to the Cross with them. I hid them at Talbot's for a short while, then decided they would be better off out of Sydney altogether. The police are searching high and low for them. Especially round the Cross. They are absolutely livid. So I sent them to our dear friend Bernard in Lorne. I know we promised that dimwitted Bishop Elsworthy we would never go near Father Shipley again. But what can he do? And I'm sure Bernard will look after them. I sent him a letter with the paintings. Poor bloody Father Shipley.

Fancy trying to save the Witch of Kings Cross when he was in Sydney. God we gave him a mass to remember. Black, white and every colour of the bloody rainbow. Photos to prove it, darling. So that's where they are, and nobody knows except you, me and dear Father Shipley. Aren't you proud of me?

Also, Normo and Dobbo were in town and left a painting each for you at Talbot's. So did that drunken bullshit artist Jacques San before he left. I put them around yours for protection and bound them all securely with that heavy, green canvas Talbot kept in his garage. The other paintings are framed, but they didn't weigh all that much and I was able to send them by post. If I remember correctly Bernard's address in Lorne is Father Bernard Shipley, Church of the Blessed Madonna, 2 Corio Crescent, Lorne, Victoria.

Well Rosa, I did my best to be brief, so I'd better sign off and also, I want to get this in the post before the boat leaves tomorrow morning. I could have left it with Talbot, but he's such a nervous Nellie, I fear if the police knock on his door he'll piddle his pants and give it to them.

In a way, I'm looking forward to the voyage home. I managed to get some good opium in Chinatown for my headaches so the trip should be quite relaxing, if nothing else. I'm certain I can get some in Auckland, too. In the meantime, take care of yourself, Rosa. I hope everything goes well with your exhibition in Melbourne and I hope there are no complications with the abortion. It is a late one this time.

I will write to you again when I get settled. Write to me care
of the post office at Te Aroha. That way I know I'll get your
letters. Oh and do me one favour will you, darling? When
the time comes, will you make sure that cunt McBride finds
out it was me who stole the paintings.

Till we meet again. With love, your friend forever,
Emile Decorice.

Everyone in the kitchen finished reading the letter at the same
time. Les placed it carefully on the kitchen table alongside the
envelope and turned to the others.

'Well, what do you make of that?' he said.

Warren shook his head. 'I'm not sure what to make of it.
It's … it's weird.'

Clover pointed to the name on the front of the envelope. 'He
called her the Witch of Kings Cross. Who was she? I've never
heard of her.'

'Me either,' said Les. 'And I've been working up there for a
while. But she must have been an artist and this Emile bloke's
gone in and got her paintings.'

'Yeah, why would they want to burn them?' said Clover.
'That's a bit heavy, isn't it?'

'Because she was a witch, I suppose,' said Warren.

'Very funny, Warren,' said Clover.

'Shit! What a letter,' said Les. 'It's all in there, isn't it. Witches,
a black mass. A priest, a bishop.'

'Opium, abortions, Callan Park,' said Warren.

'I wonder how old the letter is?' said Clover. 'I wonder if they're all still alive?'

'I'd say it's pretty old,' said Les. 'The trams stopped running years ago, for a start.'

'Yeah,' agreed Warren. 'And no one catches boats to New Zealand anymore.'

'What about Emile?' said Clover. 'I wonder who he was. Her boyfriend?'

'Sounds like it,' answered Warren. 'He's got her up the stick and pissed off to New Zealand when they let him out of the rathouse. The swine.'

'Except it turned out he had a brain tumour. Poor bugger,' said Clover.

'Where's Lorne?' asked Les.

'The other side of Melbourne,' said Warren. 'On the Great Ocean Road. We shot a Holden commercial down there once. It's nice.'

Clover shook her head slowly. 'You know, I'm getting a weird sense of deja vu about this letter.'

Les shook his head firmly. 'No. There's definitely no deja vu about it,' he said. 'But something like this did happen to me once before.'

'Yeah,' nodded Warren. 'Like when you sent me a postcard from Cooktown and you got here before it did.'

'I'll tell you what,' said Clover. 'Warren dearest, why don't you go and have a shower first, and I'll see if I can trawl something up on the internet.'

'Good thinking, Ninety-Nine.' Warren took a last look at the letter then headed for the bathroom.

'You reckon you'll find anything, Clover?' asked Les.

'You never know. Something might turn up.'

'Okay Clover. Have a nice time in cyberspace,' said Les.

Clover turned for Warren's room to fire up his computer. Les flicked through the old letter again before folding it up and replacing it carefully back in its envelope on the kitchen table. He got another beer from the fridge then took it into the lounge room and switched on the TV.

Well, if that old letter don't beat all, Les mused as he sat down to watch the ABC news. It could only happen to bloody me. Les had almost finished his beer when Clover walked into the lounge room.

'How did you go?' he asked her.

Clover shrugged and handed Les a single sheet of paper. 'That's all I could find.'

Just then Warren called out from the hallway. 'Righto. I'm finished.'

'I leave you with it.'

'Okay. Thanks, Clover.' Les began to read what was on the page.

Rosa-Marie Norton. The notorious Witch of Kings Cross. Born an only child in Wanganui New Zealand in 1920, she came to Australia with her parents in 1929 and went to school in Apollo Bay, Victoria, where her father worked as an engineer. When her parents moved to Sydney in 1934, she went to school at

Asquith and studied art at East Sydney Technical College before moving to Kings Cross when her parents returned to New Zealand in 1940. Rosa-Marie then went on to become a bohemian artist and gained notoriety as the Witch of Kings Cross, where she painted macabre, satanic paintings and held black masses in her Roslyn Gardens apartment, much to the consternation of the church and the ultra-conservative Australian establishment of that time. She was arrested on numerous occasions and is the only Australian artist to have their paintings confiscated and burnt. Despite her dubious reputation, Rosa-Marie Norton was popular within the Australian art community and corresponded with famed overseas artists like Yves Tanguy and Salvador Dali, as well as occultists like Aleister Crowley. And studied the works of Eliphas Levi. Rosa-Marie Norton died in Sydney in 1951 leaving very little money. Yet one of her paintings, *Sleeping Beast*, was sold in Sydney recently for $50,000. Further information can be found in *The Mystical Mind of Rosa-Marie Norton* by Kenneth Raymond. At the bottom of the page was a fuzzy printout of a slender woman with dark hair.

Les read the page again then went back to watching TV. A few minutes later, Warren walked into the lounge room with Clover. Clover had the same clothes on except for a black satin jacket and a pair of tan Doc Martens. Warren was wearing a dark blue, chalk-stripe, double-breasted suit, a dark blue shirt with a maroon, yellow and white tie, blue and white two-tone shoes. Sitting squarely on his head was an oyster grey snap-brim fedora with a blue hat band.

'My God!' said Les. 'It's *Natural Born Killers* meets *Bonnie and Clyde*.'

'Don't sweat it, pal,' said Warren out the side of his mouth. 'Punks like you are a dime a dozen where I come from.'

'Did you read the printout, Les?' asked Clover.

'Yeah. There wasn't a great deal,' replied Les. 'But thanks anyway, Clover.' Les offered the printout to Warren. 'You want to have a look, Woz? Sorry, I mean Archie.'

Warren's head shook slightly beneath his snap-brim fedora. 'Ain't got time, pal. I gotta go and close the Sorrelli case.'

Les drew back the sheet of paper. 'I should have known.'

Clover made an open-handed gesture. 'We have to go.'

'Okay. Have a good night,' smiled Les.

Les heard the door close and went back to the TV. After a while he tossed his empty beer bottle in the kitchen tidy and made a delicious. Warren had brought a video home from the agency, *O Brother, Where Art Thou?* Les slipped it in the VCR and settled back on the lounge.

Les enjoyed the movie. George Clooney and his two dumb mates were a hoot as the escaped convicts bumbling around the deep South during the Depression. The music was good, the singing was great and when the Soggy Bottom Boys finally got up on stage, Norton cracked up. He made a point to buy the CD with the soundtrack from the movie. But as much as Les enjoyed watching the video, every so often his eyes would drift back to the printout Clover had given him. When the video finished, Les made a mug of Ovaltine, washed up, then read both the letter

19

and the printout again before switching off the lights and taking the letter and printout into his bedroom with him.

After he climbed into bed, Les scrunched his head back into the pillows and stared up at the darkened ceiling. What happened today had to be more than coincidence, he told himself. A letter like that doesn't just get lost in the system for years then turn up out of the blue. Was it an omen? A voice from beyond the grave? Divine intervention? Les needed to know more about Rosa-Marie Norton, the Witch of Kings Cross. And the best way to find out was to get that book by Kenneth Raymond. After a while Norton's eyes started to flicker and he drifted off into the cosmos.

Wednesday was a little warmer and the northerly had swung round more to the west. Norton was up around seven; Warren was still in bed snoring. Les changed into his old blue tracksuit, had some tea and toast then tossed his training gear and a towel into an overnight bag and drove down to North Bondi to meet Billy and Eddie for a workout. Billy was leaning against the railing opposite the Surf Club wearing a tracksuit much like Norton's and a pair of sunglasses.

'Where's Eddie?' asked Les.

'Something's come up and he had to go round to Price's,' answered Billy.

'Did he say what it was?'

Billy shook his head. 'No. He probably just wants Eddie to shoot the local fire chief.'

'Yeah. And old Karl that owns the restaurant.'

'If there's any real drama, we'll find out tomorrow night, I imagine.' Billy nodded to the Surf Club. 'What do you want to do first? Have a run?'

'Righto,' said Les. 'Then we'll get on the skis. You fancy a bit of breakfast at Speedos after?'

'Okay.' Billy feinted a left rip into Norton's ribcage and they walked across to North Bondi Surf Club.

They jogged six laps of Bondi then paddled four laps on their skis. After that they smashed into each other with a medicine ball inside the Surf Club. During the run Les decided not to say anything about the letter for the time being. In fact Les didn't talk about anything much when they were running, because Billy kept the pressure on. After the workout they strolled across to Speedos, found a table inside and had a late breakfast of mineral water, OJ and a pile of scrambled eggs and bacon washed down with creamy flat whites. On the way back to their cars Billy said he wouldn't be able to train the next morning as he was going to the dentist. Les said okay. He'd see him at work tomorrow night. They got in their cars and drove off.

Les stopped for the *Telegraph* on the way home, then changed into his blue shorts and a white Roosters T-shirt and had a read while his laundry was going around. The two water dragons were sitting under the Hills Hoist; he fed them a few grapes before going back inside to read the old letter and the printout again. Les had a think for a moment then wrote something down on a piece of paper, put it in his overnight bag and drove up to Bondi Junction via Birrell Street. He fluked a parking spot in Denison Street, right opposite Waverley Library. Norton had held a library card for as long as he could remember. On a rotten, cold, boring day in winter, Les liked nothing better than to kill a few hours in the library, going over big old books about ancient ruins and other countries and their people. And the new, fully modernised cream and brown building now housing Waverley Library was bigger and better than ever, plus the staff were always helpful and patient. Les locked the car and walked across to the tiled courtyard of the Ron Lander Centre.

The double doors swished open, Les turned left at the wide, flat marble-and-stainless-steel statue in the foyer and through the two security gates inside. There was a man standing behind a counter on the left and two women seated at their desks in the corner to the right: a blonde in a grey cardigan and a brunette in a maroon shirt with matching earrings. Les approached the lady in the maroon shirt.

'Yes. Can I help you?' she asked.

'Yes please,' answered Les, placing a piece of paper on the counter. 'I'm after this book. Do you have it?'

The woman looked at the name on the piece of paper then punched it into her computer. 'Yes we do,' she smiled. She pointed to the rows and rows of books behind Les and the section Ra–Sh. 'Just over there.'

'Thanks very much.'

Les started running his eyes up and down the spines of all the books. Raymond's book was a large coffee-table type sitting between *Belle On A Broomstick* by Pat Richardson and *Just Another Angel* by Mike Riley. Les took the book over to the self-checker, placed his library card in the slot, pressed the book's spine against the red tape, there was a thump as it registered and Les picked up his printout receipt. Before he dropped the book in his bag, Les had a closer look at the cover.

The book itself was wide and long. The cover was a fiendish yet beautiful woman's face, in all the swirling, devilish colours of the rainbow, looking at you from above a darkened skyline of burning buildings. She had gorgeous lips and sinister emerald eyes that leapt from the cover and transfixed the viewer with an hypnotic gaze. In striking red and white print, it said, *The Mystical Mind of Rosa-Marie Norton by Kenneth Raymond.* Les zipped his bag closed and walked back to his car.

Despite getting caught in a gridlock of cars near Waverley College and nearly getting T-boned at Ocean Street by a woman in a 4WD talking on a mobile phone, Les was whistling happily when he pulled up outside Chez Norton and stepped inside. Finding Raymond's book was easier than he expected. He looked at his watch and thought: why not? It was getting cloudy outside. He got a bottle of Warren's beer from the fridge and settled back in the lounge room with his book.

On the inside cover was a photo of Rosa-Marie Norton wearing a military-style shirt and a hand-painted tie. She was very attractive with thick, shiny black hair, sensuous lips and plucked eyebrows that arched up giving her a sinister haughtiness. But it was her eyes, dark and lidded, that exuded a tigerish sexuality that bored deep inside you.

Amongst the printed matter were pages of her paintings. Some were black and white, but most were done in wild swirls of fantastic burning colours and flames, like the face on the cover. The subject matter was mainly esoteric satanism. Devils with four eyes, faces that turned into tarantulas, snakes with cat's heads. Genies coming out of buildings, buildings walking away on chicken's legs. Camels with heads for humps, superbly muscled men with horse's or goat's heads and penises with snake's heads. Except for one painting of a baby on a bed of pink flowers surrounded by buck-toothed rabbits titled *Tanybryn*, it was paintings of horned men and panthers making love to beautiful, cloven-hoofed women, more devils and demons, piranhas with forked tongues and werewolves holding magic wands; with titles like *Snake Blood, Demon at Rest, Love in Hell, Tarantula Power, Hair Hair the Storm Demon*. The painting on the cover was titled *The Temptress*. Les had a last look at the cover, then turned to page one and read the first paragraph.

Rosa-Marie Norton occupies a position unique in the annals of Australian art history: that of Australia's most persecuted — and prosecuted — female artist. Amongst the incidents which contributed to this dubious honour were her position as the only woman artist to be charged with 'having

exhibited obscene articles', the only artist in Australia to
have had a book of her works prosecuted for 'obscenity', and
also — and most outrageously — the only Australian artist
(male or female) to have had her works destroyed by judicial
sanction.

Les spent the rest of the day poring over Raymond's book. A stiff neck later and as the sun was starting to set, Les finished. He stretched, made a cup of tea and placed Raymond's book on the kitchen table next to the letter. Between the two, Les felt he'd been given a small window into Rosa-Marie's amazing life. Many people in the past had voiced their opinions on Rosa-Marie Norton, the Witch of Kings Cross. Les sipped his tea, sat back and tried to draw his own conclusions from what he'd read in Raymond's book.

She was years ahead of her time. And although totally outrageous, also an extremely talented artist. If she had been alive today she'd be rich and her works appreciated. Behind the devil and demon subjects of her art, the colours she created were brilliant and dazzling. One fellow artist had described her as a 'female van Gogh'. She disliked children and preferred cats to people, yet lived life to the full and, sexually, would be in anything. From sado-masochistic orgies to bondage and devil worship. Drink, drugs. You name it. Rosa always brought plenty to the party and would be the first there and the last to leave, in her colourful clothes, twirling a jewelled cigarette holder. She entertained local artists of both sexes and her fame and notoriety were well known overseas. If you could handle a brush and palette, liked kinky sex, drink and drugs and staying up for days on end, call in to Kings Cross and see Rosa. American, English and European artists would visit her and literally kneel at her feet. Men fell in love with her one after the other. She modelled for Norman Lindsay, and Jacques San was an American artist who fell passionately in love with her on a brief visit to Australia. When Rosa-Marie cast him aside, he almost drank himself to death before he packed up his paintings and returned to New York. She always had trouble selling her paintings. Yet a Bishop Thomas Elsworthy from Victoria bought two, supposedly to show his parish exactly what evil and depravity was all about. And from the sale of the two paintings Rosa was able to buy a car and spend an entire summer travelling around country New South Wales and Victoria.

Emile Decorice was a homosexual poet who shared a house with Rosa and was one of her closest and most devoted friends. The police persecuted him as well as her and had him committed to a mental institution. He went back to New Zealand only to catch pneumonia during the voyage and died a week after the boat docked in Auckland. Talbot was Talbot Houlcroft, the editor of an avant-garde magazine, *Guichet*. He, too, was a good friend of Rosa's and published her art and articles she wrote. He even published an expensive book of her art, but went broke when the authorities declared it 'offensive to public chastity and human decency' and had it banned. McBride was Sergeant Arthur 'Buster' McBride, a Kings Cross detective who constantly harassed Rosa-Marie and Emile. The newspapers and any muck-raking journalists of that time rarely left her in peace. They made headlines out of her smallest misdemeanour and wrote anything they could think of about her, mostly lies and sensationalism. According to Raymond, however, she gave an interview to a university paper in which she said she studied occultism and eastern philosophy and claimed she went along with the Witch of Kings Cross infamy because she enjoyed being a nonconformist in a conservative, Christian country like Australia. Plus it drew attention to her art, and any publicity was better than none.

She opened an exhibition in Melbourne that turned out a complete disaster and saw her once again charged with obscenity. One critic described her art as 'Stark sensuality running riot'. Another said, 'Rosa-Marie Norton paints with a lurid brush dipped in nightmares.' When the exhibition virtually closed overnight, Rosa-Marie was said to have broken down, then she disappeared from public view till she was arrested at Apollo Bay for urinating in a public place. She later showed up in Sydney and died not long after when she fell out of a tram in Taylor Square one night and broke her neck. Naturally this made headlines and a huge crowd of people and various identities from the art world and around Kings Cross attended her funeral. Her ashes were sent back to her family in New Zealand and most of her paintings simply disappeared. The biggest irony Les found was that, although she died broke, as well as that one painting selling for $50,000, the owner of a restaurant in Kings Cross that used to be a bohemian coffee lounge in the fifties found one of her paintings in an attic and knocked back an offer of $85,000 for it.

Les tapped his fingers on the book and looked at his watch. Warren would be home soon and the beer had put an edge on Norton's appetite. He got a pile of vegetables and rice together, then marinated some lamb chump chops in Taka Tala sauce. While the rice was cooking, Les perused Emile Decorice's letter again and did a little deducing.

Rosa-Marie and Emile had probably caught Father Bernard Shipley with his pants down somewhere, taken photos and decided to blackmail him. Bishop Elsworthy had bailed his priest out by buying two of Rosa-Marie's paintings. Rosa or Emile probably still kept a couple of photos, which was why Emile sent the paintings to Father Shipley for safekeeping. Rosa-Marie never got the letter Emile sent telling her. Emile died not long after he sent it. Rosa-Marie died not long after that. And Father Shipley still had the paintings. When he found out Rosa-Marie and Emile were both dead it would have been a blessed relief. No more connection with the Witch of Kings Cross and her deviate friend. There was no next of kin that Father Shipley would have been aware of and he was the only one who knew about the paintings. He could have destroyed them. But then again, he might not have. Les picked up the old letter and tapped it softly against the table. Well, if that's the case, he surmised, hidden somewhere in Lorne, Victoria, still bundled up in heavy green canvas quietly gathering dust and cobwebs, are two hundred grand's worth of paintings. Possibly under an old church. Les slipped the chops onto the griller as the front door opened and Warren walked into the kitchen wearing a white-on-white shirt and a pair of black jeans.

'Woz,' said Les. 'How are you mate?'

'Rooted,' yawned Warren. 'I must have drunk enough margaritas last night to fill a bathtub.'

'Good turn eh?'

'Too fuckin good,' Warren yawned again.

'Hey have a look at this,' said Les. 'I got a book on Rosa-Marie Norton.'

'You did?'

Les showed Warren the book he got from the library and the printout Clover had given him. Warren read the printout and started flicking through the book.

'Christ!' he exclaimed. 'What about some of these paintings.'

'Yeah. She was a wild woman all right,' said Les. 'Wait till you read her story.'

'I'm going for an Edgar. I'll flick through it before I have a shower.'

'Okay. You hungry?'

'Reckon. I had fuck-all for lunch.'

Warren went to the bathroom. Les set the table and got the dinner together. Warren eventually walked back into the kitchen freshly shaven, wearing his grey tracksuit. He put the book and printout on the table, got a beer and smiled at Les.

'What a gal,' he said. 'I didn't read all of it. But didn't she like a root?'

'Yeah,' laughed Les. 'Rosa would have been in a shit sandwich if you cut the crusts off.' He moved the book and started serving up the rice. 'You know, Warren, I've got a bit of a theory.'

'What? About Rosa-Marie Norton?'

'Yeah. I'll tell you about it while we're eating.'

While they were having dinner, Les referred to the book and the letter and told Warren his theory about what happened to Rosa-Marie's paintings. Warren hadn't read all the book and couldn't remember everything that was in the letter. But he agreed Norton's theory did hold water.

'What about those artists that gave her a painting?' said Warren. 'Normo and the other bloke. Who were they?'

'Don't know,' answered Les. 'There's nothing in the book about them. And that Yank, Jacques San, was just a pisshead she ate up and spat out.'

Warren picked up the book again. 'Look at that cover. Shit! She sure had an eye for colour.'

'Yep,' agreed Les. 'She was a female van Gogh.'

When they'd finished eating, Warren made a pot of coffee and they had a cup each while the food went down.

'So what's doing tomorrow, Woz?' Les asked.

Warren shook his head. 'Don't ask. I have to be up at six. We're doing a shoot at Whale Beach in the morning.'

'Who for?'

'A rock band called Knife Edge.'

'Never heard of them,' shrugged Les.

'You're lucky,' said Warren. 'A greater bunch of no-talent, shit-for-brains adolescents with attitude I've yet to come across. I know what I'd like to shoot the pimply-faced cunts with. An AK-47.'

'Of course they won't look like that after you've finished with them,' said Les, sipping his coffee.

Warren looked Norton straight in the eye. 'Les. When you see this ad on TV, you'll think they're silverchair, the Rolling Stones and Oasis all rolled into one.'

'TV commercials,' said Les. 'The science of arresting human intelligence long enough to get money from it.'

'Right on, baby,' said Warren. 'And talking about TV. There's not a bad movie tonight on the ABC. The original *Thing From Outer Space.*'

'Shit! That old black and white clunker,' said Les. 'I remember my old man saying he saw that in Brisbane when he was a kid. And it scared the shit out of him.'

'That's understandable,' said Warren. 'If you get too frightened, you can sleep in my room.'

'Be a bit crowded in there with the three of us, wouldn't it, Woz?'

They washed up, then made a delicious each and took it into the lounge room. Warren produced his bong and packed a couple of cones, pulling them in with relish. He offered some to Les. Les shook his head and sipped his delicious. While they were waiting for the movie to start, Les turned and looked at the boarder.

31

'Hey Warren,' said Les.

'Hey yeah,' replied Warren.

'What do you think of this for an idea?'

Warren picked up his drink. 'Go on.'

'What if I was to go down to Lorne in Victoria. Take that old letter with me. Find Father Shipley. And tell him Rosa-Marie Norton was my mother. I'm the only son. I've come to collect my mother's paintings.'

Warren looked at Les and gave him a long, slow double blink. 'What did you just fuckin say?' he asked deliberately.

Les repeated what he'd just said. 'My name's Norton,' he added. 'I could show him a heap of ID. Plus I got my mother's letter … Who's to say I'm not telling the truth? He'd probably be glad to get rid of the horrible bloody … creations of the devil.'

After the two cones, Warren started laughing that hard he had a coughing fit. 'I don't fuckin believe you. That has to be the stupidest idea I've ever fuckin heard,' he spluttered. 'You're completely fucked.'

'Okay, sorry,' shrugged Les. 'It was just a thought.'

'Just a thought?' said Warren. 'And you've got the hide to bag me about making TV commercials. You fuckin moron. Get fucked!' Warren swallowed some of his drink. 'Jesus! What next?'

'All right,' said Les. 'Don't shit your pants. It was just an idea. I'm sorry I bloody asked.'

Suddenly Warren changed tack. 'No wait,' he said. 'I'm wrong. It's a good idea. Do it. Fly down to Melbourne. Hire a car and drive down to Lorne. I'll even see if I can work you a deal through the agency on a car. That's a terrific idea, Les. You're a genius.'

Les looked at Warren suspiciously. 'Yeah that'd be right. You only want to get me out of the house so you and Clover can play chasings up and down the hallway. You two-faced little cunt.'

'Shit Les. Whatever gave you that idea?'

'Yeah. I'm awake up to you. No, fuck you. I'm not going now. You can get fucked.'

'Gee! That's nice, isn't it,' said Warren.

'And just for that, I'll have some of your pot, too. Fuck you.'

Les pulled a couple of cones while Warren watched him out of the corner of his eye and laughed. Then they settled back to watch the movie.

Half stoned and half pissed, the old black-and-white clunker wasn't bad. Even for another 'America saves the world' saga. The dialogue was snappy, it had plenty of pace and the music did add a sense of menace. It wasn't scary. In fact when the thing showed up at the end, it reminded Les of the camp android in *Red Dwarf.* It finished and Warren stood up.

'Okay Les,' he said. 'I'm hitting the sack. I'll see you in the morning.'

'Not if you're getting up at six o'clock you won't,' yawned Les, switching off the TV. 'I'll probably see you before I go to work tomorrow night.'

'Whatever,' said Warren. 'Hey. I still reckon that's a good idea, going to Lorne to get those paintings. You should do it.'

'Yeah. Thanks Warren,' answered Les. 'I'll give it some more thought.'

Warren went to the bathroom, followed by Les, then they both went to bed. The booze and the cones had made Les tired and he always enjoyed an early night when he wasn't working. His head had hardly hit the pillow when he was snoring soundly.

Les slept in the next morning and got up around eight. Warren was long gone when Les walked into the kitchen and made some tea and toast. Outside it looked a little cloudy and the wind had come up. Les decided to brush the beach and have a run in Centennial Park. He got into his shorts, trainers and T-shirt, and drove up, parking outside the gates in York Road.

Not having to keep up with Billy, Les took his time jogging around the trees, nodding to the rangers and anybody else who cared to pass the time of day. While he was trotting along, Les figured Warren was right. It would be stupid going to Victoria looking for a batch of paintings that could be anywhere after all these years, and he deserved to be laughed, chaffed and poked shit at. It was a thought, though. Albeit a devious one. But Les was still curious about Rosa-Marie Norton. And if there was one person who'd know about Rosa-Marie Norton it would have to be Price. Les decided he'd bring the subject up when they had a drink after work, then casually produce the old letter from inside his jacket and see what sort of reaction he got. Les finished his run with a few sprints, did some crunches and drove home.

He didn't get cleaned up straightaway. Instead, he guzzled down a bottle of mineral water, put some old clothes and a pair of protective sunglasses on, and whipper-snipped the patch of lawn at the front of Chez Norton. When he'd finished there, he did Mrs Curtin's across the road and finished up doing Mrs Beaty's next door to her. They thanked Les and made him a 'nice cup of tea' then gave him GBH of the earhole about the cost of living and the local council. Before they could get too much of a roll on, Les said he had things to do, said goodbye then went inside and got cleaned up.

Les drank some more mineral water and changed back into his shorts and T-shirt. While he was having another glass of water Les had another quick look through the book. The author's Melbourne address was in the back. The Obelisk Bookshop, Brunswick Street, Fitzroy. Les decided he had to have a book for himself. He rang assistance, got the number and rang Melbourne.

'Good morning. Obelisk Bookshop,' came a man's voice on the other end.

'Yeah. Is Kenneth Raymond there please?' asked Les.

'Speaking.'

'I'd like to order a copy of your book, *The Mystic Mind of Rosa-Marie Norton.*'

'No worries. I have some in stock.'

'Okay. I'm ringing from Sydney. Can you send me one?'

'No worries. It'll be forty-five dollars with postage.'

'No worries,' smiled Les. He gave the author his name, address and credit card details.

'You say your name's Norton?' asked Raymond.

'Yeah. That's right,' said Les.

'No relation — surely?'

'No,' laughed Les. 'But I'm interested in her art. And her.'

'Yes. She was a fascinating woman all right,' said Raymond.

'She sure was,' agreed Les. 'How long before it will get here?'

'Oh. It should be there within a week.'

'Okey doke. Thanks a lot.'

'No worries.'

Yeah. No wuckin furries, Les smiled to himself. Good old Melbourne. Les got some money and left the house, locking the door behind him.

He went to the photo shop in Hall Street and xeroxed a copy of the letter, plus the envelope. Then Les went to the Hakoah Club and had a meal of matso ball soup, and veal schnitzel with creamed spinach and veg. Washed down with a coffee and a quick flutter on the keno in the Maccabi Bar. After losing a few dollars, Les walked home, full, contented and on top of the day. After putzing around the house sorting out his washing and a few things, it was time to iron a shirt, put on his black trousers and bomber jacket, have a cup of tea and get ready to be at work by seven-thirty. Warren wasn't home when he left. Les tucked the old letter inside his jacket, locked up and went out to his car. The traffic wasn't too bad and Les was parked in an office driveway down from the club and jogging up the club's stairs a little before seven-thirty. Billy was inside, dressed pretty much like Les, talking to Price and George. Price was wearing a single-breasted, cream suit with a yellow silk tie, George was in a blue yachting jacket, grey trousers and a regimental striped tie. Around them the staff were preparing for another night of gambling. Everybody said hello to Les. Les said hello back then stopped to take in the new two-tone blue carpet and the distinct smell of freshness in the air.

'Very nice, Price,' said Les. He pointed to the ceiling. 'You've even shouted the club a new chandelier.'

Price made a magnanimous gesture. 'You know me, big fellah. Money's no object when it comes to providing the best for my customers.'

Les nodded. 'Yes. It's doubtful Saddam Hussein would have spent as much on one of his palaces in Baghdad. Do you and Saddam have the same insurance company, Price?'

'No. Just the same accountant,' replied Price.

Les smiled. 'Hey. There's something I want to see you about after work, too.'

'Good. Because I want to see you about something myself. Has Eddie rung you at all?'

'No.'

'Doesn't matter. He'll be here later.'

Norton's antenna went up and started turning. 'You want to see me? Eddie was going to ring me? What's going on?'

'Nothing. You'll find out after work,' said Price.

'Okay.' Les turned to George. 'I like the yachting jacket, commodore. All you need is a monogrammed pocket and you'd look like a poker machine supervisor at the Double Bay Yacht Club.'

'All you need with that nose of yours is a white glove and you'd look like Michael Jackson,' replied George.

Les gave them all an indignant once up and down. 'Well I didn't come in here to be insulted by riff raff. I'm going down to the foyer where it's more suited to a man of my congeniality and bearing.'

'Yeah. Ball bearings,' said George.

Les turned and walked down to the foyer, pleased he'd managed to get a rise out of George so early in the night. Although Les had to admit, George didn't tap dance too bad and often gave as good as he got. Straightaway, a team of Hungarian Jews, very astute German whist players, came up that Les recognised. There were smiles and high-pitched Hungarian greetings all round as Les welcomed them inside, then they walked up the stairs just as Billy came down.

'So how was the trip to the dentist?' asked Les.

The boys had been going to a Vietnamese dentist at Double Bay named Jim Ho, who they called Uncle Ho. He was a fantastic dentist. An artist. And with a great sense of humour.

'How was it?' said Billy. 'An hour of misery and pain. And

then you have to pay for the privilege. But check this crown.' Billy showed Les his new tooth in the front. It looked better than the original.

'Jees, he does a bloody good job,' agreed Les.

'Yeah. His wife just had a baby so he shouted me another shot of novocaine. I didn't feel a thing to be honest. Until I got the fuckin bill.'

Les had a stretch. 'So what's going on with Eddie and Price? You heard anything?'

Billy shook his head. 'No. Nothing.'

'Oh well,' said Les. 'I'll find out soon enough, I suppose.'

As usual the night went smooth as silk. The punters soon arrived to get in as much card-playing as possible before the club closed at twelve-thirty. Price only had a midnight licence, which suited everybody. But in that short space of time, hundreds of thousands, even millions of dollars changed hands on credit. The only drama was the usual hassle with young techno-heads coming up full of Ebeneezer thinking the Kelly Club was an exclusive disco. They'd all be dressed beautifully in expensive clothes, wearing the best cologne, their hair gelled up in the latest style, and Billy would tell them they couldn't come in because they didn't look cool enough and their clothes were so five minutes ago. Another of his put-downs was to tell them Kylie and Russell were inside with Nicole and Jodie. And if they saw people like them in the club they'd never come back. The ravers would leave absolutely shattered, wondering just how exclusive can one nightclub be? An hour before closing Eddie arrived wearing a black leather jacket, a char-grey polo shirt and black jeans.

'Hello ladies,' he said breezily as he stepped into the foyer. 'Sorry I couldn't make it on Wednesday. What's doing, anyway?'

'Not much, Eddie,' replied Billy. 'What's doing with you?'

'The same,' shrugged Eddie. He caught Norton's eye and smiled. 'Sort of.'

'I believe Price wants to see me after work,' said Les. 'Your name was mentioned too, Edward.'

'Yeah?' replied Eddie. He feinted a left hook to the big Queenslander's chin. 'We'll talk about it when we knock off.'

Eddie disappeared up the stairs and Les left it at that. A few more members arrived for a late flutter and before Les knew it they had the club emptied, the staff had gone home, the front door was locked and they were sitting in Price's office talking easily about this and that. Les was drinking Fourex, the others were drinking beer, scotch and vodka while Eddie was sipping a bottle of Pellegrino. They were talking about one of the Hungarians winning almost a hundred thousand and a likeable, retired Italian baker winning fifty thousand, when the conversation dwindled off. Les had a mouthful of Fourex, eased back in his seat and looked at Price.

'Okay, Price me old mate,' said Les. 'Let's get down to business. What did you want to see me about?'

Price took a sip of Glenfiddich and soda, then placed the glass on a coaster on his office table. 'Do you know a bloke called Latte Lindsey?'

'Latte Lindsey?' Les had to think for a moment. 'Yeah. I think I do,' he nodded. 'Tall, sort of sallow-faced dork, around thirty, with an egg-shaped head. Got a real slimy smile. Poses as an art dealer or something.'

'That's him,' said Price. 'Oily as a kerosene lamp.'

'Isn't he the bloke used to go training with Killer and the boys down at City Tatts? And they caught him nicking their dough out of the locker room.' Les turned to George. 'Your nephew Kevin marked all the money and he got sprung when they were having a shout.'

'You got him,' nodded George. 'He bolted out of the joint, otherwise they would have kicked the shit out of him.'

'Bad luck they didn't,' said Billy.

'How did he get the nickname Latte Lindsey?' asked Les.

'His parents are Poms, and he grew up in Pyrmont,' said Eddie. 'But he likes to swan around the coffee shops in Double Bay sucking down lattes. Always with his little finger sticking out.'

'Yeah, I know him,' said Les. 'I said hello to him one day up Bondi Junction, and he looked straight through me. Guess I was beneath his standing.'

'That's Latte,' nodded Eddie. 'The fuckin poser.'

'So what's Latte done to incur your wrath, Price?' asked Les.

'What's he done?' scowled Price. 'He sold my sister-in-law Kitty a painting for twenty-five grand that turned out to be a dud. It's worth about two fuckin mintie wrappers.'

'Nice,' said Les.

'I won't go into it,' said Price. 'But I want him shortened up.'

'And you want me and Eddie to do the shortening?' said Les.

'That's right,' said Price. 'There'll be a drink in it for you.'

'Shit! You're not gonna kill him, are you?' said Les. 'Honestly. I'm not into murder right now. And killing him won't get Kitty her twenty-five grand back.'

'No,' said Eddie. 'Not murder. Just a severe shortening up.'

'I don't expect to get Kitty's money back,' said Price. 'But Latte wears a twenty-five thousand dollar Bvlgari watch, and a twenty thousand dollar diamond pinky ring he snookered off a dope dealer who's in the can. I'll settle for that.'

Les thought for a moment. 'So what did you have in mind?'

'Latte's train's run out of track up here,' said Eddie, 'and he's living in Melbourne. I'm not sure where. But I know where he's putting his slimy head into an art sale down there this Saturday night.'

Les sipped his beer. 'Go on.'

'So I thought you and I might fly down to Melbourne on the weekend,' said Eddie. 'Discuss the finer details of Rembrandt and Picasso with Latte. Then fly straight home again.'

This was entirely unexpected and Norton's mind went into overdrive. But he had to be cool. Very cool.

'Shit I don't know,' he said, shaking his head reluctantly. 'I'm not all that keen. Things are going good up here at the moment. And I can't say I'm over-rapt in Melbourne.'

'Christ! It's only for a couple of nights,' said Price. 'You go down tomorrow. Eddie'll meet you on Saturday. You sort

Shithead out and fly back Saturday night. And a nice drink for your trouble.'

'I can get someone else,' said Eddie. 'But I'd rather have you.'

'You fly down business class,' said Price. 'I'll put you up in a top hotel.'

'And you can go shopping in Melbourne,' said George. 'Think of all the grouse clothes you can buy. You won't have to get around looking like a grave robber anymore.'

'Shit! I'll go if you don't want to,' said Billy. 'There's a good night scene in Melbourne. It shits on Sydney.'

Les shook his head and looked at the floor. 'All right,' he finally nodded. 'I'll go. But on one condition.'

'What's that?' said Price.

'Arrange a rental car and book me into a pub at Lorne till Friday.'

'Lorne? What's the big attraction in Lorne?' asked Price.

'Nothing really,' shrugged Les. 'But I've always wanted to see the Great Ocean Road. And I've heard Lorne's a nice spot.'

Price shrugged and looked around the office. 'Done,' he said. 'George. Sort that out with Gary.'

'I'll ring Travelabout first thing tomorrow,' said George.

'I imagine,' drawled Les, 'you've already taken my answer for granted.'

Eddie grinned and handed Les an airline ticket from inside his leather jacket. 'I knew you wouldn't let me down. You're on the twelve-thirty flight with Qantas tomorrow. You're booked into the Southville in Collins Street. A limo'll pick you up at the airport. I'll be there Saturday afternoon around five. Call in to Gary's and pick up the other bookings on your way to the airport tomorrow.'

Price smiled and pushed two thousand dollars across his desk to Les.

'And that should keep you in sandwiches and flavoured milk till you get back.'

Les picked up the money and the airline ticket and pocketed them inside his jacket, next to the old letter. 'Okay,' he shrugged. 'Like they say in Melbourne, no worries.'

'The limo driver's name's Perry,' said Eddie. 'He's a mate of mine. He'll be coming with us on Saturday night. I'll explain everything when I see you down there.' Eddie smiled and wiggled his eyebrows. 'You'll like it.'

'It couldn't be any worse than nearly getting eaten by fuckin sharks,' replied Les.

'Okay,' beamed Price, rubbing his hands together. 'That's settled.' He picked up his drink and turned to Les. 'Now, Les. What was it you wanted to see me about?'

Les looked at Price. 'See you about? Oh, yes. I was thinking about getting my place re-carpeted. And I was wondering who you used here? They did a terrific job.'

Price turned to George. 'George. You know who they are.'

'Achmet's Flying Carpet Service,' said George. 'I've got their card here somewhere.'

'Unreal,' said Norton. 'Thanks, George.'

They had one or two more drinks, then locked up the club and went their separate ways. Eddie told Les he'd see him in

Melbourne. Les told the others he'd see them when he got back from Victoria, and drove home.

Shortly after, Les was sitting in the kitchen at Chez Norton sipping on a mug of Ovaltine. The old letter was on the table in front of him next to the airline ticket and the two thousand dollars. Well, if that's not divine intervention, he asked himself, what is? That nutty idea I had earlier has just fallen into my lap, thanks to you-know-who. And even if it is nutty, what have I got to lose? Six days living it up in Victoria, courtesy of Price. Les smiled and raised his mug. To divine intervention — and Price Galese of course.

Les finished his Ovaltine, got changed and went to bed. As he buried his head into the pillows, he briefly pondered what clothes he should take. Knowing Victoria, plenty of warm ones. Les gave a final yawn and before long he was snoring peacefully.

Friday was mild and clear when Les got out of bed around eight. He changed into a pair of shorts and a T-shirt, cleaned up and walked into the kitchen. Warren was seated in a pair of jeans and a red and brown striped shirt, finishing a cup of coffee before he left for work.

'G'day Woz,' said Les. 'How's things?'

'Great,' replied Warren. 'I'm even starting to believe there is a God after all.'

'Oh?' replied Les. 'How's that?'

'Knife Edge's bass player got electrocuted in Melbourne last night.'

'Electrocuted? Shit! Is he dead?'

'Unfortunately no. But they say he's got a wonderful glow about him.'

'You're a bloody sadist.' Les checked the plunger. The coffee was still warm so he poured himself a cup. 'Anyway, talking about Melbourne, Woz. Can I borrow that suitcase of yours with the wheels on it?'

'Sure. It's under my bed. I'll get it for you.' Warren looked at Les. 'What's that got to do with Melbourne?'

'Woz, I'm taking your advice. I'm flying to Melbourne. Renting a car. And I'm driving down to Lorne to find those paintings.'

'You're what?'

Les took a sip of coffee and a faraway look appeared in his eyes. 'Warren. I firmly believe that letter was more than just a letter. It was a message. A message from beyond. You say you're starting to believe in God, Warren. Well, glory be. So am I. And God has spoken. Telling me to seek the path to Lorne, and find those paintings.' Les stared fervently at Warren. 'Woz. There's a spiritual connection between me, Rosa-Marie Norton and those paintings. They were meant for me. And through the power of the Lord, and divine guidance, I'm going to take back what's mine. Warren, I'm on a mission from God. Oh glory hallelujah!'

Warren stared at Les in disbelief. 'You've gone mad, you fuckin ratbag.'

Les shook his head sincerely. 'Nay Warren. Not mad. Just guided by unseen forces. Mysterious forces, Warren, that you and I know nothing about. Praise the Lord.'

'Jesus Christ!' exclaimed Warren.

'Him too.' Les took another sip of coffee. 'Anyway, what are you blowing up about, you little prick? I won't be back till Friday. That gives you and Clover a week to run around the house dressed up as Adolf Hitler and Eva Braun. And whatever else you get up to when I'm not here.'

'I'll get the suitcase.' Warren went to his room and came back carrying a black suitcase with rollers and a folding handle and put it in the kitchen. 'There you are, Frodo. That should help you on your quest. Do you want something to bring the paintings back in too, young hobbit?'

'No, great wizard Gandalf. I'll manage, thank you,' replied Les.

Warren glanced at his watch. 'Well, I have to get to the pickle factory.' He looked suspiciously at Norton. 'You are going to Melbourne, aren't you? This isn't just a gee-up?'

'Fuckin oath I am, sinner. Rosa-Marie's calling out from heaven.'

'Heaven? She was a fuckin devil-worshipper.'

'Makes no difference to me. I'm on a mission from God.'

Warren shook his head. 'I'll see you when you get back.'

'See you then, Woz.'

The door closed, Les opened the fridge and organised two toasted ham and tomato sandwiches. He ate them with another cup of coffee, then took Warren's suitcase into his room, put it on the bed and started filling it with whatever he thought he'd need for the trip, including his mini-ghetto blaster. Halfway through packing, Les thought of something and looked at his watch. He walked out to the lounge room, found the number still sitting next to the phone and dialled Melbourne.

'Hello, Obelisk Bookshop. Kenneth Raymond speaking.'

'Yeah. It's Les Norton in Sydney. I ordered that book off you about Rosa-Marie Norton.'

'Oh yes, Mr Norton. I remember.'

'Don't bother sending it. I'm coming down to Melbourne on business. I'll pick it up.'

'Oh all right, Mr Norton.'

'I might even call in this afternoon.'

'No worries.'

'Exactly.' Les hung up and went back to his bedroom.

Norton finished packing, had a quick shower then changed into a pair of jeans, a denim shirt and his blue cotton bomber jacket. He checked to make sure he had his travel documents and everything else, put them in his overnight bag and rang a taxi. It didn't take long to arrive. Les had a last look around the house then locked up, took his luggage out to the taxi and gave the driver directions how to get to Travelabout in Clovelly and to wait outside. Gary was seated at his desk opposite the two girls in their red uniforms, looking his dapper self in a maroon shirt and a blue silk tie. He smiled his usual warm smile when Les walked in and sat down.

'So what have you got for me, Gary?' asked Les.

'Mate. For about an hour's notice I've got you the grouse. I've booked you into the Otway Plaza Resort in Lorne. Your own modern apartment just across from the beach. The Erskine Hotel's on the opposite corner.'

'Sounds all right,' said Les.

'And you pick up a Mitsubishi Magna from Thrifty at twelve o'clock on Sunday. You know where you're staying and all that?'

'Yeah. Eddie gave me my ticket last night. You wouldn't have a map showing how to get to Lorne, would you?'

'Sure have.' Gary handed Les two brochures and a folder. 'There you go. Everything you need's in there.'

Les took the folder and stood up. 'Thanks Gary.'

'Have a lovely time in Victoria, Les,' smiled Gary. 'The garden state.'

'No worries.' Les walked back to the taxi and they drove on to Kingsford Smith Airport.

There were no dramas checking in. Les bought the *Telegraph* and next thing he was in the Qantas Club, seated on a comfortable lounge chair, reading the paper, checking out the punters and stuffing himself with tea, sandwiches and little pieces of cake. Eventually, it was time to board QF 283 for Melbourne. Les grabbed a lolly on the way out and next thing he was sitting in business class sipping a mineral water.

By the time Les finished his mineral water the plane was airborne and a flight attendant handed him a menu. Les was that full of sandwiches and cake he didn't bother to look at it. Instead he went through the two maps Gary had given him. Lorne wasn't far from Melbourne. Through Geelong and follow the road past Torquay. Apollo Bay was a little further on. Fitzroy wasn't far from his hotel in Melbourne. He had plenty of time to pick up his book after he checked in. Les put his maps away, asked the attendant for another mineral water and took out the book he was reading. *Hell's Angel: The Life and Times of Sonny Barger and the Hell's Angels Motorcycle Club.* By the time the plane was getting ready to land, Les was convinced Sonny and his Hell's Angels were just a fun-loving bunch of lads who liked to take dope, sell dope, bash, stab and kill people and root sheilas and have barbecues. The only time Sonny ever got mildly upset was when somebody from another club stole his motorbike. So Sonny and his friends went over to the other club, bull-whipped each member one at a time, bashed them with spiked dog collars and broke their fingers with ballpeen hammers. Then stole their bikes, sold them and disbanded their club. The Angels even had a member called Norton Bob. How good was that? Les put his book away, got off the plane and walked to the baggage collection. Well, here I am in Melbourne, he thought, as he passed an advertisement for Four'N Twenty Pies.

At the bottom of the stairs were several limo drivers in black suits and caps holding signs, with one saying NORTON. The driver was in his forties and not as tall as Les, but very stocky, with a hard face and eyes like onyx ball bearings. His suit was immaculately cut and he was wearing three hundred dollar Mellers shoes.

'Are you Perry?' said Les.

'Yeah. You must be Les.' The limo driver offered a quick smile and shook Norton's hand. 'Let's get your luggage.'

They followed the other passengers around to the carousel. When they got there, Norton's bag was already on the conveyor behind several others.

Les went to pick it up when Perry took it easily and nodded for Les to follow him. They stepped through the sliding glass doors then turned left towards a car park. It was cloudy outside, but Les was surprised at the heat; much warmer than Sydney and punishingly humid. When they came to the shiny black BMW limousine, Les had a sweat up, however Perry still looked cool when he placed Norton's suitcase in the boot. He opened the back door and Les climbed into the beemer's air-conditioned comfort.

Les peered out the window as they drove along a flat stretch of open road and under a circled green and yellow sign saying CITY 43. Further on a sign to the left said BULLA RD and a blue sign said CITY SOUTH-EASTERN SUBURBS. Perry hardly spoke, but every now and again his mobile would ring. He'd listen, then whisper a few taciturn words. Watching in the rear-vision mirror, Les noticed the onyx ball bearings rarely moved more than a centimetre. They passed a long yellow girder jutting out over the road on the left, and on the right what looked like the bones of a gutted whale painted red. Les wasn't sure if it was modern art or something that had fallen off a Jumbo jet.

'Eddie tells me you'll be coming with us on Saturday night,' said Les.

Perry nodded. 'Yeah. I'll be doing the driving.' Then his phone rang again.

Further on it was houses and trams and Les noticed a long park on the left. 'Is that Albert Park?' he asked.

Perry shook his head. 'No, Royal Park. That's where the nuthouse is.'

'Right,' nodded Les.

Further on Les saw what looked like a bunch of hippies hanging around the front of a black and silver coffee shop. Perry said the university was just up the road. He pointed out an old cream and brown building as Melbourne Baths, then they were right in the centre of the CBD with its traffic and pedestrians. Perry swung into Collins Street and pulled up on the left outside a small lobby with a blue sign above saying SOUTHVILLE HOTEL.

'Here you are,' he said.

'Thanks.'

Les got out of the car. Perry opened the boot and took out his suitcase.

'I'll see you on Saturday night, Les,' he said.

'Yeah. See you then, Perry.'

The limo drove off and a porter in a blue vest took Norton's bag and details. Les perused Melbourne's hustle and bustle for a moment, then followed the attendant into a small lobby with two lifts. Les took the lift to reception and stepped out facing the windows to a bar and restaurant; reception was down to the left. Les walked up and put his folder on the desk. A polite young lady in blue got him to sign in, gave Les his swipe card and told him his bag would be up shortly. Les walked to another two lifts a little further on the left and noticed the hotel was built around several storeys of shopping arcade. The light pinged, Les took the lift to the twelfth floor and stepped out, almost running into a blonde woman in a yellow skirt and jacket, who seemed to be lost. She looked left then turned right; Les checked the room numbers arrowed on the wall and started following her.

The way to his room seemed to go on forever, and a metre or so in front of him, Les could sense the woman in yellow getting nervous. They went left, then right, left again, took another right then followed a long, quiet, deserted corridor. Norton's room was at the very end, the woman's was next door. Les passed her and swiped his lock while the woman fumbled with hers.

'I didn't mean to frighten you,' smiled Les. 'But this is my room.'

'Oh … that's all right,' said the woman, still trying to swipe her lock. 'I wasn't all that worried.'

Les caught her eye. She was around thirty, with a soft face, a thin nose, pouty red lips and green mascaraed eyes. 'Well, you're a better woman than I am, Gunga Din,' said Les. 'Because if I had a big ugly gorilla like me stalking me down a corridor, and no one around, I'd be absolutely shitting myself.'

The woman returned Norton's smile then gave him a quick once up and down before he stepped into his room.

Norton's softly lit room was quite nice. Blue carpet pushed against white walls and on the left a white bathroom faced a wardrobe with full-length mirrors. There was a bench table and TV opposite a queen-size bed with a blue douvet, and at the far end, a set of blue curtains were drawn across a window looking down on the arcade. Les tossed his overnight bag on the bed, got a mineral water from the bar fridge and checked out the in-house dining menu. He was thinking the beef tenderloin with Bernaise sauce didn't sound too bad, when there was a knock on the door and his suitcase arrived. The porter placed it on a rack next to the wardrobe, Les thanked him, gave him two bucks and he left.

Les decided to have a beer while he unpacked. He took off his bomber jacket, got a can of VB from the bar fridge and was sipping it as he started hanging a few things up when there was another knock on the door. It was the woman he'd followed down the corridor. She still had her yellow skirt on, but she'd taken her jacket off and was wearing a thin, lacy white top, unbuttoned enough to show a nice pair of boobs tucked into a thin, lacy white bra.

'Hello,' said Les. 'Is there something I can do for you?'

'Yes,' replied the woman. 'I can't seem to get my suitcase open. Could you please help me?'

'Sure.'

Les took his swipe card and followed the woman into her room. It was identical to Norton's except for a red carpet and a red douvet. Sitting on her bed was a brown suitcase the same size as his.

'What's your name?' asked the woman.

'Sonny,' replied Les.

'I'm Sonia.'

'Nice to meet you, Sonia.' Les ran his hand over the suitcase. 'Where's the key?' he asked.

'Here you are.'

Sonia handed Les a small key. Les clicked open the locks then ran the zipper around the sides and opened the suitcase. All Sonia's clothes were packed neatly inside, and sitting on top was a huge pink vibrator shaped like a cock, with two stubby balls at one end under a black plug for the batteries.

'Hello,' said Les. 'What's this for? Protection? Shit, I'd hate to get hit over the head with it.'

'No,' smiled Sonia, turning to Les. 'It's for enjoyment. And I know where I like to get hit with it.'

'Oh? And just where's that?' asked Les.

'Right about here.'

Sonia lifted up her skirt to reveal she was wearing no knickers. Just a neatly trimmed ted like a tiny brown pine cone. Les gave it a double, triple blink and shook his head.

'I don't quite know what to say, Sonia,' he smiled. 'But from where I'm standing, that looks good enough to eat.'

'Well what's stopping you, Sonny?' Sonia smiled back. 'You're not on a Jenny Craig diet, are you?'

'Are you kidding?' answered Les. 'I'd give Henry the Eighth a run for his money.'

Les pushed Sonia's suitcase off the bed, eased her back down on the douvet then buried his face in her business and went for it like a Rottweiler eating topside mince.

Sonia howled and shook and grabbed Les by the hair, pushing his face in harder. Les licked and sucked and it wasn't long before Sonia's gargling had turned Les on and Mr Wobbly wanted in on the action. Sonia spread her legs as wide as she could without dislocating her pelvis while Les undid his belt. Suddenly Sonia gave a squeal of rapture and emptied out into Norton's face. Les came up for air, and before Sonia knew it Les had his fly undone and Mr Wobbly in her mouth. Sonia didn't mind one bit and sucked Mr Wobbly hard enough to drain the marrow out of Norton's bones. Sweat running down his face, Les slipped a pillow under Sonia's behind then slipped Mr Wobbly in and started going for it. He figured Sonia had got her rocks off quick enough and now it was his turn. He gave a succession of solid thrusts, then stiffened his legs and emptied out in a panting, snorting blaze of glory. Sonia yelled some more, shook a few times then lay back on the douvet in a mess of damp hair and crumpled clothes. Well that was okay, thought Les, getting his breath back. Now, let's see how this thing works.

Les reached down and got Sonia's vibrator from her suitcase. A twist of the black plug at the end and it started pulsating smoothly in Norton's hand. Les slipped it in between Sonia's legs and started running it over her clit. Sonia closed her eyes and settled back against the pillows. Les zapped away for a while then slid the monster vibrator inside her. Sonia gave a little squeal of joy and Les started pumping away.

Sonia's eyes began to flutter, her tongue lolled over her lips and her face twisted into a look of excruciating ecstasy. Les pumped the vibrator with great gusto before Sonia finally let go a scream loud enough to wake the dead and got her rocks off again. Les dropped the vibrator back in her suitcase, wiped Mr Wobbly on her skirt before tucking him back into his jeans then stood up, leaving Sonia lying on the bed looking like she'd been washed up on a beach.

'Well, Sonia,' he said, zipping up. 'I might go back to my room and finish unpacking. If that's all right with you.'

'Unnhhh, ghhh. Okay.'

'If you have any more problems with your suitcase, or anything else, you know where to find me. Just knock.'

'All right Sonny,' muttered Sonia, without opening her eyes.

'Goodbye Sonia.' Les bent down and gave her a kiss goodbye.

'Bye Sonny.'

Les left her and let himself out.

Back in his air-conditioned room, the unfinished can of VB was still reasonably cold. Les downed it in one go and opened another. He had a mouthful, belched, then walked into the bathroom and splashed some water on his face before staring at himself in the mirror. What did Clover say after we read that old letter? She felt a sense of deja vu. *The last time I was in Melbourne I wasn't in my room five minutes and that motel owner — Mrs Bloody Perry — threw me up in the air. And if I remember right, she wasn't wearing any fuckin knickers either.* Les shook his head. *Buggered if I know.* He finished his beer, stripped off and got under the shower.

After he towelled off, Les put on a pair of blue cargoes, a Blues Festival T-shirt and his trainers. He stuck his Bugs Bunny cap on, dangled his sunglasses from off the neck of his T-shirt, then tossed his camera into his overnight bag and took the lift to reception and the other lift to the lobby. Outside it was still oppressively hot. Les was going to catch a taxi but decided on a tram. He turned to a porter standing just outside the lobby.

'Hey mate! How do I get a tram to Brunswick Street, Fitzroy?'

The porter pointed to a tram stop in the middle of the road. 'Over there. Take the 112. I think there's one coming now.'

'Thanks mate.'

Les jogged across the road as the tram pulled up and climbed aboard a side door. The tram lurched off as he grabbed for a strap only to land against a ticket machine dotted with coloured numbers and directions. After he regained his balance, Les looked blankly at the machine before pushing two dollars in a slot and pressing a button marked Section Two. He took his ticket and while he was strap hanging, watched the people fanning themselves with newspapers. *That's another bloody* thing, thought Les, the last time I was in Melbourne, it was bloody hot like this too. The tram swayed up Collins Street, angled around further on, then swung left into a wide thoroughfare flanked with side streets.

The busy road was full of brightly coloured clothing shops, record stores, coffee lounges, restaurants, bars and whatever. On one corner stood a drab-looking hotel and Les noticed a bar with flames on the window called The Bar With No Name. The street had an old-world charm about it and reminded Les of King Street, Newtown and Oxford Street, Paddington. He watched the numbers on the shop fronts, then alighted near a record store. The Obelisk Bookshop was back a little from a side street on the left, between a clothes store and a bottle shop. It had a blue-tiled front, purple doors and a white awning, and on either side of the front door were two large windows piled with books. A sign in one window said THE OBELISK BOOKSHOP. In the other, SECOND-HAND, OLD & RARE BOOKS. Les had a quick look at some of the titles and stepped inside.

The bookshop was deceptively big, with blue carpet, wood-panelled walls and high ceilings. Around the walls were rows and rows of ancient hardbacks and in the middle were tables full of books, surrounded by glass cabinets crammed with more old hardbacks. A doorway down to the left opened into another room and there was another room behind that. Just inside the door on the left was the counter and on the wall behind hung a framed print by Rosa-Marie Norton. Seated at a computer in a corner was a portly man with a young face and untidy dark hair. He was wearing a maroon shirt over a red T-shirt and as Les approached the counter, he looked up and smiled.

'Yes. Can I help you?'

'Are you Kenneth Raymond?' asked Les.

'That's me,' replied the owner.

'My name's Les Norton. I rang you from Sydney.'

'Oh yes. About the book on Rosa-Marie Norton. I have it right here.'

'Good on you,' said Les.

As the owner rummaged under the counter for the book, Les noticed a rack of Rosa-Marie Norton postcards. He picked out four and placed them on the counter.

'There you are,' said the owner, placing Norton's book on the counter.

'Unreal,' said Les, having a quick look. 'I'll take these postcards too.'

'No worries.'

'I'm Les anyway,' said Les, offering his hand.

The owner shook Norton's hand. 'Ken.'

'Nice to meet you, Ken.' Les watched as the owner put the postcards and book in a plastic bag. 'So you're an expert on Rosa-Marie, Ken.'

'Not really an expert,' replied the owner. 'But I've always admired her art. And I've almost finished a longer, more detailed biography on her.'

'Fair dinkum?' said Les. 'I enjoyed the book you've already

done. Actually I borrowed it from a library. And I had to get one for myself.'

'Thanks. Though it really doesn't do her justice,' said Ken.

'Oh, I don't know,' said Les lightly. 'But she certainly was something else.'

'Yes,' agreed Ken. 'She certainly was. So how did you find yourself interested in Rosa-Marie?'

'Through the name at first,' smiled Les. 'Plus I work in Kings Cross and I've read a few articles about her. I've never seen any of her paintings though.'

'No. Most of them are in private collections,' said Ken.

Les handed the owner his Visa card. 'Ken. Do you mind if I ask you a few questions?'

'No. Not at all.'

'Rosa-Marie sold some paintings to a bishop. Is that right?'

'Yes. Bishop Thomas Elsworthy of Prahran. He bought them to show his parishioners exactly what the devil's work was all about. Then he threw them in the Yarra.'

'Was there ever any mention of a priest? Father Bernard Shipley? From Lorne?'

Ken shook his head. 'Not that I know of.'

'Okay,' said Les. 'Ken. You know when they were going to burn her paintings that time?'

'Yes. I certainly do.'

'I read where three of them went missing.'

Ken looked surprised. 'If they did, it's news to me. Where did you read that, Les?'

'Oh, just an article in a little paper up the Cross,' replied Les.

Ken shook his head. 'I doubt it. But if it is true, you'd never know. The police and the authorities at the time would never admit it.'

'Yeah, right,' nodded Les. 'Shit! She had some dramas with the police, didn't she? Especially a Detective McBride. Why was that?'

'Mainly because Rosa was considered a threat to the conservative establishment at the time,' said Ken. 'But McBride was high up in the vice squad and just hated Rosa and all her friends. He came to her house one morning with a warrant and Rosa was upstairs in the bathroom. She looked out to see who it was, and emptied a chamber pot over him.'

'She what?' said Les. 'Emptied a piss pot over him?'

'That's right. And when they charged her with assault police, she beat it. She said she was about to flush the contents. And when she looked out the window to see who it was downstairs, the po accidentally slipped on the sill.'

'She sounds like my kind of woman,' chuckled Les.

'She was something else all right,' said Ken. 'There was an American artist called Jacques San,' he continued.

'Yeah. Who was he?' asked Les.

'No one knew for sure,' said Ken. 'He wasn't in Australia long and claimed he was from New York. But he was an awful drunk and totally in love with Rosa-Marie. He grabbed a carving knife at one of her wild parties one night and threatened Rosa with it, yelling he was Jacques the Ripper.'

'Jacques the Ripper?' said Les.

'Rosa hit him over the head with a bottle,' laughed Ken. 'Took the knife off him and said, "No you're not. You're Jacques the Dribbler. Now fuck off." And he did. Back to America with all his paintings. Broken-hearted.'

'Fair dinkum? You said in your book, though, she had a way with men,' said Les.

'They absolutely fell at her feet, Les,' replied Ken.

'Would you know who two artists were, Ken, called Normo and Dobbo?' asked Les.

Ken thought for a moment. 'Can't say I do,' he replied. 'There was a coffee shop in Kings Cross called The Dobruja, that hung some of Rosa's paintings. Rosa and her friends used to call it "Dob's" for short. But I don't know of any artists by that name. Though Rosa would have known scores of artists that just came and went.'

'And she never mentioned a Father Shipley?'

'No. Not to my knowledge.'

'She had an exhibition in Melbourne, too,' said Les.

'Yes,' said Ken. 'It was an absolute disaster. Christ! She thought she had troubles in Sydney. They almost burnt her at the stake down here. She had the absolute audacity to show a woman's pubic hair in her paintings.'

'How disgraceful,' chided Les. 'And what happened when it folded?'

'Rosa just disappeared. Till she was arrested in Apollo Bay.'

'Yeah. For pissing in the street.'

'Actually, she collapsed and wet herself,' said Ken. 'But being who she was, they charged her with drunk and disorderly. There was a lot of rubbish written about her.'

'What was she doing in Apollo Bay?' asked Les.

'Probably staying with some old school friends and getting away from everything after what happened in Melbourne. She went to school in Apollo Bay where her father worked for a company laying telegraph cables. He was an engineer.'

'Right,' Les nodded slowly. 'And not long after that she fell out of a tram in Sydney and broke her neck.'

'Yes. Quite sad really,' replied Ken quietly.

'Yes it is,' agreed Les.

Les enjoyed talking to Kenneth Raymond. He was good-humoured and patently enthused in his world of old books and Rosa-Marie Norton. Plus he liked to share his knowledge with people. Especially any who were like-minded.

Ken turned to the painting hanging on the wall behind the counter. 'Poor Rosa. Apart from being a trifle eccentric, Les, she was just a brilliant artist. Years before her time.'

'A female van Gogh,' said Les.

'Yes. That's as good a description as any,' agreed Ken.

'And like van Gogh, she had trouble selling her paintings.'

'Yes. Ironic isn't it,' said Ken. 'And would you believe, Les, one of her paintings sold in Brisbane recently for one hundred and fifty thousand dollars.'

Les gave Ken a double blink. 'How ... much did you say, Ken?'

'One hundred and fifty thousand dollars.'

There was a movement at the doorway and an elderly lady dressed in all white walked in. She looked at Les then turned to Ken standing behind the counter.

'Can I help you?' Ken asked her.

'I'm after a book of Beardsley prints,' the woman said.

Ken pointed to one corner in the shop. 'Have a look over there, under B. I'll be with you in a moment.'

'Thank you.'

Les watched the woman shuffle off then turned to the owner. 'Well, Ken,' he said. 'I'd better let you get back to work. Thanks for your help and everything.'

'No worries, Les. It was a pleasure,' smiled Ken. 'How long before you go back to Sydney?'

'Tomorrow,' replied Les.

'Call in again if you've got time. I'll be closing early tomorrow. We're having a soiree here tomorrow night.'

'A soiree?' said Les.

'Yes. Rare books and documents,' replied Ken. 'I've got one of Governor Phillip's diaries. Sketches by Banks the botanist. Some original Henry Lawson manuscripts. All that sort of thing. Very wine and cheese and a little social. But,' Ken shrugged and rubbed his hands together, 'it should turn a nice dollar.'

'Oh. Well good luck with it.' Les shook the owner's hand again. 'Nice to have met you, Ken. I'll see you again.'

'You, too, Les. Enjoy yourself in Melbourne.'

'I have so far.' Les put the plastic bag in his overnight bag and left Ken to attend to the woman in white.

There was a sudden screeching of brakes and the irritated beeping of a car horn as Les almost walked under a taxi crossing the street. He gave the cab driver a sheepish look and, still doing mental arithmetic, joined the other pedestrians walking along Brunswick Street. According to Norton's reckoning, 150,000 × 3 equalled 450,000. His nutty idea didn't sound so nutty after all. And that old bishop tossed two of her paintings in the river. One thing for sure, thought Les, when I get to Lorne, I'll find out what happened to those bloody paintings. Even if I've got to knock on every door in the joint.

Still plotting and scheming, Les walked on in the heat. Neatly dressed people were coming and going or seated in swish restaurants and coffee shops eating excellent cuisine while they sipped bottles of fine wine. Jewellery shops, music shops and clothes stores appeared to be doing good business and Les got another angle on Brunswick Street and its old-world charm. Double Bay with grunge. He stopped outside a trendoid clothing shop playing house music loud enough to give you internal bleeding and wiped the sweat from his eyes while he debated whether to take a couple of photos of Brunswick Street, when a tram suddenly clanged to a halt in front of him. There was a pool back at the hotel and more cold beers in the bar fridge. Les climbed aboard and when he was flung against the ticket machine after the tram took off, found another two dollars for his fare.

Back at the hotel Les changed into his Speedos and shorts and took the lift down to the swimming pool. The open-air pool area was at the end of another long stretch of corridors overlooking the arcade and Les had it all to himself. The pool was only small, but there was a sauna, and a weight station with mirrors stood on a floor of astro-turf. He left his towel on a banana-lounge and started pushing and lifting various pulleys, then did a set of crunches and sit-ups. When he finished, Les gulped down several plastic cups of water then flopped his sweaty body into the pool and just drifted.

Norton rolled on his back and spurted a mouthful of water into the air. Well, he thought, it's kind of hard to believe I'm in Melbourne. And it's harder to believe I've been tossed up in the air already. I wonder what Sonia's story is? But what a nice bloke that Ken Raymond was. Bad luck he couldn't lay any more informaish on me about those paintings. But at least now I've got my own book on Rosa-Marie Norton. Les closed his eyes, duck-dived to the bottom of the shallow pool and came up again. So what will I do now? I could go and check out the punters and the office girls. But I don't really feel like sitting in the heat and car fumes drinking coffee. And I don't feel like plonking my arse down in a smoky bar and getting half pissed either. It's not getting any earlier. Why don't I stay in my air-conditioned room, have a few cool ones, then order up some food and watch TV? Later on take a taxi or the 'bread and jam' back up to Brunswick Street and see what goes on there at night? I won't have a late one, though. I'd better be on the ball when Eddie arrives tomorrow. Les flopped around in the pool till a shy young Japanese couple joined him, followed by a pale, flabby businessman with a comb-over like several tufts of flattened roadkill sitting on his head. Norton smiled, let them have the pool and returned to his room.

After a shave and a shower, Les got back into his shorts and T-shirt, got a Crown Lager from the bar fridge and looked at the in-room dining menu. He went for a caesar salad, braised lamb shanks with veg and mash, sticky date pudding with butterscotch sauce and ice-cream plus coffee and rolls. Room service said that shouldn't be long. Les finished his first beer then had a bottle of Heineken and switched the TV on. By the time he'd finished his Heineken the food arrived. Les tipped the girl two bucks and ripped in.

There wasn't much on TV. Les checked the in-house movies and settled on *Monsters Inc.* For an animated movie, it was an absolute hoot and the take-outs at the end were an even bigger hoot. But the look on the little girl's face when the big monster frightened her, almost brought a tear to Norton's eye. Les got involved in the movie and by the time it finished, he'd knocked over another Heineken plus three mini-bottles of vodka and bourbon. He switched off the TV, pushed his dinner tray into the corridor then changed into a pair of Levis and the light blue T-shirt Grace had given him with a dark blue, short-sleeved hemp shirt over the top. He gave himself a last detail, got his camera and took the lifts down to the foyer. There was a taxi waiting out the front. Les piled in and before he knew the driver let him out in Brunswick Street, opposite the old hotel he'd noticed earlier.

The street had really come to life now. There were people everywhere and when Les walked into the large bar area of the hotel it was packed. He squeezed through the crowd, ordered a delicious and checked out the punters. They were all around thirty, casually dressed and what you'd expect to see in any popular hotel, anywhere in Australia. Two dumpy girls, one wearing a Union Jack T-shirt, the other a black vest and matching headband, commented on Norton's T-shirt. They were English tourists and pleasant to talk to. But it was just too hot and noisy in the hotel. Les bought them a drink and took their photo, then said he might catch up with them later and drifted off into the night.

After that Les roamed from bar to bar. They were all good, the people were friendly, plenty of attractive girls and the drinks were okay. There was no hassles about having to eat. You just walked in, had a delicious or three and walked out again. Billy was right when he said Melbourne had a good night scene.

Les lost count of how many bourbons he had roaming from bar to bar. But he was getting quite a glow up when he wandered into one that reminded him of Florida, and the old bordello they'd turned into a bar in Siestasota. Crystal chandeliers sparkled from under a red ceiling and gilt-edged mirrors and old paintings decorated the maroon walls. Antique furniture and plush velvet curtains added to the bar's elegance, and near the entrance was a beautiful fish tank surrounded by statues of Grecian women supporting urns filled with healthy indoor plants. Les got another delicious and noticed three people, two men and an older woman, sitting on a red velvet lounge under a frilly white lamp. One man, wearing a gold lamé suit and a pink shirt, had his face painted like a geisha and a pair of red horns on his head. The other man was wearing a multi-coloured kaftan and a snug, brightly feathered hat. His face was painted white also, except for a wide area across his eyes squared off in light blue and edged with red. The woman was wearing an emerald green crushed velvet dress adorned with layers of coloured beads. Les couldn't help himself. He walked straight up, said he was from Sydney and would they mind if he took their photo? They were only too delighted. Les snapped off two photos, thanked them, took a couple of the fish tank then finished his delicious and left.

Les ended up in The Bar With No Name. It was smaller and quieter than the others with comfortable old lounges and soft lights. Les got one more delicious and as it was going down, decided it was time to sling his hook. He told himself earlier he'd go easy. But Brunswick Street was such a good scene, what could he do? He finished his delicious and walked outside to get a taxi just as a tram pulled up. This'll do, thought Les, and climbed aboard, grabbing hold of a strap before he got speared into the ticket machine. While he fumbled around for a two-dollar coin, Les checked things out. There was only a handful of people seated up front. But sprawled at the rear were ten members of a pseudo-American street gang, dressed in baggy jeans, sloppy T-shirts, Snoopy Dog jackets, caps on back to front and gym boots. They were all around eighteen and full of attitude, and the only difference Les could tell from street gangs he'd seen in Sydney was this lot had pimplier faces and paler skin. A tall dark-haired one seated in front with his legs stuck out wearing baggy black jeans and a St Kilda FC cap, appeared to be the leader. A couple of the gang gave Les an indifferent once up and down, then ignored him. Les gave the gang a desultory once over and decided to ignore them as well. He fumbled around some more for a two-dollar coin, then didn't bother. If he got pinched for fare evasion, stiff shit.

The tram rattled and clanged on into the night, some people got off, then two stops later another street gang got on. They were dressed much the same as the gang already on the tram and they also appeared to have a tall dark-haired one as leader; only he was wearing baggy denim shorts and a Hawthorn FC cap. The two gang leaders made eye contact and from the 'giddy-up' it was obvious there was no love lost between the two gangs.

The leader of the first gang leapt to his feet. 'What the fuck are you doin' here?' he scowled.

'Fuck you cunt,' the leader of the second gang scowled back.

Les remembered Eddie once saying that when it came to hostilities and violence in Melbourne, they didn't muck around with Mexican stand-offs. The leader of the second gang aimed up a right-cross and punched the leader of the first gang straight in the mouth, splitting his lip. St Kilda cap cursed and immediately came back with a straight left, giving Hawthorn cap a bloody nose. Once the reception formalities were over, it was choose your partner and dance.

The two gangs ripped into each other at the back of the tram in a fury of punches, kicks, knees and elbows, with Norton hanging from a strap in the middle. They were all evenly matched and although they weren't inflicting any serious injuries, they were giving each other plenty of split lips, bloody noses, black eyes and ripped clothes. Hey, this is all right, thought Les, and whipped out his camera. He got off two photos when instinct made him turn around just as a member of the second gang threw a quick right and punched him in the jaw. It stung and Les didn't like it. In return, Les threw a wicked short right that was nothing like any of the other punches being thrown in the tram. It slammed into the kid's face, knocking out all his front teeth, before dumping him on his backside out cold. Half full of bourbon and livened up from the whack on the jaw, Les thought he might as well join in the festivities, too. He slung his camera round his neck, hung off the strap with one hand and started belting gang members from both sides with the other; they were all too busy fighting to see who was doing all the damage.

Les sunk a right into another kid, pulverising his bony jaw. The unfortunate gang member slid down the one he was fighting, who looked up, straight into another short right from Les that smashed the kid's nose across his face and dumped him out cold on the floor of the tram, along with the others. Two gang members were wrestling around in front of Les. Les sunk a short right into one's ribs and smiled as he felt them crack under his fist and heard a howl of pain from the hapless gang member. The kid slumped to the floor gasping for breath as Les changed hands on the strap and smashed a left hook into the other kid's face ripping apart his lips. Blood dribbling down his chin, the kid bounced off the gang members fighting behind him into another left from Norton that opened his right eyebrow to the bone. Les watched him fall to the floor then punched another gang member in the kidneys. The kid snapped to his feet, Les swapped hands on the strap again and decked him from behind with a right backfist, dislocating the kid's neck.

Les didn't feel like a hero thumping into the gang members. Quite the opposite if anything. They were all too busy fighting each other to know what was going on and he was bigger than any of them. But he and Billy had seen smartarse street gangs strutting around Bondi and Kings Cross causing trouble, and they always felt like sorting a few of them out. So although it mightn't have felt brave flattening one gang member after another, shit, it felt good.

Les swung around on the strap and sunk his right boot into one kid's balls then brought his knee up into his face, smashing his nose and knocking out several teeth. A spray of blood hit Norton and as the gang member hit the deck, his opponent looked up and saw who did it. Les poked his fingers in the kid's eyes, then kneed him in the balls. From side on Les left-hooked another gang member in the ear. Seeing stars, the kid wobbled and reached out with his left hand to hold onto a seat. Les grabbed the gang member's arm, brought his right knee up and broke it at the elbow. The kid yelped then fell down amongst the other gang members moaning and bleeding all over the floor.

The people up front had been yelling for the driver to stop the tram. But he kept going and the tram lurched down Collins Street. Les decked another three gang members and the fighting began to slow down, except for the two gang leaders still going for it in the aisle hammer and tongs. Les grabbed the pair of them by the scruff of the neck, pulled them apart and banged their faces together, smashing both their noses. Then he whacked their heads together, splitting Hawthorn cap's scalp open before dropping them on the floor with the others. The remaining gang members stopped fighting and stared at Les like he was The Thing when it smashed through the door of the ice station in the old movie he saw with Warren. Les looked down at the blood and broken bodies lying around him on the floor and figured it might be a good time to split. He turned to the gang members still staring at him in horror and took out his camera.

'Righto fellahs. How about a smile.'

Les took several photos of the gang members left on their feet and the ones lying on the floor, when the tram came to a stop near Melbourne Town Hall. The door opened, Les climbed over the bodies and stepped out. Coming up the road he could see police uniforms. Les went round the back of the tram and quickly crossed Collins Street, ducked over Swanston then hurried down Collins Street to the hotel, past the porter standing outside the lobby and into a waiting lift. The bar upstairs was empty, the woman at reception had her back turned and Les stepped into the lift. A few minutes later he was safely in his room.

Les didn't need any more booze. He got a bottle of mineral water and had a look at himself in the bathroom mirror. Apart from a few sore knuckles and a bruise on his jaw, he didn't have a scratch on him. But blood had spattered down his jeans and onto his T-shirt. Les stripped off, threw them in the shower and got in. He rinsed out all the blood then gave himself a good scrub and hung his clothes up on the pull-out line above the bath. After changing into a clean pair of jox and a T-shirt, he sat down on the bed, yawned and stared at the floor. Now that he'd settled down, Les realised how much booze he'd drunk. He yawned again then turned out the lights and got under the bed covers. That's another bloody thing, he pondered as he shoved his head into the pillows. The last time I was down here and caught a tram at night, I ended up in a fight. Les gave his head a shake. I don't know. It's got me stuffed. Next thing, he was snoring.

Les woke up late the next morning and a bit seedy. He climbed out of bed, got a bottle of mineral water from the bar fridge and switched on the electric jug. He saw his camera sitting next to the TV, rubbed his jaw and half smiled when he recollected the previous night's events. After getting cleaned up, he climbed into his Speedos and old shorts and made a cup of instant coffee, which went down well with a hotel biscuit. A run to sweat out last night's drink would have gone well. Instead, Les went down to the pool area, did a few sit-ups and stretches by himself and had a sauna. When he got out, he could smell the stale booze trickling down his body before he splashed into the pool. Starting to feel half human again, Les went back to his room and changed into his blue cargoes and a white Rip Curl T-shirt, ready for breakfast. He got his cap and sunglasses, tossed his overnight bag across his shoulder and caught the lift down to the lobby.

It was hot outside and Melbourne's CBD had come to life. Cars and trams were honking and clanging along the streets and crowds of people were cruising the footpaths. Over from the hotel was a small arcade. Les wandered across the road and walked inside. It was mainly clothing or jewellery stores before it angled right into a narrow lane with several cafes on either side. Les chose one with small round marble tables and wicker chairs outside and ordered scrambled eggs, bacon and a flat white from a waiter in a red T-shirt. The food arrived and there was plenty of it. But the chef had scrambled the eggs in an oily pan and they didn't go down too well in the heat. While he was eating, Les decided not to tell Eddie about what had happened last night or about the girl in the hotel. Knowing Eddie, he'd probably start banging on her door wanting a piece of the action, and it wouldn't have been any laughing matter if Les had got picked up after what happened on the tram. He had another coffee to cut the greasy eggs, paid the bill and walked back round to Collins Street. He had a quick look around, adjusted his cap and sunglasses and decided to spend a leisurely day shopping and wandering around the CBD before Eddie arrived.

It didn't take long for Les to understand why Melbourne was said to be the best place to shop in Australia. As well as the enormous variety and the quality, the streets and footpaths were wide and level, making it a breeze to get around. He walked down Elizabeth Street and found where he had to pick up his car the next day, and on the way back stopped at a small art gallery where some black T-shirts with a colourful little devil on the front caught his eye. Les bought one for himself and one each for Warren, Grace and Clover. A little further on was a coffee shop specialising in fruit juices. Les took a seat and ordered a Brazilian Special. It was pink and delicious with a hint of ginger and mint. He had two. He roamed through a huge department store into the shirt section. The best ones were around two hundred dollars, yet they were all made in China. Someone must be cleaning up, mused Les and bought six at a clothes store on a corner where you paid for two and got one for free.

In the heat, Les drank more fruit juice then found a newsagency selling Sydney papers. So he had a bowl of won ton in a noodle shop and a read. He watched a busker in a turban going for it on some strange instrument in a wide boulevard with a statue of a purse on the footpath. He handed his camera to some Japanese tourists and got his photo taken in the middle of three skinny bronze statues of three weird men with briefcases. A few slices of ham and some potato salad from David Jones food hall, a perv and a takeaway coffee later, and Les couldn't believe the day was shot. He had another fruit juice from a shop across the road from the bronze statues and went back to the hotel to put away his purchases and get out of the heat. His bed had been made and they'd restocked the bar fridge. Les opened a mineral water and started unpacking when the phone rang. It was Eddie.

'Eddie. What's happening mate?' said Les.

'Not much,' replied Eddie. 'I'm here. But I've got a couple of things to sort out. I'll be about an hour late.'

'No worries. This is the earliest you've been late for ages anyway.'

'Yeah, right,' said Eddie. 'So what have you been up to?'

'Not much,' lied Les. 'Had a couple of drinks last night. Did a bit of shopping today. I'm hanging in ready for tonight.'

'Good. We might have dinner at the hotel and I'll tell you what's going on then.'

'Okay. So I'll see you in about an hour. In my room?'

'Yep. See you then.'

Les hung up and had a mouthful of mineral water. An hour, he mused. When I put all this away, I've got time for another swim. Les finished unpacking then put his Speedos and old shorts on and caught the lift down to the pool. Again he had it on his own.

Les flopped around just cooling off. When he'd had enough he went back to his room, showered and shaved then changed into his spare jeans, trainers and a yellow polo shirt. He put his ghetto blaster on and got some station playing golden oldies, and with Norman Greenbaum pumping out 'Spirit in the Sky', lay back on the bed and started reading *Hell's Angel*. He was into a part about a fun-loving member of the club called Doug 'The Thug' Orr, who could snap a pair of handcuffs and shot his girlfriend through the head before they put him in the Napa Valley Madhouse, when there was a knock on the door. It was Eddie, wearing black jeans and a grey shirt with a button-down collar.

'Hello mate,' said Les. 'Come in.'

'Fuck! How hot is it?' said Eddie stepping into Norton's room.

'Yeah. I've been hitting the hotel pool. You want a beer or something?'

Eddie shook his head and pulled up a chair. 'I wouldn't mind one down the bar before we have dinner.'

'Suits me,' said Les, sitting down on the bed.

'So you met Perry,' said Eddie.

'Yeah. He doesn't say much,' replied Les. 'What time's he picking us up?'

'Nine. Out the front.'

Les glanced at his watch. 'We got plenty of time.' He gave Eddie a thin smile. 'So what's the story?'

'We're going to sort Latte out in Fitzroy. It's not far from here.'

'Fitzroy? I was up there yesterday,' said Les. 'Whereabouts in Fitzroy?'

'At a bookshop in Brunswick Street.'

'A … bookshop?' said Les.

'Yeah,' answered Eddie. 'Called the Obelisk. It's right up one end.'

'I thought we were going to an art exhibition?'

'So did I. But they're selling a whole lot of rare books and stuff. Shithead's going to be in there with a dodgy plan of Burley Griffin. I got the listings.'

'Shit! Won't somebody recognise us?' said Les.

'I got disguises,' said Eddie. He peered quizzically at Les. 'You look a bit worried, big fellah. What's up?'

'Oh nothing, Eddie. I was expecting an art gallery. That's all. You know, more room to get around. A bookshop sounds a bit … poky.'

'All the better,' said Eddie. 'I've checked this place out. Most of the action's going to be in the front room. We just run in. Do the biz. And run out again. Easy.'

'Yeah okay. If you say so, Eddie.'

Eddie looked at his watch. 'Anyway. Let's go and have a beer and a bite to eat. By then it'll be time to go.'

'Okay.' Les stood up. 'What I got on do?'

'Sensational.' Eddie followed Les and they got the lift down to the lobby.

The bar was roomy and bright and predominantly red and cream with red furnishings and a black and white mosaic floor.

Windows on the left overlooked the arcade, the restaurant was on the right and the wooden bar faced the lobby area. Seated around the bar and tables was a small crowd of neatly dressed men and women. Eddie got two pots of VB and they chose a table with red velvet lounge chairs in a corner looking down on the arcade. They clinked glasses then took a sip each. Les tried not to appear trepidatious. But having to belt Latte in the bookshop had thrown him out. Ken the owner would have to be blind not to recognise him.

'Okay Eddie,' said Les. 'Fill me in a bit more about tonight. And what are these disguises?'

Eddie rubbed his hands together. 'Who's got everybody shitting themselves these days?' he asked Les.

'I don't know,' shrugged Les. 'The taxation department? Marilyn Manson? Osama bin liner or whatever his name is.'

'Right on, baby,' said Eddie. 'So we're going in dressed as Muslim terrorists.'

'We're what?' said Les.

'We're getting done up as Muslims. Perry's got the Arab gear waiting for us in his garage. And two Groucho masks.'

Les stared at Eddie in disbelief. 'Eddie. You are joking, aren't you?'

Eddie took a sip of beer and looked directly at Norton. 'Les. You can't tell me, when Saddam Hussein sucks on a cigar in those horn-rim glasses and his moustache, he doesn't look like Groucho.'

Les thought for a moment. 'A bit,' he conceded from over his beer.

Eddie raised his glass. 'There you go. What did I tell you?'

'So we're going to run into the bookshop and bash Latte. Wearing tea towels on our heads and Groucho masks.' Les closed his eyes. 'I don't believe it.'

'Hey. We're not going to bash him,' said Eddie. 'I'm going to cut his fingers off.'

'You're what?' said Les.

'Well, I got to get that pinky ring off his finger,' gestured Eddie. 'This is the quickest way. And while I'm at it, I'll cut his other one off too. You just hold him.'

'Shit!'

'Besides,' said Eddie, 'if we give him a hiding, it's only going to heal up. This is a little more permanent.' Eddie smiled and wiggled his eyebrows. 'See how Latte likes sucking on his lattes with a couple of Manly Warringahs missing.'

Les shook his head. 'Eddie,' he said, 'you are a deadset evil little cunt.'

'No I'm not,' replied Eddie. 'I'm a force technician.' He finished his beer and nodded to the bar. 'Your shout, dude.'

Les got another two pots, Eddie went to the gents and saw the head waiter about a table on the way back. They drank their beers and talked about this and that. Eddie said there were a couple more things he wanted Les to do when they hit the bookshop; he'd explain when they were getting changed in Perry's garage. They finished their beers and went round to the restaurant.

The head waiter, wearing a high-collared white shirt and black vest, was Tim. Tim was very friendly and sat them down at a polished wooden table near the centre of the restaurant, across from a section of curved windows overlooking Collins Street. The restaurant was almost full and softly lit, with tasteful furnishings and the same mosaic floor pattern as the bar. Next to where they were seated, a huge vase of flowers sat on a solid wooden table that doubled underneath as a wine rack. Les went for a dozen oysters and the veal cutlet on citrus risotto. Eddie had a dozen oysters and Moroccan spiced chicken on mashed potato with coriander salsa. They drank mineral water with their meal; no sweets, just coffee. The food was delicious and very filling with crispy bread rolls, and they were too busy enjoying it to say a great deal. But they did agree that although twenty-five thousand dollars was just a bet to Price, Latte Lindsey must be living in another world if he thought he could get away with dudding a member of Price's family for even a postage stamp. Latte should have stuck to robbing people he knew. They finished their coffees, charged the meal to Les's room then gave the waiter a twenty and caught the lift down to the foyer. They were there a minute when the BMW limo pulled up out the front. A porter opened the rear doors for them and they climbed in the back and drove off.

'How are you, Perry?' said Les.

'I'm all right, Les,' replied the driver, glancing at him in the rear-vision mirror. 'How's yourself?'

'Good.'

'Perry's is only a few minutes over the bridge from here,' said Eddie.

'Righto,' nodded Les.

Not a great deal was said in the limo. Perry and Eddie exchanged a few words. Les stared out the window at the passing cars and darkened buildings not having a clue where he was, except the water below when they crossed Queens Bridge must be part of the Yarra. They went under a freeway then down a long wide street flanked with neat houses, flats, small hotels and busy restaurants. They turned into a smaller street and pulled up in front of a wide cream-painted double garage under a red-brick two-storey house with an enclosed verandah. The garage door on the left swung up, the limo glided inside and a light came on when the door closed. They got out and Les had a look around.

Perry's garage was neat and tidy with white-washed concrete walls. A double fridge sat in one corner, there were drawers and cupboards and a long white workbench ran along one wall beneath a tool rack. A meat hook hung from the ceiling and in one corner was a battered green punchbag. In the other parking bay on the right sat a blue Holden sedan with tinted windows.

'Do a bit of bag work, Perry?' said Les, nodding to the punchbag in the corner.

'Perry used to be amateur welterweight champ of Victoria. Didn't you mate,' said Eddie.

Eddie threw a couple of left jabs at Perry. The limo driver weaved expertly and countered Eddie with a left and right to the mid-section.

'A while ago,' smiled Perry.

'Not that long ago, if you ask me,' said Les.

Perry took off his coat and cap and Les followed Eddie over to the workbench. Sitting near a lathe were two neat piles of clothes and two Groucho masks. Eddie picked up one pile of clothing and handed it to Les.

'Righto Fred Astaire,' said Eddie. 'Here's your top hat and tails.'

Eddie handed Les a red and white cotton headscarf edged with small white tassles, plus a ring of thick black cord that doubled over and secured it to your head. Along with a long-sleeved collarless brown cotton shirt that reached the floor and buttoned up to your chin.

Les turned to Eddie. 'What the …?'

'The head gear's called a kofia. The shirt's a dajdaja,' said Eddie. 'Put it on over what you're wearing.'

Les was sceptical. 'Yeah righto,' he said.

Les slipped the dajdaja on and was surprised how easily it fitted over what he was wearing. He buttoned it up then put on the kofia, doubling the ring of black cord above his forehead.

'And now,' said Eddie. 'The piece de resistance.'

Eddie handed Les one of the Groucho masks. He'd tinted the rubber nose darker, glued hair to the plastic moustache and changed the horn rims into sunglasses. Les put it on and turned to Perry, who was now wearing a hooded black tracksuit top and a blue baseball cap.

'How do I look, Perry?' asked Les. 'I feel like a nice Beechams Pill.'

'Have a look.'

Perry opened a wardrobe near the fridge. Les had a look in the full-length mirror behind the door and was pleasantly surprised. The Groucho mask didn't look that ridiculous and with the sunglasses hiding his eyes and the kofia masking both sides of his face, his own mother wouldn't have recognised him. Les stepped back from the mirror.

'Not too bad, I suppose. All I need is a pair of white shoes and I'd pass for a second-hand camel dealer.'

Eddie put his outfit on and walked over for a look in the mirror. He had the same red and white patterned kofia, but his dajdaja was white.

'Pretty good if you ask me,' said Eddie. 'What do you reckon, Perry?'

'Terrific,' said Perry. 'Laurel and Hardy of the Sahara.'

Perry closed the wardrobe door and Eddie turned to Les. 'Righto Les,' he said. 'Here's our game plan. As soon as we spot Latte, I'll give him a whack in the guts to settle him down. You grab him by his right arm and pin it down palm up on the nearest table full of books.'

'Okay,' nodded Les.

'I'll lop his right little finger off first and get the ring. Then you grab his left arm and pin it down. And I'll lop the other finger off and grab his watch.'

'Sweet as a nut.'

'Now all the while,' said Eddie, 'I'm going to be yelling and screaming and carrying on like a madman.'

'That's nothing new,' said Les.

'And I want you to just keep yelling out Aieee! Aieee!'

'Aiee? Aiee?' said Les.

'Yeah. You've seen those ratbags on TV when they're all running around screaming. Death to Israel. Death to America.'

'Yeah,' nodded Les.

'Same as that,' said Eddie. 'Only louder.'

'AIEEEE! AIEEE!' howled Les.

'That's it Les,' said Eddie. 'Beautiful.'

'AIEEE! AIEE!'

Perry opened a drawer and handed Eddie a cleaver. It was small but quite heavy with a black plastic handle. 'Here you are, Eddie,' he said.

Eddie slipped it under his dajdaja. 'Thanks mate.'

Perry gave them both a quick once up and down. 'You right?' he said.

'Yeah. Let's get going,' answered Eddie.

'Why not,' said Les. 'Aiee! Aiee!'

Perry opened the doors of the Holden and got behind the wheel. Les and Eddie piled in the back. The other garage door swung open and they drove off into the night. They went back over the river, through the CBD, and next thing they were following the traffic down busy Brunswick Street. The Obelisk Bookshop was all lit up when they went past, there was a reasonable crowd inside, and standing at the door was a dark-haired woman in a black dress meeting and greeting. Perry swung the Holden into the side street ahead on the left and stopped in a no parking zone on the corner with the engine running.

'Righto,' he said. 'Good luck, boys. I'll wait right here.'

'We won't be long,' said Eddie.

'Two snips of a lamb's tail,' smiled Les. 'Aiee! Aiee!'

They got out of the car and walked towards the bookshop. There were people around and Les expected Saudi Arabia's answer to Laurel and Hardy would get some strange looks. But compared to the two Grand Viziers whose photo Les had taken the night before, they were small potatoes and barely rated a second glance. Sitting on the footpath just before the old bookshop was a skinny old white dog with a happy slobbery face. It saw them and started to wag its tail.

'Hello, old fellah,' said Eddie as they strode past.

'G'day mate,' said Les and gave the old dog a pat on its bony head.

They reached the bookshop and the woman on the door must have thought they were wealthy Middle Eastern buyers; she ushered them inside with a slight bow of her head.

'Good evening, gentlemen,' she said.

'Yashmak,' grunted Eddie.

'Shalom,' smiled Les.

The front room of the Obelisk looked very wine and cheese, exactly as Ken the owner had said. The men were all wearing well-cut suits, the women were dressed in style, and everybody was sipping on a glass of white wine while a string quartet creaked out Mozart in the next room. Ken the owner was standing on the left in a dark blue suit with a red tie talking to a woman in yellow. Les gave a double blink from behind the sunglasses. It was Sonia, the girl next door. The owner saw Eddie and Les, gave them a second look then turned away, knowing it was impolite to stare. Over to the right, wearing a three-piece grey suit and a regimental striped tie windsor-knotted into a blue shirt with a white collar, was Latte Lindsey. There was no mistaking his egg head, jowly face and oily smile as he escorted a woman in a red floral dress across the room. He was walking measuredly, his left hand flat across his stomach and his right arm bent by his side with his index finger drooped towards the floor. He looked like the Duke of Bedford strolling through his drawing room about to take tea with the Duchess of Crawley. Eddie spotted him the same time as Les, gave Les a nudge in the ribs and went into action.

'There he is!' shrieked Eddie, in a whiney, high-pitched voice, pointing at Latte. 'The one who fornicates with dogs and desecrated the tomb of Kareem.'

'AIEE! AIEE!' howled Les.

'Seize the infidel,' yelled Eddie.

'AIEE! AIEE!'

The band played on out the back, but everything in the front room stopped as all eyes fell on Les and Eddie. Latte had a look of outraged indignation on his face when Eddie strode across the room and sunk a left rip into his solar plexus. Lindsey went white, his knees buckled and he started gasping for breath as Les grabbed him by his right arm and pinned it down on a stack of books piled on a table behind him.

'This man is a thief, a liar and a desecrator,' shrieked Eddie, pointing Latte out to everyone in the room.

'AIEE! AIEE!' howled Les.

'Death to thieves and liars,' shrieked Eddie. 'And all those who would desecrate the tomb of Kareem.'

'AIEE! AIEE!' yelled Les.

'Hold out the hand of the infidel desecrator,' yelled Eddie, whipping the cleaver out from under his dajdaja.

'Aiee! Aiee! Death to the infidel,' said Les.

Latte went even whiter when he saw the cleaver in Eddie's hand. 'Help me, somebody. Please,' he whined.

'Silence, dog,' shouted Eddie.

Les pushed Latte's right hand down on the books palm up, Eddie brought the razor-sharp cleaver down with a solid crunch and Latte's right little finger came off, spurting blood and shreds of nerve endings all over *Key to the System of Victorian Plants*, Von Mueller, black bound.

'Oh my God,' screamed Latte.

Everybody in the shop either gasped or screamed as Eddie quickly removed the ring, left the finger where it was and raised the cleaver again.

'Now hold out the other hand of the infidel,' shrieked Eddie.

'AIEE! AIEE!'

Les changed sides and forced poor Latte's left hand down amongst the books on the table. Eddie whipped off Latte's watch and brought the cleaver down again. Latte's other little finger came off and a gush of blood spurted across *In the Wake of the Windships*, Frederick William Wallace.

'Ohhhh, God help me,' Latte's anguished cry was pitiful to hear.

Eddie slipped the watch and ring under his dajdaja then picked up the two fingers as Les let go of Lindsey. Moaning with pain, Latte slumped on his backside against the book table, spurting blood all over the carpet.

'Let this be a lesson to all thieves and liars,' shrieked Eddie, holding the two fingers up in front of the horrified people in the shop. 'And all those who would desecrate the tomb of Kareem.'

'AIEE! AIEE!' howled Les.

Eddie gave Latte a parting smack in the teeth with the blunt edge of the cleaver, then slipped it under his dajdaja before turning to Les.

'Come, my brother. Now we must leave.'

'AIEE! AIEE!'

Les followed Eddie past the ashen-faced woman at the door and into the street. The old white dog was still sitting on the footpath. It saw them coming and started wagging its tail again.

'There you go, mate,' said Eddie, and tossed the fingers to the dog.

The old dog snapped them up, and started chewing hungrily.

'Good boy,' said Les. He gave the old dog a pat on the head, then followed Eddie back to the car and jumped inside.

'How did it go?' asked Perry, as they drove off.

'Easy as shit,' replied Eddie. He turned to Les. 'Mate. You were fuckin unreal back there,' he said, slapping Les on the back. 'Good on you.'

'I did my best,' shrugged Les. 'And I think I learned something tonight, too.'

'Yeah. What was that, Les?'

'If you know what's good for you, don't fuck with the tomb of Kareem.'

'Or the club of Galese,' winked Eddie.

Les and Eddie took their Groucho masks off as Perry swung the Holden into another side street then headed towards the CBD. Before long they crossed the Yarra again and were back inside Perry's garage. Les and Eddie got out of the car and removed their blood-spattered Arabian clothing while Perry unscrewed the number plates on the Holden and changed back into his driver's suit and cap. They left the two outfits on the floor then washed any blood off themselves in a sink near the fridge. Eddie washed the cleaver, then rinsed Latte's watch and ring and looked at them sitting in the palm of his hand.

'Hard to believe that ring's worth twenty grand, isn't it,' said Eddie.

'Yeah,' agreed Les. 'Not a bad-looking watch, though.'

'I have to drop Eddie off at the airport,' said Perry. 'What do you want to do, Les?'

Les thought for a moment. 'I don't feel like going straight back to the hotel. And Fitzroy's definitely brushed. There's a hotel on the water at St Kilda. I did a TV commercial there the last time I was down here.'

'The Boulevard?' said Perry.

'That's it. Can you drop me off there?'

'No worries.'

Perry got behind the wheel of the BMW, Eddie got in next to him, Les piled in the back and Perry reversed out of the garage.

Eddie and Perry were talking business in the front so Les just sat back and watched the cars and buildings go past, pleased how smoothly the night had gone and glad it was all over. Before long they were cruising down a wide, flat boulevard with houses on the right, trams in the middle and crowded bars, restaurants and hotels on the left. A tram rattled by at the end and Perry swung the limo left past several blocks of flats. Les got a glimpse of the darkened ocean before Perry pulled up in front of the old hotel.

'All right, Les,' he said. 'Here you are.'

'Thanks, Perry.' Les shook the driver's hand before he got out. 'Nice to have met you, mate.'

'You too, Les.'

'I'll see you back in Sydney, Les,' said Eddie. 'Have a good time in Lorne. Hey. And thanks for everything, big fellah. You're the best.'

'Any time, Eddie,' winked Les. 'I'll see you and the others when I get home.' Les watched as the limo drove off into the night then turned to the Boulevard Hotel.

It was the same as the last time Les was there. Big and white, windows overlooking the bay and stairs out the front. Only this time there were a lot more people around. Les walked up the stairs past two security men in jeans and T-shirts and stepped through the door.

Inside was crowded with casually dressed punters. The lounge area on the right was packed and a band on stage had just finished a bracket. People were swarming everywhere or seated under the stairs at the end or at what tables there were. On the paint-chipped walls were posters for different bands. Bugdust, The Chucky Monroes, They Might Be Vaginas. A girl with spiked dark hair walked past wearing a black T-shirt under a white singlet with I LIKE HARLOCKS SACKS across the front in red. There was a small bar on Norton's left with a sign above saying TONIGHT, BOB MARLEY BIRTHDAY BASH, CONRAD ROOM. Les went to the bar, got a delicious and stepped back into the crush. The Conrad Room was down to the left, and Les thought he'd check out the Bob Marley Bash.

The gig was down the end of a corridor and seven dollars in. It was hot, smoky and absolutely jam packed; you couldn't swing a mouse, let alone a cat. On stage at the far end a DJ in a Jamaican beanie was playing Bob Marley's 'Lion In Zion'. Les got pushed and shoved and the ice in his delicious melted before he had a chance to drink it. Les drank some then put the glass on a table and left the Bob Marley fans to it.

Back at the bar Les ordered another delicious. By the time he'd drunk half he'd had enough. It was a good night in the pub if you wanted to get half full on ink and rage. But being on his own and after what happened earlier, Les wasn't quite in the mood. He finished his drink and walked outside.

Still looking for a quiet sort of drink, Les noticed the other bar to the right of the stairs and decided to have a look in there. It was just as crowded as upstairs and in a corner on the right as you walked in, a three-piece punk band and a singer were all screaming their heads off under a sign saying 102.7 FM TRIPLE R. The band were all stripped to the waist and covered in tattoos, the bearded singer was wearing a buffalo-skin hat and a black and white dress that looked like it was made from an old string shopping bag. It was all 'Oi, oi, oi' head-banging, loud and fast. Les walked straight back outside, gulped in some fresh air and cleared his head. He was thinking of having a look in the bars he'd seen round the corner driving there, when a taxi cruised up out the front. It wasn't getting any earlier, and the bar might still be open at the hotel. Les got in and told the driver to take him to the Southville in Collins Street.

The taxi ride home was uneventful and after getting hosed the night before, Les felt he was doing the right thing having an early one. This time tomorrow I'll be in beautiful down-town Lorne, he yawned as they approached the lights of the CBD. The taxi pulled up in front of the hotel, Les paid the driver then returned the porter's greeting as he stepped through the lobby and into the lift. The bar was still open and about a dozen people were seated around the various tables. Alone at the bar a woman was staring balefully into her drink. There was no mistaking the yellow outfit and neat blonde hair. It was Sonia. Les walked over and stood next to her.

'Hello, Sonia,' he said. 'How are you?'

Sonia gave a start and looked up. 'Oh, Sonny. Hello.'

Les gave her a smile. 'So what's a nice girl like you doing in a place like this?'

Sonia stared into her drink and shook her head. 'Sonny. You wouldn't want to know,' she replied.

Les immediately took this as an invitation for him to stick around while she poured her heart out. He ordered a delicious then turned to Sonia. 'Okay if I join you?'

Sonia indicated to the bar stool alongside her. 'No worries.'

'Thanks.' Les sat down and had a pull on a particularly excellent delicious.

'Where have you been tonight, Sonny?' Sonia asked.

'I had dinner in the restaurant earlier,' answered Les. 'Then I went to St Kilda for a Bob Marley night. But it was too crowded, so I came back to the hotel. What about yourself?'

Sonia drew in a deep breath. 'I just saw one of the most awful things I've ever seen in my life.'

'What? A car accident?'

'If only.' Sonia stared directly at Les. 'Sonny. I just saw two Muslim terrorists chop a man's fingers off.'

'What?' Les looked horrified. 'You're joking,' he said.

Sonia shook her head. 'I wish I was,' she replied, and gulped down a mouthful of her drink.

Les took a sip of his delicious. 'Tell me what happened?' he asked.

'I was at a rare book sale in a bookshop at Fitzroy,' said Sonia.

'A rare book sale?'

'Yes. I work for a firm of solicitors in Geelong. They sent me down here to bid for a rare book.' Sonia indicated with her glass. 'That's why I'm staying at the hotel.'

'Go on,' said Les.

'I was standing in the bookshop talking to the owner, when these two Muslims came in and started screaming and carrying on like madmen.'

'What did they look like?'

'Like … Muslims. Arab headgear, long shirts. Thick moustaches. A tall one and a short one. And they were both wearing sunglasses.'

'Sunglasses.'

Sonia nodded. 'The short one did all the talking. The big one just ranted like a lunatic and waved his arms around, yelling Aiee! Aiee!'

'Aiee! Aiee?' said Les.

'Yes,' nodded Sonia. 'Then they grabbed this poor man. Screamed out he was an infidel and a thief. Then held his arms down and chopped his fingers off.' Sonia shuddered. 'It was horrible. I've never seen so much blood in my life.'

'How many of his fingers did they cut off?' asked Les.

'I don't know. They took the fingers with them. But it was a lot. They were brothers, too. Because I heard the small one say to the big one, "Come on, brother. Let's get out of here."'

'Good heavens,' said Les, taking a pensive sip of his delicious. 'What's the country coming to?'

Sonia shook her head. 'They got some tablecloths and tried to patch the poor man up till the ambulance came. But you should have seen the blood. It was everywhere.'

'I can imagine, Sonia,' said Les. 'Shit! That must have been terrible for you.'

Sonia gulped down some more of her drink. 'It was. But you know the funny thing, Sonny?'

'No. What?'

'The man they attacked went into shock. And while we were waiting for the ambulance, the owner loosened his tie and took his coat off. And a Cayman Islands bank cheque fell out.'

Les stopped himself from sputtering into his drink. 'A Cayman Islands bank cheque?'

'Yes. And not only that,' said Sonia. 'They checked the item he had up for sale. And it turned out to be a bit foreign, too.'

'You're having me on.'

Sonia shook her head. 'No. The police came and took down all the details. I only just got here a little while ago. I had to give a statement.'

'Great day in the morning,' said Les.

'Yes. But not a very nice night.' Sonia drained her glass.

Les finished his delicious and pointed to Sonia's empty glass. 'Would you like another one, Sonia?'

'Yes. Thank you, Sonny. Brandy and lemonade.'

Les ordered two more drinks, clinked Sonia's glass and tried not to burst out laughing. Listening to Sonia relay the events at the bookshop had made his night. But the final wash-up with Latte was the icing on the cake. Price and Eddie would crack up when they found out.

'Well if you ask me,' said Les, 'maybe the bloke was a thief and an infidel and he got what he deserved.'

'Yes, but these people can't just come out here to Australia and make their own rules,' said Sonia.

'You're right, Sonia,' nodded Les. 'And I don't want to get into it, because you'll only think I'm prejudiced.'

'Oh. Why's that, Sonny?'

'Why? Because I'm Jewish. That's why.'

'Jewish?'

'Yes. Sonny's just my nickname. My real name's Solomon. Solomon Klinghoffer.'

'Oh,' replied Sonia, taking a thoughtful sip of her drink. 'So are you from … Melbourne, Solomon?'

Les shook his head. 'Sydney. My family owns a supermarket at Rose Bay. And call me Sonny.'

'Okay. So what brings you to Melbourne, Sonny. Business?'

'No. Holidays. I just stopped in Melbourne to do a little shopping. And tomorrow I'm off to Lorne for a few days.'

'Oh? Geelong's not far from there. I'll have to give you my phone number. Maybe we could catch up?'

Les gave Sonia an oily smile. 'I'd very much like that,' he told her.

'Yes. There's some nice hotels there. Good restaurants. Where are you staying?'

'Otway Plaza Resort.'

Sonia looked impressed. 'Oh, lovely.'

With a couple of brandies under her belt, Sonia started to relax. After a couple of nice bourbons on top of what Sonia just told him, Les was beginning to feel the same way.

'Sonia', said Les. 'There's something I'd like to ask you.'

'Sure,' smiled Sonia. 'What is it, Sonny?'

'Well. Yesterday. I wasn't in my room five minutes and you knocked on my door with that … Well, let's face it. That line about your suitcase. I mean. What was that all about? You certainly took me by surprise.'

Sonia looked a little embarrassed. 'Do you ever experience deja vu, Sonny?'

'Sometimes,' answered Les. 'But there's never any future in it.'

'Yes, okay. Well a year ago, the same thing happened to me in another hotel. This man followed me to my room and started to attack me. Luckily an army officer came out of his room and the man ran off. But I've been really scared when I'm alone in hotels ever since.'

'That's understandable,' said Les.

'When you were following me down the corridor. I was absolutely terrified. I thought I was going to faint at one stage. Then when you opened the door to your room, and you said what you did about … me being a better woman than you are Gunga Din and all that. When I got inside I started laughing and couldn't stop. I was so relieved. It was like a huge weight off my shoulders. Then I just felt. I don't know. I just felt like confronting my fears. So I thought, bugger it.' Sonia smiled. 'And I knocked on your door. If that sounds stupid, I'm sorry.'

Les shook his head. 'No. It doesn't sound stupid, Sonia. I think it's great the way you buried your demons.' He clinked Sonia's glass. 'Good on you.'

'Thank you, Sonny.'

'The other thing I wanted to ask you, Sonia,' said Les.

'Yes.'

'What's with … Señor Buzz? Where did he come from?'

Sonia blushed coyly. 'That's my woman's home companion, Sonny. I call him Max.'

'Max?'

'Yes. Short for Maximus.'

'Fair enough,' said Les.

'Geelong's not all that big, Sonny. And if you like a bit of nooky, like I do, it doesn't take long to get a reputation. So …'

'Hey. Nothing wrong with masturbating, Sonia,' smiled Les. 'You're always in good company.'

'Right on, Sonny,' said Sonia. 'And might I say, Solomon, you handled Max wonderfully.'

Les made an open-handed gesture. 'What can I say, Sonia? Max did all the heavy lifting. I just gave directions.'

The barman told them they were closing now and would they like any last drinks. Les looked around and he and Sonia were the only ones left. He asked Sonia if she wanted another brandy. Sonia declined. She'd had enough, it had been a traumatic night and she was getting up early in the morning. But she was glad she had run into Sonny again. Les put the drinks on his tab and smiled at Sonia.

'Well, Sonia. Would you like me to walk you home? Or will I ring you a taxi?'

Sonia put her hand on Norton's knee. 'Why don't you walk me home. I might even get you to check my suitcase again.'

'Still giving you trouble, is it Sonia?' asked Les.

'It's a bugger, Sonny. I should never have bought the cheap darn thing in the first place.'

They caught the lift to their floor. Sonia put her arms around Les when the door closed and they slipped into an extremely passionate embrace, with lots of tongues going everywhere and plenty of heavy breathing. They were still going for it when the door opened on the twelfth floor and they continued to grope each other all the way to Sonia's room. As soon as they got inside, Sonia started getting her clothes off and Les got out of his jeans. They finished in the nude and Sonia didn't have a bad little body. Her bum was tight, her boobs sat neatly and there was even a hint of six pack. Mr Wobbly had one look and he was up and at 'em and rearing to go.

'You know, Sonny,' said Sonia, putting her arms around Les. 'We really shouldn't be doing this. I'm not on the pill ...'

'Yeah and I'm not wearing a raincoat,' said Les. 'But I've got a simply splendid idea.'

'What's that, Sonny?'

'I'll get Max. And we'll have a sixty-niner.'

'Ooh yes,' squealed Sonia. 'I'd like that.'

Sonia got the vibrator from her suitcase, put a little hand lotion on it and handed it to Les, then they got on the bed. Les swung himself around and next thing he was looking into Sonia's neatly trimmed lamington. He switched Max on and started buzzing it around Sonia's clit when he heard her laugh.

'What is it, Sonia?' asked Les.

'I was just thinking, Sonny,' chuckled Sonia. 'You definitely are Jewish.'

'Shalom.' Les started buzzing away then shuddered as he felt the sweet sting of Sonia's mouth around Mr Wobbly.

Les quite enjoyed his anomalous sixty-niner. Sonia's warm tongue and lips felt sensational and it was fun watching the vibrator sliding in and out of her ted. Sonia sounded like she was having a great time too and over the soft buzz of the vibrator Les could hear her snorting and moaning away. Les held off for as long as he could, but eventually he began to approach critical mass. Beneath him Sonia started getting her rocks off too. She gripped Norton's thighs, kicked her legs and the moaning turned into muffled growling noises. Les kept giving it to her with the vibrator when suddenly the kicking stopped and Sonia raised her pelvis, let go a muffled scream and fired off a rattling great broadside. Les screwed his face up in sweet pain and with a roar like a bull emptied out into Sonia's mouth a moment or two later. After they'd both orgasmed, Les climbed alongside Sonia and shakily placed Max near the clock radio next to her bed.

'Shit,' panted Les. 'That was an Exodus I won't forget in a hurry. I feel like the Red Sea just parted right up my blurter.'

Sonia's eyes were still rolling around in her head like marbles. 'God! What a way to go,' she spluttered. 'Mamma Mia!'

'And my mother wanted me to be a dentist,' said Les. 'Oi vey! If she was alive now, she'd roll over in her grave.'

Les lay on the bed for a while then gave Sonia a kiss on the lips, got up and climbed unsteadily back into his jeans. Sonia reached out to the hotel biro and writing pad next to the bed, wrote something down then got beneath the douvet. With his trainers and shirt in one hand Les sat down on the bed.

'Well I'd better get going, Sonia,' he said. 'I got a long walk home. And you have to get up early in the morning.'

'Okay, Sonny,' said Sonia. 'There's my phone number in Geelong.'

'Thanks.' Les pocketed the piece of paper and kissed Sonia again. 'I'll ring you when I'm settled in at Lorne.'

'Okay Sonny.' She returned Norton's kiss. 'I'll see you through the week. Don't forget to ring me.'

'No. I'll remember. See you then Sonia.' Les blew her a kiss and let himself out.

Back in his room, Les got out of his jeans, used the bathroom then cleaned his teeth. When he'd finished he gave the mirror a tired smile.

Hello Sol. How are they hanging, baby? Long and loose and out of juice?

Les turned off the lights, yawned and climbed under the sheets. What about Sonia, he mused as he closed his eyes. Even she's into this deja vu. Come to think of it, I lied my head off to those two women poets in the Blue Mountains and got a blow job. Les scrunched his head into the pillows. Include me out of deja vu. It's too spooky. Who wants to recollect on what might be waiting for you round the corner. The big Queenslander yawned again then he was snoring.

Les woke up the next morning, had a look at his watch and pushed his head back into the pillows. He generally slept in on Sundays, so he stayed in bed and dozed back off into dreamland before finally getting up and drinking a bottle of mineral water. He decided to have breakfast in his room then pack his gear and check out. He rang room service and ordered Bircher muesli, fruit, eggs Benedict and coffee, then climbed into his old shorts and went down to the pool. He splashed around and got the cobwebs out then by the time he caught the lift back to his room, changed into his blue shorts and a white Bob Dylan T-shirt Clover had given him, breakfast arrived. Les tipped the girl then started eating while the same radio station ran 'Love is in the Air' by John Paul Young into 'You Can Call Me Al' by Paul Simon.

The breakfast was very good. Les drank the last of the coffee then got his clothes from the bathroom and finished packing. He tossed a hotel biro and some stationery into his overnight bag, had a last look around then picked up his suitcase and got the lift to reception.

Yes, he told the smiling girl behind the counter, he enjoyed his stay at Southville, the food was great, the bed was comfortable and he'd recommend the hotel to his friends. After charging everything to Price, Les took his suitcase down to the lobby and told the porter he had to pick up a car; he'd be back later. No worries, Mr Norton. The name's Klinghoffer. Solomon Klinghoffer, squinted Les, as he flicked his sunglasses open and walked out into another hot sunny day.

If Melbourne's CBD was crowded the day before, Sunday was even busier. Every little cafe or restaurant was crowded, bookshops were doing a roaring trade and all the trendy clothing stores were full of customers with the techno music pumping at warp nine. At minute intervals a tram would clang to a stop and more people would get off armed to the teeth with credit cards, cash and cheque books. Maybe it's the heat's bringing them out, thought Les, flicking some sweat from his eyes. He cruised around killing time before walking up to the paper shop he had found yesterday and buying the *Sunday*

Telegraph. A support lead on the front page of the Melbourne *Sunday Age* and two identikit drawings caught his eye. BRUTAL ASSAULT IN FITZROY. MUSLIM TERRORISTS ATTACK MAN AT RARE BOOK SALE. Les lowered his eyes and bought the *Age* then walked up to the fruit juice shop, got a Brazilian Special and sat down.

'Two terrorists, apparently Muslims, were involved in a violent confrontation at The Obelisk Bookshop in Brunswick Street, Fitzroy last night in which a man's fingers were hacked off.'

The story must have broken late because there were only a few paragraphs and the paper hadn't had a chance to beat it up yet. It just said how shocked onlookers saw the men run in shouting slogans denouncing Zionists and infidels before chopping the man's fingers off. There were a couple of eyewitness accounts fairly similar to what happened and at the end it said, *'The injured man, a resident of Brighton, is in a stable condition at Royal Melbourne Hospital where he is currently helping detectives with their inquiries.'* I'll bet he is, thought Les. There were a few more paragraphs and two identikit photos like Groucho Marx minus the cigar. Les kept the front page and tossed the rest of the paper into a bin. As he placed it in his overnight bag something ominous struck him. Oh no, he said to himself. I'm not saying nothing about anything. But the last time I was down here I made headlines when I blew up that church in Whittlesea, and I was described as 'solidly built of Middle Eastern appearance'. And what else did it say? *'The evil octopus of international terrorism has spread its tentacles from the Middle East to sleepy Whittlesea in Victoria.'* Les looked up at the sky. Sorry boss. But I ain't saying nothing to nobody. Les got another Brazilian and started on the *Telegraph*.

By the time Les finished the paper and two cappuccinos, it was time to pick up the car. Thrifty was a short walk along Elizabeth Street.

The car rental was busy, but before long it was Norton's turn. No worries, Mr Norton, smiled a polite lady in blue. Your car is waiting. May we see your licence and how much insurance do you want. Les showed his licence and wanted maximum insurance. More smiles and paperwork later and Les found himself behind the wheel of a silver Mitsubishi Advance with a map from Thrifty marked in highlighter showing how to get onto the M1 and out of town. Les followed the traffic up Elizabeth then turned into Collins and pulled up in front of the hotel. The porter had his suitcase waiting and Les was on his way.

The Advance handled smoothly and was very comfortable with plenty of zip. That was the good news. The bad news was, there was no cassette player, only a radio and CD player. Which meant Les couldn't listen to his tapes. Les left the radio off till he figured out where was what. But there were no dramas and before long he was down Collins, found Flinders, yada-yada-yada and he was on the M1 with the other Sunday drivers, going through Altona Meadows towards Geelong.

At a sign saying POINT COOK RD, Les put the radio on and got some station playing classical dirges: moaning cellos and creepy violins. It sounded like backing music to the shows on SBS about the Holocaust. Les brushed it and flicked round the dial. He saw a sign saying LITTLE RIVER and thought of the old LP *Diamantina Cocktail* when he hit on PBS Station 106.7 FM and got some good blues music. The DJ announced some tune Les had never heard before, Geoff Costanza and Jerry Lou, 'Jive Samba'. More good music and very few ads later and Les was driving past brown and grey countryside with few trees. 106.7 changed disc jockeys and went on a jazz trip. Near Geelong Les brushed Miles Davis and found 96.3 Reema FM. It was all soul music and seemed to be a happy-clapping, praise-the-Lord station. Les blew Sonia a kiss as he crossed a bridge bypassing Geelong and further on the road veered left at sign saying THE GREAT OCEAN ROAD, LORNE 62 KMS. Les drove past Geelong airport and the scenery changed to wide, flat plains running off to hills in the distance and lines of trees on either side of the road.

The traffic increased going through Torquay and besides the houses and shops, Les noticed all the huge surf outlets. Norton was right in the heart of waxhead territory. Some radio station was playing 'Baby Love' by Diana Ross and Les started singing along as he went past the turn-off to famous Bells Beach. He got a glimpse of the ocean then it all opened up into red and brown cliffs and scrubby green hills on one side of the road. And on the other, shallow reefs and long golden beaches dotted with surfers taking advantage of the offshore wind. Driving past on a beautiful sunny day, Les was impressed. The Great Ocean Road truly lived up to everything he'd heard about it. Les was crooning along behind the wheel to some other pop song when suddenly the radio station sprung Celine Dion on him wailing 'I Drove All Night'.

'Ohh shit!' howled Les. 'Where's the cyanide pill? Give me a razor.'

Les turned the radio off and drove on in silence. He went through Anglesea before arriving at a sign saying WELCOME TO LORNE, SURF COAST. In the distance Les glimpsed a town and a long pier running out to sea from a rolling green headland.

'Hello. Looks like I'm here,' smiled Les.

Les eased the Mitsubishi around several hairpin bends then drove on past houses nestled into the green hills on his right, with wide bay windows facing the ocean before a long curve of golden sand opened up on the left. Further along a small white suspension bridge crossed over a wide brown creek running into the sea, then the traffic slowed down as Les passed a supermarket set back amongst trees on the right. Next to a tiny alcove of shops and a caravan park to the right, the road crossed the Erskine River and turned left. On a corner next to some colourful studio apartments with weather vanes on the roof sat two Rubenesque statues of a bug-eyed blue woman and a bug-eyed green one. Les drove past them and a row of buildings being demolished then, opposite a resort on the beach, the road swung right into Mountjoy Parade: Lorne's main street.

The traffic was heavy and crowds of people were either lying on the beach, taking a swim or walking around in the sun. Through the trees Les could see the ocean on his left and roughly a kilometre of shops and buildings on the right. An old two-storey picture theatre faced an open-air swimming pool and steep side streets ran up to the forested hills overlooking the town. A car park and a modern surf club sat inside the headland where the beach ended and on the other side of a roundabout in Mountjoy Parade, the Otway Resort faced the Erskine Hotel on the opposite corner. The mustard-coloured resort was three rambling storeys of sundecks facing the ocean and looked very swish. The olive-coloured hotel had a beer garden on top full of sheltered tables surrounded by glass railings and a lounge underneath encased in smoked-glass windows, all built to take advantage of the view. White marble steps ran up to the entrance and there was a drive-in bottle shop underneath.

Les drove past a white church set amongst trees on the right then followed the road alongside the ocean for another kilometre to the wooden pier he'd seen in the distance. It started at a seafood restaurant and a fish co-op then ran out towards a low headland where a handful of surfers were catching waves off a point break. At the end of the pier a number of people were fishing near a crane and boats chocked up on the wooden pylons. Across the road from the pier was another hotel that had been beautifully restored back to its old-world charm. Huge windows surrounded the entrance, beneath sweeping verandahs with yellow wrought-iron railings that faced the ocean. On top was a steep, tiled roof with a large windowed loft and two smaller ones. Lorne ended at a block of holiday units, a small restaurant and more homes built into the hills. Les pulled over opposite the hotel and did a U-turn then crawled along with the

Sunday traffic back to the roundabout between the first hotel and the resort. He took a left at the start of a steep hill then swung right into the resort's driveway.

There was a circled flowerbed in the middle and plenty of room. Les got out of the car, stretched his legs and walked into reception, where a dark-haired man in a blue suit was standing behind a brightly lit desk talking to a beefy woman in white shorts. Les waited his turn and had a look around. Outside were more gardens and landscaped walkways running by an enclosed pool and a gymnasium. Everything was mustard-coloured stucco, quite modern and very well maintained. The beefy woman departed and it was Les's turn.

Not a problem, Mr Norton, smiled the man in the blue suit. Your room is on the second floor on the Anchorage level. Parking is underneath. One key opens the roller door, the other your room. The lift is down the end of the hallway. Thank you, Mr Norton. Enjoy your stay at Otway Resort. Sitting on a wooden table next to the reception desk was a bowl of Roma apples. Les took one and started chomping on it on the way back to his car. It was that crisp and full of juice he went back for another before driving down to the parking area and finding a spot near the lift. He got his bag from the boot then caught the lift to the second floor, found his room easily and let himself in.

Les was surprised to find his room was a modern one-bedroom unit. The bedroom was off the corridor on the right, then the bathroom and after that you stepped down past a modern kitchen into a large air-conditioned lounge room with two comfortable lounges and a TV. A sliding glass door opened up onto a sundeck with a great view of the beach. The unit was done out in beige and pastel colours with thick blue carpet, white curtains and prints on the walls. Les got his suitcase from where he left it near the front door and tossed it on the bed along with his overnight bag. There was another TV in his room and a desk with a lamp. He checked out the cream-tiled bathroom. There were plenty of soaps, shampoos and bath gels and at one end you stepped down to a spa bath and shower. Les felt one of the fluffy towels then walked out to the kitchen. There was plenty of room and everything else, plus a nice big fridge, and every appliance imaginable for preparing meals. And if you didn't feel like cooking, there was an extensive room service menu. Les got a drink of cold water from the fridge and looked around. Shit! How good's this, he thought. Gary's done it again. Les went back to the bedroom, opened his suitcase and took out his ghetto blaster. He set it up in the lounge room, chose a tape and with the Jive Bombers thumping 'JB Boogie' through the unit, started to unpack.

When he'd finished, Les was looking forward to a swim. He put his Speedos on under his shorts, tossed a towel and his camera into his overnight bag then took the lift to the lobby. From the resort it was just a short, sloping walk to the corner then across the road to the beach.

The beach was crowded and it was high tide with a nice wave running between the flags. Les asked a family stuffing themselves with sandwiches under a beach umbrella if they'd watch his bag then jogged down to the water's edge and dived in. The water was chilly compared to the last swim Les had had at Bondi. But it was all right once you got in. Les caught a few body waves, flopped around, got out and picked up his things. He thanked the family under the beach umbrella and managed to sneak a photo of them hogging into the sandwiches. He had a shower next to the car park then strolled off to take a look around and have a cup of coffee.

Lorne was a pleasant holiday resort full of boutique clothes shops and nice restaurants. It reminded him of Port Douglas, only the shops were all on one side of the road and there was a surf beach. He went into a real estate agency and helped himself to a small map of Lorne, then found a milk bar-cafe with outside seating and ordered a flat white from a pretty brown-haired girl in a black T-shirt. The coffee was that good, Les immediately ordered another and went over his map.

Lorne appeared to be split in two by the Erskine River. On one side was a golf course and a road leading out to Deans Marsh. This side was the shops and the resort. The beach sat in Loutitt Bay, and Corio Crescent where the church was, wasn't far from where he was staying. Les glanced at his watch and daylight saving in Victoria having slipped his mind, he was surprised how late it was. He paid for his coffees and left.

On the way back to the resort, some striped shirts in a window caught Norton's eye and a second-hand bookshop in a little old house up from the street looked interesting. Les bought some fruit, milk and a few things in a takeaway food store, checked out the menu in the restaurant under the resort, then crossed over to the hotel bottle shop and got a bottle of Jack Daniels, a dozen VB, ice and mineral water.

Back in his unit Les had a VB, listened to some music and put everything away. He didn't have a clue what was on TV, so he checked out the in-house movies then perused the room service menu. He rang down and ordered a prime rib steak with potato lasagne, a side salad, a caesar salad and oven-roasted asparagus with shaved parmesan. While he was waiting, Les had a hot shower and a shave, put his blue shorts back on and changed into a grey Winnipeg Blue Bombers T-shirt. The food arrived and the waiter placed it on the table near the balcony. Les tipped him, put the caesar salad in the fridge for later then sat down and ate the rest watching the movie he chose: *Billy Elliot*.

The movie was a ripper. By the time the kid got into ballet Les finished eating and had his first delicious. When the kid did a routine with the woman dance teacher to Marc Bolan's 'I Like to Boogie', Les got up and started dancing round the lounge room and Les almost burst into tears when the kid, now all grown up and starring in the Royal Ballet, leapt out onto the stage at the end. It was the feel-good movie of all time and after several Jack Daniels, Norton was feeling very good indeed.

Les put his tray out on the landing, finished another delicious and contemplated his navel. He could have an early night and maybe watch another movie. Or he could go and have a drink. The hotel was just across the road. Les decided to go for a stroll down the other end of town and walk the meal off then come back to the hotel. He locked the unit and, taking his camera with him, caught the lift to the lobby.

Outside, the evening felt pleasant and the sky was full of stars, however most of the daytrippers had gone home and there weren't many people around. Les strolled past the shops and several restaurants still ticking over then shuddered when he went by the old picture theatre and saw the feature movie was *The Two Towers*, the second part of *The Lord of the Rings*. Further on he found some unexpected action. A restaurant with a white front, a white door and wide windows facing the street, was going off. There were chairs and tables along the footpath with people seated having a drink and music was coming from inside. A blue sign above the door said: ROSA'S. The name alone told Les he had to have a drink there, so he stepped inside to get a cool one.

Rosa's had soft lighting and pastel tiles with pink and black murals on the walls and people were seated drinking coffee or finishing bottles of wine after their meals. A square of bar sat opposite the kitchen and in a corner on the right a young DJ was playing ambient house music. Les got a delicious then went back outside and sat down at an empty table to have a look around.

There were a few people on his left. But to Norton's right, a crowd of casually attired drinkers faced each other over a long wooden table. Les overheard their conversations and gathered

116

most of them worked in the local catering industry. Everybody was drinking and nattering away, except for a girl seated at the end of the table next to Les, staring pensively into an empty glass. She had spiky black hair and soft grey eyes set in a pretty, if slightly hard-boiled, face and was wearing a black cotton jacket over a long-sleeved yellow T-shirt tucked into a short tartan dress, and black gym boots. On the table in front of her was a well-worn leather handbag and near her feet sat a blue travel bag. Les would have put her age at around twenty. Seated next to her was a tall girl with a long face and long brown hair, wearing a white jacket and Levis. The girl with the spiky hair seemed oblivious to the people around her as she stared into her glass and Les didn't have to be a mind reader to tell something was wrong. He had another mouthful of bourbon and took out his camera.

'Excuse me,' he said to the girl at the opposite table. 'Do you mind if I take your photo?'

The girl moved her eyes from her glass to Les. 'Did you say something?'

'Thanks,' said Les, and fired off a photo.

The girl blinked at the flash. 'What was that all about?' she said.

'Nothing really,' answered Les. 'It's just that I'm having such a good time sitting here. And you looked like you were having such a good time too. I had to take your photo.'

The girl stared wryly at Les. 'Having a good time? Are you fuckin kidding?'

'Okay,' shrugged Les. 'Maybe I'm a bad judge. But that's how it looked to me.' He finished his bourbon and stood up. 'Anyway. I'm going for another cool one. Can I get you something?'

The girl looked at Les for a moment. 'All right,' she said. 'Jack Daniels and soda, with a slice of orange.'

'That sounds all right,' said Les. 'I might have one of those myself. Watch my camera for me, will you.'

Les walked into Rosa's and got two bourbons. When he returned the girl was still staring into her glass so he put her drink in front of her.

'There you go,' said Les, taking his seat.

'Thanks,' replied the girl.

'No worries.' Les reached over and clinked her glass. 'Cheers,' he smiled.

The girl couldn't quite manage a smile. 'Yeah, cheers,' she said.

'So what's your name?' asked Les, after they'd each taken a sip of their drinks.

'Stepha.'

'Nice to meet you, Stepha. I'm Les.'

The girl gave a little nod and turned to Norton. 'Where are you from, Les?'

'Sydney.'

'Yeah? What brings you down here? I suppose you're a waxhead.'

Les shook his head. 'No. Just a holiday. Till Friday. What about you, Stepha? Where are you from?'

'Melbourne.'

Les nodded to Stepha's travel bag. 'You on holidays too? Or have you just been kicked out of home?'

'Yeah,' nodded Stepha derisively. 'You could bloody say that.'

Suddenly the long-haired girl next to Stepha put her head in. She was waving a glass of wine around and looked drunk. 'Oh, Stepha,' she said. 'I see you got a drink.'

'Yes,' answered Stepha. 'Les got me one. Les, this is Trish.'

Les raised his drink. 'Hello Trish.'

Trish gave Les a half once up and down. 'I suppose Stepha's been telling you all the trouble she's in,' gabbled Trish.

Les shook his head. 'No. We were just talking, that's all.'

'Well she's in some, aren't you, Stepha?'

'Yes, Trish. I suppose I am,' Stepha replied wearily.

Les smiled at Stepha. 'And I suppose it's none of my business, either.'

Trish turned to one of the windows and noticed something inside Rosa's. 'Nicole wants me,' she said. 'I'll be back.'

Les watched her leave then turned to Stepha who looked a little embarrassed. 'All right, Stepha,' said Les. 'I know it's none of my business. But what sort of trouble are you in? Are you involved with all the North Korean heroin they found in Lorne? Have you murdered someone? Done a kidnapping?'

'I'd settle for any of the above three,' replied Stepha.

'Fair dinkum? Shit! You must be in strife.' Les gave Stepha a congenial look over his glass. 'Do you want to tell me your troubles, Stepha? I'm a good listener.'

Stepha stared at her drink for a moment, then took a deep breath and turned to Les. 'All right, Les,' she said. 'If you want to know, I came down here to work the holiday season for three months.'

'Doing what?'

'Waitressing. The money's always good and so are the tips. Anyway, I met this guy and moved in with him. He seemed all right at first. Then he thought he owned me.'

'A control freak,' opined Les.

Stepha pointed to her eye and Les noticed a slight mouse. 'You better fuckin believe it.'

Les nodded slowly. 'I see. So what does this ... chap do?'

'Burne. He's a bar manager. And he sells dope. Which I didn't know about at the time.'

'What? Smack? Coke?'

'Eccy mainly,' said Stepha. 'Plus speed. And a bit of hash.'

'The Lorne cartel,' said Les. 'So what's all the drama with the bar manager?'

'I got out of the house,' replied Stepha. 'I decided to leave Lorne early and I'm getting the bus back to Melbourne tomorrow morning. But when Burne finds out he'll come looking for me. As well as owning me, he reckons I stole some money off him too.'

'Right.' Les nodded to the bar. 'What about your girlfriend? Can't you stay with her?'

'Trish?' Stepha shook her head. 'She's not my girlfriend. And nobody else wants to get involved. Not with Burne.'

'Sounds like one tough hombre,' said Les. 'So what's the bottom line, Stepha?'

'The bottom line, Les?' Stepha had a mouthful of bourbon. 'The bottom line is I've got nowhere to stay tonight and Burne will finish work soon and come looking for me. All the cheap motels are booked out. So I'll most likely finish up sleeping on the beach. Then he'll probably be waiting for me at the bus stop in the morning.' Stepha raised her glass. 'Life's fuckin great, isn't it, Les.'

'Can't you go to the cops?' suggested Les.

'What are they going to do?' shrugged Stepha.

'Fair enough, I suppose.' Les shook his head then smiled at Stepha. 'Well. All I can say is, Stepha, I feel your pain, matey. I've got a bit of a problem myself.'

'You? What's your problem?'

Les nodded to his left. 'I'm staying in a fully furnished unit at the Otway Resort. Besides my bedroom, there's two big lounges. Two TVs, music. I've got a fridge full of beer, a bottle of Jack Daniels and a bag of ice. Tea and coffee. Oh, and there's bloody room service if I want it, too.' Les sipped his drink and stared into the glass.

Stepha peered derisively at Les. 'You got a fuckin unit in the Otway, with all the trimmings. And you call that a problem. Are you all right in the head?'

'I don't know,' answered Les. 'It's just that I got it all to myself. And it's too bloody big.'

Stepha moved a little closer to Les. 'You've got the place all to yourself?'

'That's right,' nodded Les. 'All on my lonesome.'

Stepha fished into her battered leather purse, came up with a twenty-dollar bill and looked pleadingly at Norton. 'Les. I haven't got a real lot of money on me. But I'll give you twenty dollars if you'll let me sleep on your lounge for the night.'

Norton took a sip of bourbon and looked evenly at Stepha. 'Make it twenty-five.'

Stepha fished out a five-dollar bill and handed the money to Les. 'Okay. Twenty-five it is.'

Les pocketed the money. 'Righto. When did you want to move in?'

'Now,' replied Stepha.

'Now?'

'Yeah right fuckin now. Before Burne shows up.' Stepha drained her drink and stood up. 'Come on let's go. There's nothing happening here anyway.'

'What about in the morning?' asked Les.

'I'll worry about that when the time comes,' replied Stepha, picking up her bag. 'At least I'll be safe tonight.'

'Okay,' shrugged Les. He finished his drink and stood up also. 'Do you want a hand with your bag?'

Stepha shook her head. 'No, I'm fine, thanks.'

Without saying goodbye to anyone, Stepha started off towards the resort with Les at her side. Les didn't quite know what to say. He felt like a heel taking the poor girl's money. However, there were no complications that way and if she got smart he could give it back and kick her arse out the door. But

Stepha seemed all right and it was an awful predicament she was in. Nonetheless, Norton would be sleeping with his car keys, money and credit cards under his pillow. They walked on and by the time they passed the garage and got to the picture theatre on the opposite corner, Les found out Stepha was twenty-five and had a brother in the Navy. Les gave her the same spiel about his family owning a supermarket in Rose Bay. But added he'd just spent five years in the clergy.

'You were a priest?' said Stepha.

'That's right,' nodded Les. 'Father Les.'

'What denomination? Catholic? Anglican …?'

Les shook his head. 'I don't really want to discuss it, Stepha,' he said. 'As far as I'm concerned, it was five wasted years of my life.' He smiled at her. 'I'd have been better off joining the Navy.'

'Yeah. Vince loves it,' said Stepha. 'He's just come back from the Gulf.'

'They do a bloody good job our armed services,' said Les. 'I've got no time for people that bag the military.'

'Good on you, Les.'

'Thanks, Stepha.'

They passed some phone boxes opposite a wire fence running past a church when Stepha slowed down and the expression drained from her face.

'Oh-oh,' she said.

'What's the matter?' said Les.

'Here comes Burne. Shit! And he's with Allan and fuckin Bucky too.'

123

Les stared ahead at three shadowy figures diagonally crossing the road towards them. The tallest one in the middle was wearing a cap, the others at his side appeared bare-headed and not much shorter. Les turned to Stepha and smiled.

'You know, Stepha,' he said. 'I had a feeling this was going to happen.'

'Look Les. Don't say anything. I think I can handle it. Christ!'

'If you say so,' replied Les. 'But I can be very diplomatic in these sorts of situations. Which is who?'

'Burne's the tall one in the cap. Allan's on the left. And Bucky's the solid one on the right.'

'Okey doke,' said Les.

'But leave it to me, Les,' said Stepha. 'There's no need for you to get involved.'

'Don't worry, Stepha,' Les assured her. 'They'll hardly know I'm here. Would you mind holding my camera for me?'

The three men approached. Burne was wearing a red Quicksilver cap, black jeans, and a white shirt hanging out over a black T-shirt. Bucky was squashed into a pair of faded Levis and a black Rolling Stones sweatshirt with the sleeves hacked off. Allan was wearing a grey tracksuit and a thick grey woollen beanie. They were all around thirty, they weren't small and no one was smiling when they stood in front of Les and Stepha. Burne looked positively filthy.

'Where the fuck are you going?' he barked at Stepha. 'I've been looking for you. You fuckin little moll.'

'Burne. Look, will you just listen,' pleaded Stepha.

Burne's two friends puffed up and gave Les a menacing once up and down, then figured he looked harmless enough and there were three of them if he was stupid enough to put his head in. Les smiled at the three men and decided to put his head in.

'Excuse me,' he said politely to Burne. 'Are you talking to Stepha?'

Burne glared at Les. 'Well, I sure ain't talking to you, dopey. So why don't you fuck off while you're in front?'

'Fair enough,' nodded Les. 'But you asked Stepha a question. Perhaps I can answer it for you.'

'You?' sneered Burne.

'Yeah.' Les pointed in the direction he and Stepha were walking. 'My parents own a holiday house just up the road. Stepha and I are on our way back there. To smoke some pot, snort a few lines of coke, drop a tab of acid and do a bit of crystal meth. Then we're going to boil up some Viagra. Shoot it. And fuck each other all night. After that I'm going to order a pizza with the money Stepha stole off you. And when we've finished eating it, I'm going to invite you over. And shove the cardboard box up your fat arse.' Les smiled at the three men before turning back to Burne. 'Now you know, Burney boy. You happy?'

Stepha gave Les a double blink. The three men exchanged glances then Burne sucked in his breath and snarled a reply.

'What?'

Les knew he was in Victoria and there wouldn't be any huffing and puffing, so he whacked Burne in the face with a crisp straight left. Not hard enough to knock him out. But hard enough to stun him and make his nose bleed, giving Les a few moments with just his two mates. Les decided to get rid of Bucky first.

Bucky and Allan started for Les. Norton weaved to the side and Bucky walked straight into a diabolical left hook from the big Queenslander that had all Norton's shoulder behind it. Bucky's eyes rolled back as his front teeth fell out in a gush of blood, then his knees went and Bucky landed on his rump and one elbow somewhere between Mars and Disneyland. Allan let go a flurry of good, hard punches landing a couple on top of Norton's bobbing head. He set himself to throw some more when Les moved in and banged a short right under Allan's heart, stopping him in his tracks. Les followed up with two filthy left hooks that tore Allan's face open and almost jolted his head off, then belted another short, bone-crushing right into his ribs. Out on his feet and in an awful lot of pain, Allan closed his eyes and turned away. Using his right arm, Les grabbed him in a standing reverse headlock, bent down and sent Allan cartwheeling over his shoulder. Allan's beanie flew off and he crashed heavily on his face near the phone boxes, out cold and oozing blood across the footpath.

By now Burne had shaken away the cobwebs and noticed his two mates lying on the footpath. He snarled angrily, wiped some blood from his face and threw a solid left and right at Norton. Les caught them both on his arms, crouched slightly then moved into Burne and brought his knee up hard into Burne's groin. Burne let out a howl of pain and started to double up. Les whacked him with a couple of left uppercuts, knocking Burne's cap off, then pushed Burne's head down and smashed another two knees into his face. As Burne started to buckle, Les grabbed him by the scruff of the neck and the back of his jeans and banged his head noisily into the corner of the nearest phone booth. Burne collapsed unconscious on the footpath next to Allan, then rolled over and the metal corner of the phone booth had split his forehead open from his hairline to the bridge of his nose. Bucky was still lying on the footpath on one elbow with blood pouring out of his mouth, wondering through glazed eyes what year it was and who was prime minister. Les walked over and booted him hard in the face, leaving him sprawled on his back out cold. Les had a quick look up and down the street and noticed that luckily there were no other people around. He turned to Stepha, who was still standing near the wire fence holding his camera.

'Well, Stepha,' gestured Les innocently. 'I did my best to be diplomatic.'

Stepha looked at the bleeding, unconscious men lying on the footpath and nodded her head. 'Yeah. Yeah you did.' She turned to Norton. 'Les. Do you mind if I do something?' asked Stepha.

'No. Go for your life,' shrugged Les.

'Thanks.' Stepha handed Les back his camera then walked over and kicked Burne in the groin, then kicked him in the head. 'That's for Friday night. You fuckin bastard!' Burne didn't feel a thing. Stepha kicked him in the balls again then spat in his face. 'Arse-fuckin-hole!' She turned to Les. 'Okay. Let's go.'

Les thought for a moment. 'Yeah, righto,' he said. 'But your friends look a bit untidy lying here in the street. Hold on a sec.' The wire fence in front of the church was only waist high. Les dragged Burne, Allan and Bucky across, then flipped them over onto the other side, leaving them lying on the church grass. 'That's better.' He gave Stepha a smile. 'Now let's head for home.'

'Yes, let's.'

'You sure you don't want me to carry your bag?'

'No. It's quite all right, thank you.'

'Okey doke.'

They walked on in silence. Les wiped any blood from him with his hanky. Stepha slung her bag over her shoulder. They got as far as the resort restaurant on the corner, when Stepha suddenly dropped her bag on the footpath and stared questioningly at Les.

'All right Father Les,' she demanded. 'Just what the fuck are you? Some kind of Shaolin fuckin monk or something? And don't give me any shit about being diplomatic. You're about as diplomatic as a fuckin wrecking ball.'

'What are you talking about?' asked Les.

'What am I talking about?' Stepha pointed back to where they'd just come from. 'I've seen Bucky knock guys out with one punch. Allan does tae-kwon-do. And Burne's fitter and tougher than both of them. Which is more or less what attracted me to the prick in the first place.'

'Go on,' said Les.

'But you just bashed the shit out of them. Like they were

three girl guides selling jam lamingtons. What's your story — boy?'

'I dunno,' shrugged Les. 'I watch a lot of Jackie Chan videos.'

'Ohh fuckin bullshit!'

'All right. Don't shit your pants,' smiled Les. 'I'll tell you when we get upstairs. Anyway, you needn't talk. I saw what you did back there. You vicious little monster.'

'Vicious little? … Yeah, all right.' Stepha humphed and picked up her bag then followed Les to the resort.

A man behind the desk wearing a neat grey suit and red tie smiled up when he saw them walk into the foyer.

'Good evening, sir,' he said.

Les returned the man's smile. 'How are you, mate?'

'Evening, madam.'

'Hi,' said Stepha.

They caught the lift to the Anchorage level in silence. Les found his key, then they walked across the landing; Les opened the door and switched on the light.

'Ohh wow!' said Stepha. 'This place is really cool.'

'Yeah, it's not bad,' agreed Les, closing the door. He tossed his camera on the bed then pointed out the bathroom and kitchen to Stepha as they followed the corridor down to the lounge room. Les nodded to the lounge nearest the TV. 'I reckon that's the most comfortable of the two. I'll get you a blanket and pillows from my room.'

Stepha placed her bag near the TV and flopped on the lounge. 'Ohh yeah. This'll do me. Thanks Les.'

'No wuckin furries.' Les rubbed his hands together. 'Well, I'm going to have a drink. You want one?'

'Thanks. I might go to the loo first.'

Les made two Jack Daniels with soda and sliced up an orange. He gave them a stir and added the orange as Stepha came back from the bathroom.

'You got a spa bath in there,' she said.

'Yeah,' nodded Les. 'I haven't tried it yet.' He pushed Stepha's drink across the bar top in the kitchen. 'There you are.'

Stepha sat down on a bar stool round the other side, picked up her drink and clinked Norton's glass. 'Thanks Les,' she said.

'That's okay, Stepha,' replied Les. 'Cheers.'

'Yeah, cheers.' Stepha had a mouthful, blinked at the kick then looked directly at Les. 'Righto Mike Tyson,' she said. 'A little bit of explaining please. And forget the Jackie Chan videos.'

'All right.' Les came round and sat down on a bar stool next to Stepha. 'The monastery where I was studying was right out the back of New South Wales. A couple of the other priests were Korean and into all that martial arts stuff. So a couple of us started training with them. There wasn't much to do after prayer. And I finished up training about five hours a day for five years. Plus I'm fairly fit.' Les shrugged his shoulders. 'That's about it. No big deal.'

'No big deal?' said Stepha. 'Shit! I'm glad I'm not Burne and his mates. And how about showing me that one where you threw Allan over your shoulder. That was so cool.'

'Yeah, I might later,' said Les, sipping on his bourbon. 'But just don't ask me any more about the church. It's a bit of a sore point with me.'

'Okay. No worries.'

Les looked evenly at Stepha. 'Do you think there'll be any dramas with the police over what happened tonight?'

'I doubt it,' answered Stepha. 'The cops have got their eye on Burne. And Bucky's on bail for assault. And there's no way they'll admit just one guy beat them up.'

'Good,' nodded Les. 'And you won't have to worry about catching the bus in the morning either. In fact you don't even have to leave.'

Stepha shook her head. 'I've already lined up a job in Melbourne. But yeah, you're right. I can catch the bus in peace now.' She clinked Norton's glass. 'Thanks to Father Les. The fighting priest. Ooh, sorry. Don't mention the church.'

'That's okay.' Les walked across to the ghetto blaster. 'You fancy a bit of music?'

'All right. What have you got?'

'This.' Les pressed play on his ghetto blaster and Bernard Ellison started cranking 'Fistful of Dirt'.

'Hey. This is all right,' said Stepha. 'Rock 'n roll.'

'It's good for your soul,' smiled Les.

They chatted away about this and that as the tape played. Les bullshitted about the family store in Rose Bay and how he'd been out of circulation up until a couple of months ago. Stepha told him about life in Box Hill, where she lived in Melbourne, working in Lorne and how she wasn't much of a judge when it came to men. After a couple more drinks and knowing she was rid of the bar manager, Stepha loosened up. She also started taking a bit of a shine to Les, her knight in shining armour and new landlord.

'For an ex-priest, you sure know a lot about drugs, Les,' smiled Stepha. 'That pay you gave Burne cracked me up. If I hadn't been so worried at the time I would have burst out laughing. Boil up some Viagra. Where did you get that from?'

'I dunno,' Les smiled back. 'I was amped up, and it was just the first thing that came into my head. I'm not into drugs. Though I've smoked pot.'

'You have?'

'Yeah. It was growing all over the place out west. We used to make scones with it. I think that was what made me give up the priesthood.'

Stepha gave Les a quick once up and down. 'Would you like a smoke now? I got some hash joints in my bag. Courtesy of Burne.'

'Sure why not,' shrugged Les. 'We'll smoke 'em out on the sundeck.'

'Unreal.'

Stepha went to her travel bag, found a plastic container and came up with two small joints and a lighter. Les walked across to the sundeck, opened the sliding glass door and they stepped outside with their drinks. Stepha stuck a joint in her mouth, lit it, took a hit and handed it to Les.

'There you go,' she said from behind a curl of smoke.

'Thanks.' Les took the glowing joint and had a hit.

They finished the joint fairly quickly. Stepha stubbed it out and lit the other one.

'Drug City Mamma,' said Les.

'Just call me Amphetamine Annie,' said Stepha.

They finished the second joint and took their drinks inside. Stepha sat on the lounge near her bag and kicked off her shoes. Les sprawled back on the one opposite. It wasn't long before the hash kicked in and Les began to relax on what felt like a very comfortable lounge. The music sounded better and Stepha started to look like Miss Universe.

'So how was that, Les?' said Stepha, grinning like a Cheshire cat from the other side of the room.

'Very good,' Les nodded slowly. 'Very good indeed. Hey, if you get the munchies later, there's some biscuits in a cupboard, and a caesar salad in the fridge.'

'Thanks Les,' said Stepha.

Les started to slip deeper into the cosmos. He stretched and smiled around the unit too. 'You know, it's funny,' he said slowly. 'Just a few hours ago I was in Melbourne having a Brazilian. Now I'm in Lorne having a Jackies and smoking Johnny.'

Stepha spluttered into her bourbon. 'What did you just say you were having in Melbourne, Les?' she asked incredulously.

'A Brazilian,' replied Les.

'A Brazilian? Oh my God!' Stepha fell back on the lounge and started giggling like she was going to wet herself.

Les stared at her completely confused. 'What's the matter? Did I say something funny?'

'A Brazilian?' giggled Stepha.

'Yeah. It's a bloody fruit drink,' said Les.

'A fruit drink. Oh shit! I don't believe it.'

Les shook his head. 'Bloody hell!' he said. 'The hash wasn't that good.'

Stepha straightened up and wiped her eyes. 'Les. Do you know what a Brazilian is?'

'Yeah. I just told you. A sweet, pink, fruit drink. With mint in it. Christ!'

Stepha shook her head. 'No it's not. Well maybe. But this is a Brazilian.'

Stepha pulled up her tartan dress, took off a pair of lacy blue knickers, then lay back on the lounge with her legs apart.

'That's a Brazilian, Les,' she said. 'A waxed fanny.'

Les gave Stepha's bald ted a double blink. 'Holy mother of God,' he said. 'Where did you get that?'

'In Melbourne. Haven't you ever seen one before?' asked Stepha, holding her legs apart.

'No. I told you. I've been out of circulation for five years,' replied Les.

'It ain't just a fruit drink, baby,' said Stepha.

'Evidently not,' said Norton. 'All right if I have a closer look?'

'Be my guest,' invited Stepha.

With his drink in one hand, Les crawled across the room on his hands and knees and stared into Stepha's freshly plucked business. In his confused state Les couldn't think what it resembled. He gave it a little poke with his finger.

'What a ripper,' said Les. 'It looks like … like a plate of veal schnitzel without the crumbs.'

'Oh Lord!' squealed Stepha.

Les shook his head. 'I'll tell you what though, Stepha,' he grinned. 'It might not be the same Brazilian I was talking about. But it sure looks just as pink and sweet.'

Les took a sip of his drink then pushed his face into Stepha's lamington and found it slightly spiky. But very chewy and very delectable; and you didn't have to pick pubic hairs out of your teeth. He gave it a reasonable going over while Stepha moaned and groaned on the lounge. After a while Les came up for air.

'Hey, this is all right,' he said to Stepha. 'Forget macadamias and peanuts. From now on, I'm a certified Brazil nut.'

'Yeah, well don't stop,' panted Stepha.

Les stood up. 'Hang on a minute,' he said. 'I got an idea. Don't go away.'

Les hurried to the bathroom, had a quick leak and ran the bath. He came back into the lounge room where Stepha hadn't moved.

'Hey. You feel like a spa bath?' asked Les.

'Yes. That would be good,' replied Stepha. 'Now how about …'

'Coming right up,' said Les. 'Sorry. Make that going right down.'

Les finished his drink and got stuck into Stepha's business again, like he was the guest of honour at a cannibal feast. Stepha sighed and howled then started to kick her legs before emptying out into Norton's face. Les gave a howl of approval and came up with his eyes sparkling and his face looking like an iced Danish.

'Oh baby that's a what I like. Shake it, but donnn't break it.'

'Shit! What hit me?' heaved Stepha. 'Father Les. You're a beast.'

'Hey. What did I say,' frowned Les.

'Yeah, right. Don't mention the church.'

'Exactemondo. Now come on, Miss Brazil. Let's go for a surf.'

'Whatever you like.' Stepha smiled sweetly up at Les. 'But how about a kiss first, huh?'

'Why certainly, my child,' smiled Norton.

Les put his arms tenderly around Stepha and met her lips coming towards him. They were lovely and soft and Stepha had a hot, spicy tongue. After a while he opened his eyes and smiled into Stepha's.

'Come on,' he said. 'Let's get in the spa. It should be about ready.'

'I'll see you in there,' smiled Stepha.

Les went to his room and got out of his clothes, then padded down to the bathroom. The spa had filled perfectly and the temperature was ideal. He got a bottle of spa crystals, dumped them in the water then ran the jets and watched the crystals foam up like clouds of white fairy floss, bubbling and crackling as they burst into the steam. He put his foot in the water, then slowly climbed into the spa bath and lay back against one side, closed his eyes and sighed as the jets of water softly massaged his body.

'Ohh yeah. How good's this.'

'Did you say something?'

Les looked up and Stepha was standing by the side of the spa, naked. She had a whippy little body and pert boobs. Her skin was pale and across her ribs were several purple bruises. Norton looked at them for a moment and wished he'd smashed the bar manager's head into the phone box a couple more times. Nevertheless, the boot in the balls Stepha gave him would give Burne something to think about when he woke up.

'I was just saying,' said Les, 'how sweet it is. Give me your hand. The floor's a bit slippery.'

Stepha took Norton's hand and lowered herself into the spa. 'Ohh yeah,' she smiled. 'This is unreal.'

'All part of the service, ma'am,' said Les.

Les poked his legs out and felt Stepha's legs resting on top of his. He closed his eyes, leant his head against the side of the spa and let the sweat run down his face while the jets of water gently massaged his body. Stepha did the same. Les dunked his head under the warm water for a while and so did Stepha, then they sat in the spa smiling happily at each other. Les switched off the jets and it went quiet in the bathroom. The music drifted in from the lounge room and Les recognised the song as Johnny Lang bopping 'If This Is Love'.

'Hey Stepha,' said Les.

'Hey yes,' answered Stepha.

Les tilted his head to one side. 'How about a kiss, huh?'

Stepha batted her eyelids. 'Why Les,' she answered. 'I never thought you'd ask.'

Stepha drifted across the spa and Les put his arms around her then they got into a steamy kissing session that matched the atmosphere in the bathroom. Stepha sucked Norton's tongue and kissed him all over the face, Les kissed her neck and bit into it leaving a love bite under her ear as big as a fifty-cent coin. As Les kissed Stepha and felt her in his arms, he got the impression that beneath the bad language and the rough exterior, Stepha was just a little battler who only wanted to love and be loved in return. Plus she had a good, honest heart. She didn't have much money and she could have taken advantage of Les and put it straight on him to stay the night. But she offered Les what she could spare. Then found the extra five dollars when he niggardly asked her for it. And when Burne showed up, she told Les it was her problem. He didn't have to get involved. Les could have easily walked away and left her. And when Les didn't, she got between them and faced up to Burne, knowing she'd only cop it again. That showed plenty of heart. And a lot of honesty. Yes, thought Les, as he kissed Stepha's eyes and gave her a big, big hug. The cheeky little waitress from Melbourne was all right.

Somebody else in the spa, however, had different feelings about the cheeky little waitress from Melbourne. Mr Wobbly. He'd been sitting up under the bubbles just biding his time. Now the evil little monster wanted in on the action. And why waste another minute. Les eased Stepha against the side of the spa bath, spread her legs then got between them and entered her, finding the little waitress firm and warm. Les then did his best to return Stepha's honesty as sweet as he could, for as long as he could.

The steaming water churned in the spa, the bubbles rose and fell and water spilled over the side. Stepha held Les round the neck, sighed and went with him, kissing the big red-headed Queenslander tenderly. It was all too good; and after the hash joints, it was even better. Les got his arms under Stepha's legs, held her against the side of the spa then thrust as hard and as deep as he could, and with a moan of pure ecstasy that echoed Stepha's squealing, poured everything he had into her. The water in the spa bath swirled from side to side, bubbles went everywhere, then it all settled down just as the tape cut out in the lounge room.

They lay together in the spa and shared a few kisses till eventually the water temperature began to drop.

'Well what do you reckon, Stepha?' said Les. 'We go to bed? I'm not used to all this and I'm about knackered.'

'Yes,' agreed Stepha. 'I'm tired too.'

They got out of the spa bath, wrapped towels around themselves, Les pulled the plug and they walked out to the lounge room. Les smiled at Stepha and put his arms around her.

'Look,' he said. 'You can sleep in bed with me if you want. But I had a huge meal earlier and a few drinks. So I'll be farting and snoring all night. You'd be better off sleeping on your own. But please yourself.'

'That's all right,' replied Stepha. 'I understand. You've had a root. Now I can piss off. Would you like me to sleep out on the landing?'

'Okay. Bring the paper in with you in the morning.' Les scrabbled Stepha's hair. 'Hang on. I'll get you a pillow and blankets.'

Les went to his room and changed into a clean T-shirt and jox then came back with two blankets and two pillows from the wardrobe. Stepha put on a black Freddie Mercury T-shirt, a pair of grey tracksuit pants and woolly socks.

'Here you are Baby Bunting.' Les lay Stepha on the lounge, put the pillows under her head and tucked the blankets up under her chin. 'Now. Are we all warm and snug?'

'Yes thank you,' said Stepha.

'Good. What time does the bus leave in the morning?'

'Ten-thirty.'

'Unreal,' smiled Les. 'We can have a nice breakfast before you go.'

'Okay. Hey Les.'

'Yes.'

'Do I get a goodnight kiss?'

'Oh, I don't see why not,' replied Les.

Les lifted Stepha's chin up gently and left her with a long, lingering kiss. 'How was that?'

'That was just fine.' Stepha rolled over on her side as Les turned out the lights. 'Hey Les,' she said, from under the blankets.

'Yes Stepha.'

'I like you, Father Les. You're really nice.'

Les smiled at Stepha's silhouette in the darkness. 'Thank you Stepha. You're rather nice yourself. I'll see you in the morning.'

Les went to his bedroom, closed the door and switched off the light, not bothering to put his money and credit cards under the pillow when he got into bed. Well, apart from having to take those three mugs to task, he yawned, I'd call that a pretty good night. And I think somebody else enjoyed themselves too. Les smiled and thought about Stepha when the wind picked up across the landing and began flicking at the window curtains on the opposite side of the room. Outside Les could hear the ocean breaking along the beach. Norton yawned again and scrunched his head into the pillows. In seconds he was snoring happily.

Norton's sleep was disturbed the next morning by the sound of his door opening. He was awakened a few seconds later by something getting under the douvet and curling up against his back.

'Stepha,' blinked Les. 'What's …?'

'I just came in for a cuddle. That's all,' said Stepha.

'No worries.' Les took Stepha's arm and wrapped it round him. 'How are you this morning?'

Stepha nuzzled his neck. 'Good.'

'Did you sleep all right?'

'Yes thanks. I got up to go to the loo and found that caesar salad. Gee it was nice.'

'Yeah? Did you leave me any?'

'I meant to.'

'No wonder Burne kicked you out of the house.'

Stepha pinched Les through his T-shirt and it hurt. Les chuckled into the pillow and closed his eyes. A few moments went by then Stepha started rubbing Miss Brazil against his back. A couple of minutes of this and Mr Wobbly began to think Stepha had got into bed for a bit more than a cuddle. He was soon up and about and somehow managed to roll Les over on his back and find his way into Stepha's mouth. Stepha gave Les a diabolical polish then got on top. Les gave a shudder of delight as Stepha came down on him. It felt that good he could have kissed her. So he did. Stepha kissed him back then started grinding away. Les smiled up and watched Stepha's hair swaying rhythmically from side to side then closed his eyes and went along for the ride.

It was a fantastic way to commence the morning and Les would have liked to have gone on till lunchtime. However, Stepha revved up then came down too hard and too often in one long burst and Les let go with a howl that rattled the windows. Stepha eventually got off and lay down alongside Les. Norton's heart had settled down and Mr Wobbly was flopping around, a mere husk of his former, finely chiselled self.

'How was that?' purred Stepha.

'For just a cuddle. Not real bad,' answered Les. 'What would have happened if you'd've come in wanting a root?'

Stepha gave Les another pinch. 'You big shit. No wonder they kicked you out of the church.' She got up and dropped the douvet over Norton's face. 'I'm going to have a shower.'

Les smiled and lay under the douvet for a while then got up and sat on the edge of the bed. Shit! Am I imagining things, he shivered. Or is it cold in here? He glanced up at the windows above the TV and it looked very gloomy on the landing. Les got up, wrapped a towel around himself then walked down to the lounge room, drew back the curtains and opened the sliding glass door onto the balcony. Outside it was drizzling rain, the wind was blowing onshore and it was grey and gloomy all the way to the horizon. He closed the door and turned around just as Stepha walked into the lounge room wrapped in towels.

'What a miserable bloody day,' said Les.

'You're only saying that because I'm leaving,' smiled Stepha. 'Aren't you, darling pet.'

'You're right.' Les gave Stepha a kiss on the forehead then headed for the shower.

Stepha was standing in the lounge room wearing a pair of jeans, the same black jacket zipped up over a black T-shirt and a huge grey beanie, when Les came down wearing his blue tracksuit. His hair was combed and he'd squirted himself with deodorant, but he hadn't bothered to shave. He walked up to Stepha and put his arm around her.

'Well Stepha,' he said. 'Parting is such sweet sorrow. But we got plenty of time for breakfast. You hungry?'

'After one lousy caesar salad. What do you reckon?' said Stepha.

'Why are you such a romantic, Stepha?' asked Les.

'It's you, Father Les,' she smiled. 'You've taken away all my pain. And filled my cold, cold heart with love.'

'I'll carry your bag for you.'

Arm in arm, Les and Stepha caught the lift to the lobby, sharing a kiss or two on the way down. Rather than enter the restaurant through the resort, Les walked Stepha outside to see if the weather was as bad as it looked from the balcony. It was. And as they rounded the corner past the pine trees, the rain got heavier. They jogged up a short flight of stairs, then stepped through the chairs and tables in front of the restaurant. Les slid the glass door open and they stepped inside.

The restaurant was called Michael's. It had soft lights set in a white ceiling and was painted in shades of tan to match the resort. The counter was on the right and in the middle was a buffet breakfast. Coffee and tea was against the wall behind. Les gave the girl at the counter his room number then he and Stepha walked past the other diners and found a table in a corner facing the ocean. Les placed Stepha's bag against the wall and nodded at the buffet.

'Why don't we just attack?' he suggested.

'Good idea,' nodded Stepha. 'I'm going to get a cup of tea first.'

After tea and fruit juice they got into the Bircher muesli and fruit, then proceeded on to bacon and eggs with all the trimmings plus hot buttered toast washed down by cups of tea and coffee. From the look on Stepha's face as she ate a third piece of toast with apricot jam, she hadn't done too bad for twenty-five dollars. They talked about different things, Les got Stepha's mobile phone number and it was a very leisurely, very enjoyable breakfast. However, time always flies when you're having fun.

'Stepha,' said Les. 'You've worked down here a few times and you know your way around.'

'Yeah. That's right,' replied Stepha.

'If I wanted to find out … say something about old Lorne. Where would I go? The council? They got a historical society round here or something?'

Stepha pointed down the street. 'You know the second-hand bookshop in the laneway?'

'Yeah. The little wooden house back off the street.'

'That's it,' nodded Stepha. 'See the lady that runs it. Mrs Totten. She's lived here all her life and knows everything there is about the place. I get my books off her and she's a real old sweetheart. She'll look after you.'

'Thanks Stepha,' said Les.

Stepha looked at her watch. 'Shit! I'd better get going. The bus'll be here any minute.' She smiled at Les. 'I wish I wasn't going now.'

Les returned Stepha's smile and put his hand on hers. 'I wish you weren't either.'

They finished the last of their tea and coffee, Les picked up Stepha's bag and paid the bill while she went to fix her non-existent make-up. They walked outside and by the time they joined the other people huddled at the bus stop, the bus was coming down the hill, its windscreen wipers beating away at the swirling rain. It squealed to a halt and the door swished open, several passengers got off and the people at the bus stop filed on, happy to be getting out of the cold. Les handed Stepha her bag, put his arms around her and gave her a warm kiss goodbye.

'Listen, Stepha. Before you go,' said Les. 'I've got something for you.' He fished into his tracksuit and came up with a twenty-dollar bill. 'There's your twenty dollars back. I'm keeping the other five for the caesar salad.'

'What? You miserable bastard,' said Stepha. 'If I'd have known that I wouldn't have eaten it.'

Les fished into the other pocket of his tracksuit and handed Stepha an envelope. 'My phone number's in there. Give me a ring sometime.'

Stepha took the envelope, felt it then took a peek inside. 'There's money in here,' she said. 'Shit! Are some of those fifties?'

'They're all fifties,' said Les.

Stepha shook her head and pocketed the envelope. 'Why did you have to go and do that, Les? You big prick.'

'I dunno,' shrugged Norton. 'It's a prick of a day. And I guess you've left me in a prick of a mood. What can I say?'

The rain pattered down on Stepha's beanie, dripped onto her face and blended in with two smears of warm salty water trickling from the corners of her eyes. 'For a priest, you're certainly something else. Aren't you — Father Les.'

The other people had got on the bus and Les could see the

driver trying his best to look patient. 'Next time I see you, I'll tell you a bit more about myself.' He gave Stepha a quick kiss on the lips and pulled down her beanie. 'Now go on. Get on the bus, you little shit. Before you catch pneumonia.'

Stepha picked up her bag and got on the bus and the door swished shut behind her. She sat down at a window seat and stared out at Les. Les smiled up through the rain, blew her a kiss and waved. Stepha waved back, then the bus began to move off. She was still staring out the window at Les when it went past the old picture theatre. Les watched the bus disappear round the bend then shoved his hands in the jacket pockets of his tracksuit and walked back to the unit.

Once inside, Les switched the kettle on and walked into the lounge room, noticing Stepha had folded the blankets neatly and left them on the lounge. He stared out across the balcony at a rotten cold day and suddenly the unit felt awfully empty. The kettle boiled, Les made a cup of tea and took the blankets and pillows back to his bedroom.

Les sipped his tea, took his tracksuit top off and put on a grey sweatshirt with his GAP anorak on over the top. He tossed a few things in his overnight bag, took it out to the kitchen, then finished his cup of tea looking over the map of Lorne he got at the real estate agency. Corio Crescent was up a hill behind the main street. Okay, thought Les. Let's see how we go. He rinsed his cup, put his cap on, and caught the lift down to the car park.

The Mitsubishi purred into life, Les checked his map and tuned the radio to 106.7 FM. The reception was a little scratchy and the woman DJ was on a bluegrass trip, playing Yank Ratchell a'plunking 'Cigarette Blues'. It was a bit hokey for Norton's taste. But anything had to be better than listening to Who Da Funk, or hearing 'Hotel California' for the two hundred thousandth time between ads for junk food and electrical appliances. The roller door was up, Les drove out into the rain, went down the hill then turned left into Mountjoy.

There was hardly any traffic. Les took a left at a motel then drove up the hill and turned right at the local police station, before passing an ambulance station and a school. All the houses were spread out on hilly open blocks surrounded by trees, and Corio Crescent was a deadend running into bush. Number two was on the corner. It was a big old weatherboard building painted white and set back in a yard full of tall blue gums. A white picket fence, divided by a wooden gate framed with pine logs, ran around part of the yard, and a concrete path led to a set of steps going up to a vestry out the front. Either side of the vestry was an enclosed verandah beneath an A-frame roof with a satellite TV dish on the side. A blue and gold sign hanging above the gate said MADONNA BACKPACKERS LORNE. Seated on a milk crate beneath the apex at the top of the stairs, a woman in a red flannelette shirt and jeans was washing a small white dog in a yellow plastic bathtub. Les switched off the engine and got out of the car. He stood in the rain for a moment looking at the old wooden building before opening the gate and hurrying along the path and up the stairs out of the rain. The woman looked up as Les stepped under the apex.

'Not much of a day,' commented Les.

'No,' agreed the woman, pouring water over the dog's head. 'Chewy's enjoying it even less.'

The woman was an overweight blonde, with a plump, happy face; the dog was a Maltese terrier with a flat, miserable face. Standing reluctantly in the soapy water, it was that miserable it didn't even acknowledge Norton's presence, let alone bother to bark at a stranger.

'Chewy? That wouldn't be short for Chewbacca, would it?' said Les.

'Yes. The little shit. He rolled in something earlier. God, the stink was enough to make you sick.' She gave the dog another splash of water then lifted it out of the tub. Chewy shook himself, gave his owner a filthy look then ran off around the verandah. The woman wiped her hands on a tea towel and looked at Les. 'So what can I do for you?'

'Have you got something to do with this place?' asked Les.

'Yes. I'm the owner,' replied the woman. 'With my husband. Are you looking for a room?'

'Actually,' said Les. 'I'm looking for a church.'

The woman gave a little laugh. 'Well you're a bit late,' she said.

'Late?' said Les.

'Years bloody late.'

'Years?'

'Yeah,' said the woman. 'This used to be a church, till the priest died. Then some sculptors turned it into a studio. Before

149

me and my husband bought it and started up a backpackers. We kept the old name.'

'That's right,' said Les. 'It used to be the Church of the Blessed Madonna. And the priest's name was Father Shipley.'

The woman shook her head. 'No. It wasn't Shipley. It was Marriott.'

'Marriott?'

'That's right,' said the woman. She got up off the milk crate, rubbed her legs and looked curiously at Les. 'What did you want the old church for, anyway?'

'Well,' said Les. 'My name's Norton. Les Norton. And my late mother, Rosa-Marie Norton, had some paintings sent here from Sydney to a Father Shipley for safekeeping. It was a long time ago. But I was sort of ... hoping they might still be here.'

The woman looked at Les somewhat amused. 'Have you come all the way from Sydney to find these paintings?'

'That's right,' answered Les.

'Well, all I can say is, mate, you've come a long way for nothing.'

The woman picked up the bathtub and emptied it out into the garden at the side of the stairs. Les felt like he'd been kicked in the stomach.

'If you don't mind, ma'am,' said Les. 'What's your name?'

'Sirotic,' replied the woman. 'Maureen Sirotic.'

'Mrs Sirotic. There wouldn't be an old storage shed or something round the back would there?'

'There would,' replied Mrs Sirotic. 'But I can tell you now, there's no paintings in there. When the sculptors moved out they practically stripped the place bare. Anything they did leave, we either threw out or burnt.'

'Fair dinkum?' said Les bleakly.

'Fair dinkum,' repeated Mrs Sirotic. 'But seeing you've come such a long way, you're welcome to have a look around when my husband comes back from Geelong. But you'd only be wasting your time.'

Les looked at the owner and knew when he'd tossed tails. 'No, that's all right, Mrs Sirotic. I'll take your word for it. But thanks for your help anyway.'

'No worries,' said the owner.

The dog appeared from around the verandah and decided to bark at Les. Les felt like giving it a kick in the arse. The owner told it to keep quiet then turned to Les.

'Are you staying in Lorne?' she asked.

'Yes. Till Friday,' replied Les. 'At the Otway Resort.'

'Well, why don't you ask the priest at the church just up from there. He was friends with Father Marriott. He might be able to help you, and he lives on the premises.'

'Okay. I will. Thanks.' Les gave the woman a brief smile then turned and trotted down the stairs.

A gust of wind hit the trees and a shower of wet leaves fell around Les as he opened the car door. He got inside and stared back at what was once the Church of the Blessed Madonna. Well wouldn't that root you, he cursed to himself. I've been kneecapped right from the word go. I should have bloody known. Les started the engine, the radio came on and Harry Manx began moaning 'Lay Down My Worries'. Ohh get fucked, you whingeing hillbilly prick, Les cursed again. He reversed round and headed back into town.

Les found the church easily enough, did a U-turn and pulled up in front under a pair of towering eucalypts. It was set in neat surroundings edged with trees, and made from white weatherboard like the first building, except the vestry stood at the end and it was built side-on to the road. Stained-glass windows ran along the side, under a grey roof with a cross on top, and a sign out front said CHURCH OF THE HOLY BLOOD, SURF COAST PARISH, VICAR: ENOCH RATHBONE. There was a driveway on the left and near the driveway a man in yellow plastic coveralls, glasses and a dirty white cap was working a whipper snipper. Les got out of the car and walked over to him.

'Excuse me,' said Les.

The man turned down the whipper snipper and looked at Les. He had a three-day growth and horrible brown teeth that said he rolled his own and smoked plenty of them. 'Yeah mate,' he wheezed. 'What's up?'

'I'm looking for the vicar,' said Les. 'Is he around?'

The man indicated to the driveway. 'He's down the back.'

'Thanks mate.'

The man continued whipper snipping and Les walked up the driveway, coming to a garage at the end. To the right, a white-panelled house was built onto the back of the church, and behind the garage a permalum storage shed stood on one side of a grassy yard opposite an open greenhouse full of roses. Inside the greenhouse, a big man was standing at a table pruning a magnificent yellow rose. Les walked over and approached him quietly.

'Excuse me. Are you Vicar Rathbone?' asked Les.

The man slowly turned around and stared at Les. He had an impassive, jowly face, dark fire-and-brimstone eyes topped by thick black eyebrows and a head of unruly black hair. He was wearing a yellow shirt and black trousers under a green apron that came up to his chest and in a gloved hand was a pair of secateurs. Les gave him a double blink. Shit! Where's Warren? I've found Nero Wolfe.

'Yes. I am he,' boomed the vicar, in a voice that matched his eyes.

'My name's Les Norton,' said Les. 'Mrs Sirotic sent me around.'

'Mrs Sirotic? Oh yes. From the backpackers.'

'That's her.' Les offered his hand and the vicar gave it a quick shake.

'So what is the purpose of your visit, Mr Norton?' asked Vicar Rathbone.

'Mrs Sirotic said you were a friend of Father Marriott.'

'That's right. Father Marriott had the Church of the Blessed Madonna. Until sadly he was taken from us.'

'Taken?' said Les. 'What happened?'

'A motor accident,' answered Vicar Rathbone. 'William was knocked off his pushbike.'

'Oh. That's no good,' said Les.

'Indeed not sir. He was a good man, Father Marriott.'

Les gave an understanding nod. 'Vicar Rathbone. Would you know a priest called Shipley? Father Bernard Shipley.'

'I would,' replied the vicar. 'He had the church before William.'

'Is Father Shipley still …?'

Vicar Rathbone shook his head. 'Hardly. We laid Bernard to rest many years ago, over in Lorne cemetery. I read the eulogy.'

'Oh. What happened to Father Shipley?'

'The Lord called him,' orated Vicar Rathbone. 'And he went to his arms.'

'As good a place to be, vicar,' said Les solemnly.

'Indeed.' The vicar went back to pruning the beautiful yellow rose sitting in its pot on the table. 'So Mr Norton,' he said. 'What exactly is it you want from me, sir, on this rather inclement day?'

'All right, vicar.' Les gave Vicar Rathbone the same spiel he gave Mrs Sirotic. The vicar listened politely, although he seemed more interested in his roses than listening to Les. 'The thing is, vicar, my mother may not have been a well-known artist, but she was very gifted. And those paintings mean a lot to my family, in sentimental value.'

The vicar digested all Les said and waited before answering. 'I understand the purpose of your visit, Mr Norton,' he replied sagely. 'I also respect your family values, and you have certainly come a long way. But how can I possibly be able to help you?'

'Well,' said Les. 'I just thought the paintings might have finished up in your care. Seeing you knew both Father Shipley and Father Marriott. Mrs Sirotic suggested it actually.'

'She did?' said the vicar.

Les turned to the white permalum shed behind the garage. 'There's a storage shed over there, vicar. If I was to make a donation to the church, do you think I could have a look inside?' Les produced a one-hundred-dollar bill from his pocket and Vicar Rathbone's fire and brimstone eyes lit up like halogen lamps.

'I don't see why not,' replied the vicar. He dropped the secateurs on the table and deftly snatched the hundred from Norton's hand. It disappeared under the vicar's apron and was replaced by a set of keys. 'Follow me, my boy.'

'Thanks, vicar.'

Les followed Vicar Rathbone over to the storage shed. The vicar opened the door, found a switch on the wall and the storage shed lit up under several fluorescent lights hanging from the ceiling. There was any amount of junk and objects the church had saved, and like the vicar's roses, most of it was laid out neatly on tables. The remainder was stacked around the walls or propped up in corners.

'Start wherever you wish,' offered the vicar.

'Thanks,' said Les.

With the vicar watching him like a hawk, Les started rummaging through all the junk. There were old heaters, furniture, wicker chairs, boxes of crockery. Piles of magazines, car parts, an organ, battered violin and guitar cases and two milk crates full of old albums. Les absently flicked through a few. Patti Page, The Ink Spots, Perry Como, Bing Crosby, the soundtrack from *West Side Story*.

Next to the mandatory piles of *National Geographics* and *Reader's Digests*, were two paintings. Norton's eyes lit up as he moved them out from the wall. One was Christ on the cross. The other was the Virgin Mary, complete with a shiny white halo. Les put them back against the wall.

The more he looked around, the more Les realised nearly everything in the shed was left over from church sales. He dropped a Snoopy doll back into a box of toys and turned to the vicar still watching him from the door.

'Well, they're definitely not in here, vicar,' said Les.

'I could have told you that, Mr Norton,' replied the vicar. 'But I had no desire to curb your enthusiasm.'

Yeah. Or miss out on the lazy hundred. 'That's okay,' said Les. 'I appreciate your help anyway. Hey, vicar. There's a church down the road. Who's in charge of that one?'

'Saint Fabian's?' replied the vicar. 'Reverend Kimball Pillinger.'

'I may as well call in there, too,' said Les.

The vicar nodded sagely. 'Yes, why not. Kim knew Father Marriott.'

'And are there any other churches around here?' asked Les.

'There's one on the other side of town, in Falls Terrace. I don't know who runs it now.'

'Doesn't matter,' said Les. 'I'll call in there too.'

The vicar switched off the lights and opened the door. Les stepped outside into the rain and the vicar locked the door behind them.

'Good luck, Mr Norton,' said the vicar. 'God willing, you will find your mother's paintings.'

'Yes,' smiled Norton. 'I can see her looking down from heaven now, telling me to keep searching. Goodbye, Vicar Rathbone.'

Les walked down to the car and the vicar went back to his roses. Brown teeth had taken a breather and was standing under a tree puffing on a roll-your-own. Les gave him a nod and got in the car. Well, another out, thought Les, as he started the engine. And I got a feeling there's going to be plenty more. With the Wildwood Valley Boys howling 'Are You On The Right Road?' Les drove down to the next church, finding a parking spot between the phone boxes and the old picture theatre. He switched off the engine and got out of the car.

Walking past the phone boxes, Les noticed the rain had washed away any blood from last night's activities and in the daytime St Fabian's was a lovely old church. Built in white weatherboard like the others, it was bigger, with higher stained-glass windows and topped by a green roof with green turrets. The sloping grounds were lovingly maintained and full of beautiful flower beds and rockeries. A set of stone steps with a white railing ran up to the church and behind on the right was a white weatherboard house. A sign near a gate in the wire fence said ST FABIAN'S, LORNE,

CONSOLIDATING CHURCH OF AUSTRALIA, MINISTER: REVEREND KIMBALL PILLINGER. Where Les had dumped Burne and his mates the previous night, a man wearing a plastic raincoat was standing under an umbrella staring down at the grass. Through the plastic raincoat Les could make out a pair of black trousers, a black cardigan and a white priest's collar. I think that could be my man, surmised Les. He let himself in the gate and walked over.

'Excuse me,' said Les. 'Are you Reverend Pillinger?'

The man turned around under his umbrella. He was stockily built with thinning brown hair going grey, and came up to Norton's chin. He had a plump, ruddy face and slightly bloodshot eyes, and a thick red nose and veiny cheeks suggested the good reverend didn't mind a tipple at the altar wine now and again.

'Mmhh? What was that?' he said vaguely.

'Are you Reverend Pillinger?' repeated Les.

'Yes, yes. That's me. Are you from the police?'

'No. Vicar Rathbone sent me down,' said Les.

'Oh.'

'Why? What's the matter?' inquired Les. 'Is something wrong?'

'There was a nasty accident outside the church last night,' answered Reverend Pillinger. 'A car jumped the gutter and knocked three young men over the fence.'

'Fair dinkum?' said Norton. 'Was anybody seriously hurt?'

'Seriously enough,' replied Reverend Pillinger. 'One young man has a broken jaw and several teeth missing. The others are quite knocked about too, I believe.'

'Gee. That's no good,' sympathised Les. 'And a car accident, you say, reverend?'

'Yes. It's rather strange, though,' ruminated the reverend. 'The police thought they might have been in a fight. But one of the lads said a 4WD hit them, and sped off.'

'Did they get the number?'

'Unfortunately no,' said Reverend Pillinger. 'Actually I was just saying a prayer for the victims when you walked up.'

'Very thoughtful of you, reverend.' Les decided not to go in with the hard sell too early. 'I believe the same thing happened to Father Marriott too,' he said.

'Yes. That was quite tragic,' said Reverend Pillinger. 'Poor William was riding his pushbike at night without a light, and a tow truck hit him.'

'You can never be too careful,' said Les. 'Did you know Father Marriott well, reverend?'

'Yes. We used to study the Bible together and go fishing. He only had a small diocese. But he was a lovely man. Sorely missed.'

'What about Father Bernard Shipley, reverend. Did you know him?'

'Not very well. I hadn't been here long before he passed away. And he was often in Apollo Bay.'

'Right,' Les nodded slowly.

'So why did Enoch send you down here?' enquired Reverend Pillinger. 'And might I say, you're a fine stamp of a lad. Footballer are you?'

'Yes,' smiled Les. 'But not Aussie Rules, I'm sorry to say.'

Reverend Pillinger drew closer. 'Between you and me, I don't like rules. Kick basketball, I call it. But say that around here and they'll hang you.' Reverend Pillinger drew Les into his confidence. 'I'm a Rugby Union man myself.'

'The game they play in heaven, reverend,' said Les. 'But I have to confess. I used to play Rugby League.'

'Close enough.' Sharing his umbrella with Les, Reverend Pillinger turned and started walking up to the church residence. 'Now, where were we?' he said. 'Oh yes. Enoch sent you down. Exactly what for, Mr ...?'

'Norton. Les Norton. From Sydney.'

Les gave Reverend Pillinger much the same spiel he gave the other two. Reiterating that because of the mutual connection between the different ministers in Lorne, Shipley or Marriott might have left his mother's paintings at another church when the one in Corio Road folded. Again Les offered a donation if he could look through the church's storage area. The good reverend said that wasn't necessary, but Les insisted he take fifty dollars.

When they reached the house, it was white weatherboard like the church. There was a storage room built underneath and a set of steps ran up to the front door and an enclosed verandah. Reverend Pillinger appeared deep in thought as he stepped across to a door beneath the house.

'Paintings you say, Mr Norton?' he said.

'Yes. Six of them,' replied Les. 'Bound up in green canvas.'

The reverend nodded thoughtfully. 'You know, something like that rings a bell.'

'It does?' said Les.

'Yes, yes.'

At that moment a white-haired lady wearing a grey twin set and a kitchen apron over a checked woollen skirt came down the stairs.

'Reverend Pillinger. You're wanted on the phone,' she said. 'It's Reverend Whittle in Bendigo.'

'Thank you, Mrs Hardaker.' The reverend found a set of keys in his trousers and opened the door. 'The light switch is just inside the door, Mr Norton,' he said. 'Have a good look around. I'll be back directly.'

'Okay, Reverend Pillinger. Thanks a lot.' Les stepped into the storage room and groped around for the light switch. Shit! I wonder what he means by 'rings a bell' thought Les. Don't tell me the bloody things are in here. Les found the switch and turned on the light.

The storage room was as big as the previous one, but just a single, weak light bulb hung from the ceiling, and instead of things being laid out neatly or placed on tables, they were scattered everywhere or piled on top of each other. Old fuel stoves, wheelbarrows full of rusty tools, wooden boxes that could have contained anything. Boxes of toys, a couple of old computers, coils of chicken wire, a rusty ab-rocker, even a clothes dummy with an arm missing. Shoes, clothes, men's hats and ladies' bonnets, handbags, blankets, rolls of carpet. Junk of every description and more leftovers from church bazaars, all gathering dust and cobwebs. Next to a shelf full of Mills and Boon novels and a carton of knitting patterns were several milk crates full of albums. Les checked some out. Lawrence Welk and his Champagne Music, *Listening and Dancing*. Lester Lanin, *House Party. Cocktails and Conversation*, Jan August at the Piano. What? mused Les. No Radiohead or Groove Armada?

Les scoured through the junk finding everything from Monopoly sets to a framed photo of Mao Tse-tung. But no sign of any paintings. The cobwebs stuck to Norton's clothes, the dust made him sneeze and the dim light had him squinting. An enjoyable time it was not. Les looked at his watch, wondering where Reverend Pillinger had got to when a movement in the doorway caught his eye.

'How are you going, Mr Norton?' asked the reverend, stepping into the storage room.

'Yeah. Real good,' answered Les sarcastically.

'Sorry I'm late returning,' said Reverend Pillinger. 'But believe me, when Joe Whittle gets going, there's no stopping him. Then Mrs Hardaker insisted I have a cup of tea.'

'That's okay,' said Les.

'So, have you come across anything?'

'Not so far,' said Les. 'Hey reverend. What did you say before? About something ringing a bell?'

'Yes. Over here in the corner,' he replied. 'You did say there were six paintings bound in green canvas. Didn't you?'

'That's right,' said Les.

'Well there's something like that, been sitting here for years,' said the reverend. 'I've never bothered to see what it is.'

Norton's eyes lit up. 'Yeah?'

Reverend Pillinger led Norton over to a corner of the storage room and started pulling away a pile of rugs next to a hat stand. Beneath the rugs was a dirty green canvas bundle tied with rotting black rope. There was no name on the canvas bundle, but it was old and thick with dust and when Les gave the reverend a hand to lift it up, he could definitely feel wooden frames.

'There's a table by the door,' said the reverend. 'Help me over there with them.'

'It's okay, reverend,' said Les. 'I can manage.' Les picked up the old bundle and followed the reverend over to a table near the light switch. The reverend cleared a few things away and Les placed the bundle gently on top.

'There should be a knife somewhere,' said the reverend.

'It doesn't matter.'

Les grabbed the rope and gave it a sharp tug; it was that old it disintegrated in his hands. Brimming with expectation, Les carefully unwrapped the canvas under the watchful eye of Reverend Pillinger. When he'd finished, they both stared at the contents. Sitting on the table were eight old ouija boards.

'Damn ouija boards!' exclaimed Reverend Pillinger. 'I never knew these infernal contraptions were down here.'

'They definitely ain't paintings, are they,' gritted Les.

'My word, they are not,' declared the reverend. 'And they'll go on the fire this afternoon. The devil's work, if you ask me.'

Les felt deflated and would have much preferred not to have found anything at all. All he wanted now was to get out of the gloomy storage room with its dust and junk and away from Reverend Pillinger. Les turned to the reverend and gave him a thin smile.

'Reverend. I have to get going,' he said. 'Thanks for your help.'

'Not at all, Mr Norton,' replied Reverend Pillinger. 'Would you care for a cup of tea before you leave?'

Les shook his head. 'No, thank you. See you later, reverend.'

Norton left Reverend Pillinger with his ouija boards and stepped out of the storage room into the fresh air. He turned his collar up against the wind then strode quickly across the church grounds back to the car, pressed the remote and got inside, shutting the door firmly behind him.

The rain came down and Les stared up at the leaden sky. Bloody ouija boards. Fair dinkum, boss. Why do that to me? Les took out his hanky and wiped away the dust and rain from his face. Well, what now? The church of the great unknown, over the other side of town, and waste more of my time. Les checked his map then started the car and headed for Falls Road, while some hillbilly band called the Bluegrass Cardinals started honking a song over the radio he didn't catch the name of.

Once he'd crossed the bridge over the Erskine River and veered left onto Deans Marsh Road, Les began to see the ironic side of things and a thin smile creaked across his face. What about the boys saying they were hit by a car. Bloody Stepha. She wasn't wrong. I'll give her a ring later. Les hung a left up a hilly road and thought he might 'cruise the hood' before he found Falls Road.

It was steeper than the other side of town, with the same nice homes on big blocks of land, only with more trees. Les drove past a flock of sulphur-crested cockatoos picking at the grass on the side of the road, then the road climbed through a sloping golf course and he came to a sign on the edge of a large parking area saying LORNE COUNTRY CLUB, VISITORS WELCOME. The golf club was on the right and on the far side of the parking area was a tennis court. The rain eased off, Les parked next to a set of steps at the tennis court and got out of the car with his camera.

There was no one on either tennis court and a handful of cars in the parking area. Les walked along the back of the tennis court then stopped at the edge of the fairway. From high on the golf course the view was magnificent. Even on a dismal day Les could see right across Lorne to the jetty and the old hotel and back to the surrounding green mountains. He took a couple of photos then walked over to the car and drove back down the hill.

Les followed his little map and Lorne Cemetery appeared on the left behind a fenced-off dirt parking area surrounded by trees. All the graves sloped down to the treeline and faced the ocean and around the corner, two gates sat opposite the houses across the road. Falls Road was further down on the right. Les drove past a row of houses to a corner to where the road levelled off, and several houses along on the left was the church.

Compared to the others, it was very humble. Just a brown wooden building in a yard surrounded by trees, and a low cyclone-wire fence separating it from the houses next door. A square of yellow window panes with a white cross on them faced the street, the entrance ran up on the left and a driveway led through the trees to what looked like a rickety wooden shed at the back. Les pulled up and switched off the motor. Apart from the rain and a few magpies whistling in the trees, there were no other sounds and no one about. Les took his overnight bag from the back seat and got out of the car.

Behind the fence, the front yard was full of leaves and needed mowing and along the side were small piles of rubbish. Next to the front gate a faded yellow sign on a chipped brown background said CHURCH OF FUNDAMENTAL ADORATION, LORNE, DEACONESS: BRITNEY SKENRIDGE. Les let himself in the front gate and got a feeling Deaconess Skenridge definitely wasn't a profit preacher. He closed the gate behind him and followed the dirt driveway to the shed at the rear.

The shed was built from old brown palings, had a sagging roof and wasn't much bigger than a garage. On the side was a rickety door bolted with a rusting padlock. Les gave it a tug then glanced at another pile of rubbish stacked alongside the back fence. Beneath the bricks and rubbish was half a metre of steel rod from a building site. Les picked it up and put it in the lock, gave it a twist and the lock snapped easily. He kept the piece of metal and pushed the door open.

There was no light inside. But enough coming in to make out a dirty, concrete floor and a cobweb-strewn ceiling. Les took a torch from his overnight bag and ran it around the shed. Stacked alongside one wall were a couple of push-blade mowers, and a birdcage sitting on an old suitcase. In the middle was a canoe with a hole in it, a pushbike with two flat tyres and a coffee table stacked with magazines. Along the other walls were more piles of wood, tins of paint and a whipper snipper resting against an old table strewn with tins of screws and nails. Pinned to the wall above the table was a poster of the Geelong Cats. Les had another quick look around then turned off the torch and exited, locking the door behind him as best he could.

Before he left, Les stopped under the entrance at the side of the church and took an empty envelope from his overnight bag. He put a fifty-dollar bill inside, printed DONATION on the front and slipped it under the door. After walking back to the car, Les had one last look at the little church sitting quietly in the rain, then drove back into town. He didn't bother about the radio.

When Les turned into Mountjoy Parade, he was wet, cold and ready to kill for a cup of hot coffee. He parallel-parked facing the beach, got his overnight bag and walked across to the same coffee shop. After ordering a flat white from inside he picked a table out the front and sat down. An attractive dark-haired girl in black brought his coffee out; Les added sugar and took a very enjoyable sip. He had another sip then got a notepad and biro from his bag and jotted down a few things; all negatives surrounded by doodling.

The day had been a waste of time and money. However, Les couldn't think of anywhere else to look for the paintings except in the old churches. Les still doubted if Father Shipley destroyed the paintings, and he would never have hung them; if the customs department was going to burn them, they'd be too raunchy. There was another possibility: he left them to someone when he died. If that was the case, then the paintings could be anywhere. Talk about looking for a needle in a haystack. But Reverend Pillinger said Father Shipley was often in Apollo Bay. So tomorrow would be much like today. Visit the churches down there, give whoever the same spiel, along with a donation, and with a bit of luck the paintings might turn up. A lot of luck. Norton finished his coffee and went inside to order another.

Les resumed his seat and was wondering where the day had gone when a different girl, wearing black jeans and a black leather jacket, came out of the doorway with his coffee. She had shiny black hair cut in a fringe and appeared just as attractive as the other girl, when she came across the footpath. Unexpectedly, an elderly man wearing a hat and raincoat, darted past and knocked her from behind. The girl with the fringe slipped in the wet and Les copped most of his flat white down the front of his anorak; the rest went over the table.

'Oh shit!' exclaimed the girl. 'I'm so sorry.'

Les flicked at the coffee on his plastic jacket. 'That's all right,' he said good-naturedly. 'I'm wearing plenty of wet weather gear.'

'Look. Let me get a cloth,' said the girl.

She straightened the cup and saucer, went inside and returned with a wettex and a tea towel. Les took the tea towel while the girl wiped the table.

'I really am sorry,' she said.

'Don't worry about it,' said Les, wiping coffee off his jacket. 'I won't get you the sack.'

'There's no chance of me getting the sack,' said the girl, wringing coffee out of the wettex. 'I don't work here.'

'That figures,' said Les.

'Now don't be like that,' smiled the girl.

'So what are you doing if you don't work here?' asked Les. 'Rehearsing for a part in The Three Stooges run a coffee shop?'

'No. I just called in to see my girlfriend. She was on the phone. So rather than see a nice gentleman like you waiting out here in the rain, I brought your coffee out for you.'

'Well raise my rent,' said Les. 'Don't you know how to butter people up. You can tip as many cups of coffee over me as you like.'

'I'll get you another one,' smiled the girl.

'Thanks.'

The girl took the tea towel off Les and went inside. A few minutes later she was back with another coffee and the same thing happened again. This time it was a woman in a yellow mackintosh pushing a pram. The girl managed to straighten up and save the coffee. But it was close.

Les recoiled slightly. 'Hey listen. I was only joking before,' he said.

The girl carefully placed the coffee in front of Les. 'Golly! I don't think it's my day.'

'You're not Robinson Crusoe there,' said Les.

The girl looked at Les and smiled. 'Enjoy your coffee,' she said.

Les returned her smile. 'I will. Thanks very much.'

The girl went inside, Les drank his coffee and stared absently at the rain on the ocean. For some reason holiday resorts always seemed worse than anywhere else when the weather turned sour. His mind completely in neutral, Les finished his coffee, left some money on the table then picked up his overnight bag and walked back to the resort.

When Les got inside the unit and tossed his bag on the bed, it suddenly dawned on him that he'd left the car opposite the coffee shop.

'Shit!' he cursed. 'Now I'll have to go back and get the bloody thing.'

No, bugger it, he thought. I'm having a shower first. Les climbed out of his damp clothes, wrapped a towel around himself and walked down to the lounge room. He switched on the ghetto blaster, and with Jools Holland and Marianne Faithfull getting into 'You Got To Serve Somebody', stepped into the bathroom.

After a miserable, cold day, Les took his time under the shower. He had a few bruises on his arms and the odd lump on his head from the fight on Sunday night and he was enjoying the hot, steamy water running over his body. It would have been nicer if Stepha was in there with him, helping him save water while he showered with a friend. But it was still pretty good. Les got out and had a shave then changed into a pair of jeans and a dark blue Easts T-shirt and made a cup of tea. It wasn't cold in the unit and after he switched on the TV, Les sat on the lounge watching the news and pondered what to do. Why not ring Stepha and see how she's going? He got her mobile number from his bedroom and picked up the phone. After dialling he got the usual message saying the mobile phone he'd called was switched off. Ring back later. Les replaced the receiver and sipped his tea. Hang on. What about Sonia in Geelong? I promised I'd give her a call. He found Sonia's number and dialled.

'Hello. You've rung Sonia. I'm not home. Please leave a message and I'll call you back. Thank you.'

'Sonia. It's Solomon. How are you? I'm in room 202 at the Otway Resort, Lorne. Call me when you get a chance.'

Les rinsed his cup and thought about having a couple of nice draught beers then dinner. There was a hotel just across the road. But he had to go and get the car. Why not drive up to the old hotel near the jetty, check it out and have a couple in there? Les put his black leather bomber jacket on, locked the door and caught the lift down to the lobby.

Outside, the rain had eased off but it was still a cold, bleak night and there was no one around as Les walked briskly down to the car. He got behind the wheel and minutes later pulled up in front of the Great Ocean Hotel, which was lit up like an ocean liner in the night and looked beautiful from the road. Les locked the car and stepped up to the entrance under the archway.

Inside, the hotel had been revamped with an ultra-modern interior that contrasted tastefully with the outside. A restaurant on the right faced a roomy lounge with polished wooden tables sitting on a polished wooden floor. The walls and ceiling were ivory white and around the walls were asymmetrical mirrors, panels of black riverstone and sepia photos of old Lorne. Rear of the lounge was the bar and behind the bar, a mirror reflected back to the doorway. The bar top was perspex with coloured lights underneath. Soft lights sat in the corners next to healthy indoor plants and music was playing softly from speakers hidden in the ceiling. Despite the delightful atmosphere there wasn't a soul in the place. Les pulled up a black padded stool, sat at the bar and waited. Before long a dark-haired man in a blue shirt and black trousers appeared from a doorway behind the bar.

'Sorry mate,' he said. 'I was doing something out the back.'

'That's okay,' replied Les.

'What can I get you?'

Les looked behind the bar then pointed to a pilsener glass and a Carlton Draught tap. 'One of those full of that, thanks.'

'No worries.'

The beer arrived and it was chilled and delicious. Les left his change on the bar and the man walked out the back again. Les decided to have a wander around with his beer and look at some of the old photos.

There were shots of the old hotel, beached whales and stranded sailing ships, all blown up and clear as the day they were taken. Down a step left of the bar and along a short corridor, another room with a bar full of coloured lights looked out over the ocean. In the middle of the room several small lounges faced a fireplace. Three girls in black were seated on two of the lounges having a quiet drink and a cigarette. Les guessed by their outfits they'd just finished work somewhere. One of them turned around and caught Norton's eye. It was Trish, the girl who'd been seated next to Stepha outside Rosa's. Les blanked her. But she got up and walked over, holding a glass of white wine.

'Hello,' she said evenly.

Les looked at her like she was trying to sell him insurance. 'Hello,' he replied. 'Do I know you?'

'Trish. I was with Stepha last night. You left with her.'

Les gave her a false double blink. 'Oh yes. I remember now. I'm sorry.'

Trish gave Les a surreptitious once up and down. 'Where did you go with Stepha?'

'Go?' replied Les. 'Nowhere. I walked up the road with her and put her in a taxi. She went to a friend's house.'

'Oh? Did you hear what happened last night?'

Les looked mystified. 'No. I was only talking to Stepha for a few minutes before a taxi came along. Do you know if she got the bus all right this morning? She seemed quite worried about it.'

'Yes. Evidently she did,' said Trisha. 'So what did you do after Stepha left in the taxi?'

'Me? I went home to bed. It was getting late and I was tired.'

'Where are you staying?'

'Staying? Falls Road. Up near the cemetery. I'm down here visiting my sister.'

'And you don't know anything about last night?' said Trish.

Les shook his head. 'I wouldn't have a clue. Why, what's up? Is Stepha all right?'

'It's not about Stepha.'

'Well, you've lost me, Trish.' Les looked at his watch. 'Anyway. If you'll excuse me. I have to meet someone in the restaurant. Nice talking to you.'

'Yes,' replied Trish.

Les turned and walked back to the other bar. Fancy bumping into her, he mused. And what about the third degree. You can bet she's friends with those three dills I belted last night. They can have her. When he got to the other bar a girl wearing a black uniform was seated having a cup of coffee. It was the same girl who tipped the coffee on him earlier. Well, well, well, Les smiled to himself. Isn't it just my night for bumping into old acquaintances. He resumed his seat one stool down from the girl, where his change was still sitting on the bar.

'Hello,' said Les. 'If it isn't Larry out of The Three Stooges. I'm not going to wear that cup of coffee too, am I?'

The girl turned to Les. She had lovely hazel eyes and a

whippy body under her uniform and was even more attractive than Les had noticed earlier.

'Oh hello,' she said cheerfully. 'How are you?'

'Good thanks.' Les took a sip of beer. 'Are you working here?'

'Yes. In the restaurant.'

'Looks like you've got it easy tonight.'

'Yes. It's dead,' agreed the girl. She looked at Les over her coffee. 'So what brings you up here? It's not much of a night.'

'I wanted to check the place out. So I came up for a couple of quiet beers,' replied Les. 'I'm glad I did. It's a terrific old hotel.'

'Yes. The new owners did a great job restoring it.'

'There's nothing wrong with the beer either,' said Les.

'Hey, you were really nice this afternoon when I spilled your coffee on you,' said the girl. 'Generally if that happens, people start jumping up and down like it's the end of the world.'

'What was I going to do?' shrugged Les. 'It was an accident. And I could see you were proficiency challenged.'

'Proficiency challenged,' laughed the girl. 'You're a cheeky bugger. What's your name?'

'Les. What's yours?'

'Claire.'

'Nice to meet you, Claire.'

'You too, Les.'

'So what sort of work do you do in here, Claire?' asked Les.

'Tonight I'm in the restaurant,' replied Claire. 'Thursday night I'm singing up here.'

'You're a singer? Unreal. What? You play a guitar and all that?'

'Yep. Sure do.'

Les raised his glass. 'Good on you. It must be terrific to have talent. Any particular sort of music?'

'Oh. I do a bit of Cheryl Crowe. k.d. lang. Casey Chambers.'

'Yeah? I don't mind all three,' said Les. 'I might come up and see you.'

'Why don't you,' said Claire. 'We get a few in here on Thursday night.'

'All right. You got me,' said Les.

Claire gave Les a short once up and down as he had a mouthful of beer. 'Where are you from, Les?'

'Sydney. I'm here till Friday. I got a unit at the Otway.'

'Really? I've heard it's very swish in there,' said Claire.

'It is.' Les took another sip of beer and smiled at Claire. 'You might like to call round and hear some music. You like blues? Rock 'n roll?'

'Of course I do.'

'Well. I got a ghetto blaster and some good tapes. If you want to come back for a cool one before I leave, you're more than welcome.'

'I might just do that when I finish on Thursday night,' smiled Claire. She looked at Les for a moment. 'Do you like a little puff, Les?'

'Does a honey bee like a little buzz, Claire?'

'I'll see you up here Thursday night.' Claire glanced at her watch. 'Well, I'd better get back to work. We're doing a stock-take.'

Les pointed to his empty glass. 'Can you get me another beer before you go?'

'Sure.'

Claire got Les another beer then disappeared out the back. Les had a mouthful and looked into his glass, a tiny smile flickering around his eyes. Thursday night with Claire, eh. There's not enough O's in smooth to describe you, is there Norton. Les caught his reflection in the mirror and grinned. Queenslander.

Les relaxed with his beer and listened to the music coming out of the hidden speakers, finding it laid back and very easy to listen to. He had another sip of beer and his stomach started to rumble. He thought of checking out the restaurant menu then decided he may as well order room service back at the resort and watch a movie. The food at the resort was very good and he could have a meal at the hotel on Thursday night.

Les was halfway through his beer and he still had the place to himself when a movement in the bar mirror caught his eye. Maybe it was coincidence. Or maybe Trish had got on a mobile or something. But Bucky, the bloke he'd belted the night before, had just walked in with two other blokes. Les kept his back to the door and checked them out in the mirror as they approached the bar. Bucky looked solid in a Levi jacket and jeans, except his jaw was wired up and he had two glorious black eyes. His two mates weren't quite as solid. But they were tall and fit. One bloke with fair hair was wearing a black leather jacket and jeans. The other had a black mullet and a black leather jacket over a pair of grey trousers. They both had lean, sallow faces and hard eyes and something in their walk that got Norton's radar going. They saw Les sitting at the bar and appeared to take no notice. Les casually sipped his beer and stared ahead as the three men sat down two stools away on his right; the fair-haired bloke nearest to him, Bucky in the middle and the Mullet on Bucky's right. The man in the blue shirt came out and one of the men ordered three Bacardi and cokes. They got their drinks and the man in the blue shirt went out the back again. The fair-haired bloke gave Les an impassive once up and down then the three men settled into a quiet conversation. Well, thought Les. They haven't particularly come in here looking for me. And Bucky hasn't noticed who I am. I reckon if I keep my head down, I'll be able to finish my beer and get out of here without any dramas. And return on Thursday night looking the goods. Les finished his beer then stood up and pocketed his change, leaving something on the bar for Claire. Bucky absently noticed Les in the mirror and suddenly squeezed a painful double blink from behind his blackened eyes. He motioned to his mates, mumbled something through his wired-up jaw, and pointed at Les. Oh well, thought Norton regretfully. So much for no dramas. Because I'm not letting them follow me out to the car. Especially those two pricks in the leather jackets.

Les took a quick step across then reached down and grabbed the legs of Bucky's stool with both hands and yanked it out from under him. Bucky's legs shot up in the air and he flew back, hitting his head against the bar rail before landing under the bar seeing a lot of stars through a lot of pain. Les brought the stool up over his shoulder then swung it against the side of the fair-haired bloke's face. It knocked him violently off his stool and he slammed into the bar then fell on the floor next to Bucky, out cold. The bloke with the mullet jumped up and reached under his leather jacket just as Les hurled the bar stool into his chest knocking all the wind out of him. The Mullet clutched at his solar plexus gasping for breath and from somewhere under his leather jacket a knife fell out and clattered on the floor. Les left it there then quickly picked up the stool he'd been sitting on, raised it above him and banged it down over the Mullet's head like a mallet. The Mullet's eyes glazed over and he landed on his backside against the bar then slumped over on top of the others, out like a light. Les looked at the three men stacked neatly on the floor and brought the stool up again to give them another serve, the Mullet in particular. But there was no visible blood and no one had seen anything. Les decided to leave it at that. He replaced the bar stools, then picked up the knife and put it in his pocket just as Claire appeared from out the back. She couldn't see what was on the floor in front of the bar. But she saw Les standing there and smiled.

'You're leaving?' she said.

'Yeah,' nodded Les, zipping up his leather jacket. 'I'm driving. And it's best not to take the risk.'

'Smart thinking,' agreed Claire. She looked curiously at Les. 'I thought I heard noises out here?'

Les pointed to Bucky and his mates lying on the floor. 'Yeah. I don't know what happened,' he replied frankly. 'These blokes were sitting having a quiet drink. Then they fell off their stools. Maybe they're epileptics or something?'

Claire looked down over the bar. 'Good Lord!' she said. 'I'd better get the manager.'

'Yeah,' agreed Les. 'A glass of water might be an idea too. Okay Claire. I'll see you on Thursday night.'

'Yes,' Claire replied absently. 'I'll see you then Les.'

Norton walked back to the car, got straight in and quickly drove home. Minutes later he was standing in the kitchen having a delicious. Alabama 3 were quietly bopping 'Reachin' on the ghetto blaster and Les was softly crooning along with the lyrics, the knife sitting on the kitchen bar top. It was ten centimetres long, with a black handle and a tiny, serrated knob on the blade so you could flick it open with one hand. Well fuckin beat that, mused Les. I can't go anywhere without getting into strife. Australia just isn't big enough for me. And even though I swore I wouldn't mention bloody deja vu again, the same thing happened to me in Adelaide. Some bloke I belted turned up at a pub in Victor Harbor with his mates, and I had to fight them too. But at least they didn't have knives. Les sipped his bourbon and stared at the deadly little weapon sitting on the bar. Yeah. I knew there was something about those two blokes. If they'd have followed me outside, that could have finished up in my back. And you can bet his mate had one too. Pair of pricks. Les drained his bourbon and patted his stomach. Anyway. I got more important things on my mind than Bucky and his mates. Dinner. It's getting late, and I ain't been fed.

Les made another delicious then rang room service and ordered two dozen oysters kilpatrick, braised lamb shanks with parmesan mash and port wine jus, a side salad and oven roasted potatoes with rosemary and garlic. Plus a frozen chocolate mousse with creme anglaise. He changed into his blue tracksuit then kicked back in front of the TV while he waited for room service.

His food arrived before long. The waiter placed it on the table, Les tipped him then ripped in. It was delicious, the two beers had put an edge on his appetite and Les ate every morsel; when he'd finished he could hardly move. But he managed to make another delicious before turning on the in-house movie, *Austen Powers — The Spy Who Shagged Me.*

It wasn't the worst movie Les had ever seen. But it was up there with them. Inane dialogue and non-stop corny sexual innuendos mixed with ghastly colours and atrocious music. It was that bad it got Les in. Or maybe it was Elizabeth Hurley's boobs. Send up or not, it was a dog. And when it finished Les couldn't work out for the life of him why a good actor like Tim Robbins would take a part in such a stinkerrollah. Les shook his head in disgust then turned everything off and went to his room.

Les thought about reading for a while. But the huge meal and dud movie had flattened him. He yawned, switched off the bedlamps and got under the douvet. Oh well. Tomorrow, my quest takes me to Apollo Bay. I wonder what sort of shit I'll get into down there? Knowing my luck, deep and thick. Les yawned again, shoved his head into the pillows and before long he was sawing wood.

The rain had temporarily eased to windswept drizzle and it was another cold, bleak day when Les got up the next morning and stared out over the balcony. Although he'd slept in his tracksuit, he didn't bother changing. He just cleaned himself up, put his gym boots on then got the lift down to the lobby and took the stairway from the resort down to the restaurant.

After a fruit juice and coffee, Les had a chuckle over his breakfast as he reflected on last night's events in the old hotel. I wonder if Trish came across Bucky and his mates lying on the floor after I left? I'd like to have seen the look on her face if she did. Norton finished his breakfast with one more cup of good coffee and went back to his unit.

His sweatshirt had dried out, so he put that back on with his anorak over the top. After checking his overnight bag and taking a look at the road map, Les put his cap on and took the lift to the parking area. When he opened the car door and went to throw his overnight bag inside, he noticed the damp, rusty piece of iron inside it was rubbing against everything. Near another car were several sheets of newspaper. Les put them on the back seat and lay the length of iron on top. He started the motor and turned on the radio to find the station was playing blues music. Les drove out of the garage then took a right at the roundabout, and with Eric Clapton crooning 'Got You On My Mind', headed for Apollo Bay.

The road was even windier than driving down from Melbourne, with steeper cliffs and hills overlooking the ocean. Coming off the sea, a strong breeze was pushing the rain up against the cliffs like huge billowing clouds of steam. Les didn't see many beaches. Mainly glimpses of pretty little bays with small green rivers running into them between rocky headlands. And only glimpses. The road was full of hairpin bends and he wasn't game to take his eyes off it for a second. The surrounding hills and cliffs also made the radio reception a bit iffy. However, the rain suddenly stopped, although there was absolutely no sign of any sun.

Les drove through Wye River and glimpsed several odd-looking long-necked animals amongst some cattle high up on a hill. They were alpacas. The last time Les had seen an alpaca was in Wagga Wagga, when he was minding the Murrumbidgee Mud Crabs for Neville Nizeguy. He slowed down as he approached the small hamlet of Kennett River then slowed right down when he noticed a white police car parked near a shower block in a dirt parking area on his left. Next thing a uniform cop stepped out from in front of the patrol car holding a STOP sign. Les turned in and pulled up alongside him. The cop had a ruddy face lined from the weather with tufts of scrubby red hair poking out from under his cap, and from the way he towered over the car, Les tipped he was an Aussie Rules player.

'Good morning, sir,' he smiled. 'I'm Constable Hitchon. Apollo Bay police. Have you been drinking at all?'

Les looked up at the cop and shook his head. 'Sober as a judge, officer.'

The cop continued to smile. 'Would you mind blowing into this, sir?'

'Sure,' said Les.

The cop pushed a breathalyser unit through the car window. Les blew into it and it came up negative.

'May I see your driver's licence, sir?' asked the cop.

'Sure,' repeated Les.

Les took his wallet out from beneath his anorak and handed the cop his New South Wales driver's licence. The cop noticed all the money in the wallet and looked at Les as he carefully examined the licence.

'Are you the owner of the vehicle, sir?' the cop asked.

Les shook his head again. 'No. It's a rental. I got it in Melbourne.'

The cop handed Les his licence back, glanced at Norton's overnight bag then noticed the length of iron on the back seat. 'What's the iron bar for, sir?'

Les half turned around. 'That? I found it in the car park where I'm staying. And I've been using it to knock the mud off my shoes.'

'Where are you staying, sir?'

184

'The Otway Resort in Lorne. I'm down here on a holiday.'

'May I examine the contents of your bag, sir?'

'Sure.'

Les sat the bag on his lap and opened it up. The cop gave it a perusal noticing the torch and Norton's camera.

'A torch, sir?'

'I always carry a torch with me,' shrugged Les.

The cop nodded. 'Would you mind stepping out of the vehicle, sir?'

'If you want.' Les switched off the engine and apprehensively got out of the car.

The cop gave Les a heavy once up and down. 'Would you please open the boot, sir?' he said.

'Sure.'

Les reached into the car and pulled the button. The lid swung open and Les stepped round to the back of the car while the cop examined the boot. It was spotlessly clean and empty.

'You can close the boot, sir,' said the cop.

Les shut the boot and turned to the cop. 'Is there a problem, officer?'

'No. No problem.' The cop gave the car another once over then smiled at Les. 'Enjoy your stay in Victoria, sir.'

Les returned the cop's smile. 'Thank you, officer. I'm sure I will.'

Les got back in the car, the cop waved him on and Les drove off. In the rear-vision mirror he noticed the cop writing something down in a notebook. Well what the fuck was that all about, wondered Les as he went round another bend. Suddenly he clicked his fingers. That big heroin bust they just had down here, when they boarded that North Korean freighter. There was a body and a shitload of heroin on a beach near Lorne. And only last week they found another forty-five kilograms buried on some other beach. No wonder they're pulling cars up. And me, driving a rental and coming from New South Wales, especially with my big boofhead. I'd stick out like … like an alpaca's knackers. But, smiled Les, apart from smoking two grouse hash joints with a good little sort, I have got nothing to do with wretched drugs and the misery they bring. Les drove on with the radio playing something inaudible in the background.

The road climbed up and Les got snatches of a sensational view as he drove past Cape Patton Lookout. He drove through more tiny hamlets with names like Wongarra and Skenes Creek, then the road levelled off, curved once or twice, and just as the rain started up again a long white beach flanked by trees opened up on the left and he came into Apollo Bay.

Unlike Lorne, the surrounding hills facing the ocean were much further away from the road and the bay ended at a breakwater and harbour. A large red-brick house, built up off the road on the right with a sign out the front saying OLD CABLE STATION MUSEUM, was the first thing Les noticed as he drove by, then came blocks of land, houses, and holiday units before the shops started: a garage, restaurants, clothes stores, etc. Les passed a large, modern hotel and a park alongside the beach opposite dotted with wooden statues, before coming to an older hotel near the end of the shops. Although Apollo Bay's shopping centre was longer than Lorne's, it wasn't as developed, and still had an easygoing, country town look about it. The shops ended at a war memorial in the middle of the road near the local police station, then the road continued south. Les pulled over on a rise where a sign said MARENGO. Cattle were grazing in open marshes on the right and in the grey distance Les could see a cemetery overlooking the ocean. He did a U-turn and came back into Apollo Bay.

On the right, a golf course ran alongside the harbour, and across the road was a large red-brick church. Not far up the road from the war memorial was another church built from white weatherboard. Hello, smiled Les. We're in business already. He drove slowly along the strip then pulled up outside a coffee shop next to a real estate agency. Les got out of the car and walked into the real estate. It wasn't very big and behind a desk sat a dark-haired woman in a beige dress. Les stepped up to the counter and caught her eye.

'Excuse me,' he said. 'I was looking at some houses in your window. Would you have a map of Apollo Bay?'

The woman pointed to some flyers on a rack near the door. 'Help yourself.'

'Thanks.' Les took one out and came back and placed the map on the counter. 'Actually,' he said, 'I'm trying to buy a house for my mother who's very religious. Could you mark where the local churches are for me?'

'Certainly.' The woman got up with a biro and made three crosses on the map. 'There's two just down there. And another further round in Sandstock Road.'

'Thanks very much,' smiled Les.

'No worries.'

Les got back in the car and drove down to the big brick church he'd noticed opposite the golf course. He stopped in a driveway out front, took the piece of iron from the back seat, put it back in his overnight bag and got out of the car.

The church was high and wide and set in well-kept grounds surrounded by flowerbeds. A set of concrete steps ran up to an open door behind a white archway at the front, and next to the archway a sign said CHURCH OF OUR BLESSED LADY, MINISTER: FATHER RUPERT STRECKETSEN. Les figured there was no need to go inside the church, so he walked around the back.

Built onto the rear of the church was a red-brick house surrounded by thriving flowerbeds. One was full of huge white roses shimmering with rain drops. Opposite the house was a garage and two small toilet blocks, and near these was a brick storage shed with a green wooden door. There was no one around and no sounds coming from the house. Les walked up the steps and knocked on the door. There was no answer, so he knocked again. Les gave it a third knock then walked over to the storage shed. He had a good look around then took the length of iron from his overnight bag to prise it open. Suddenly a thought occurred to Les. When the cop pulled him over earlier, he questioned him about the iron bar on the back seat and the torch in his bag. If a local church reported a break-in, that cop would remember him for sure. And after leaving footprints, tyre prints and fingerprints all over the place, it wouldn't be five minutes before the local wallopers were banging on his door at the resort. And besides getting nicked, if he did happen to find the paintings, the police would confiscate them. All of a sudden Les was up shit creek. He was about to let go a string of expletives then remembered he was on sacred ground. He turned and walked back to the car. Les sat behind the wheel staring out the windscreen at the rain for a while, then started the car and drove down to the white-panelled church he noticed driving in. He pulled up out the front, turned off the motor and checked it out.

Two small wooden buildings, almost side by side on a neatly kept lawn, faced the street from behind a low brick wall. They both had stained-glass windows set in panels and the larger building on the right had a vestry out front. A concrete driveway ran between the two buildings to a residence at the rear, and a sign in the left-hand corner of the front yard said SAINT QUILLAN'S CHURCH, MINISTER: REVEREND BRANDER CROMWELL. Les got out of the car and walked along the driveway.

The residence was separate from the church, with windows along the side and a set of steps running up from a garden to a front door on the right. Between the residence and the smaller building on the left, was a wooden storage shed as big as a double garage with a flat tin roof and a wooden door at the end. Les checked the lock then walked up to the residence and knocked on the door. Again no answer and no sounds from inside. He knocked twice more then went back and had another look at the lock on the storage shed. It was just a lock and Les was sorely tempted. Instead, he shook his head ruefully and walked back to the car.

Oh well, thought Les, as he stared morosely out the windscreen. One church to go. And you can bet there'll be no one there either. Bloody hell! Where would anyone be, on a prick of a day like this? He checked the map and drove off towards Sandstock Road.

The last church was on an open block of land where the houses thinned out into trees running up towards the surrounding hills. It was a yellow weatherboard A-frame featuring a row of stained-glass windows along the side and a white vestry in front with a wooden cross on top. Built onto the back of the church was a residence, and a garage on the right faced a wooden storage shed on the left. A slab walkway led from a gate in a fence out front up to the vestry and the residence, and a driveway cut through the trees to the garage. The grounds were well maintained with beds of flowers running along either side of the walkway, and the church had just been given a fresh coat of paint. Les pulled up near the front gate, switched off the engine and got out of the car. On a white wooden sign board behind the gate it read CHURCH OF THE HOLY ORDER, MINISTER: DEACON LORIMER BROCKENSHIRE. Les followed the wooden walkway up to the residence and was about to take the steps to a door at the rear, when a man in a pair of khaki overalls stepped out of a side door in the garage carrying a stepladder. He had a lean, acned face with thick fair hair swept straight back from his forehead along with a fervent, God-fearing look in his eyes and reminded Les of a young Jerry Lee Lewis. When he saw Les, he stopped and placed the stepladder on the ground as if it was a shield between them and stared at Les suspiciously.

'Is there something I can do for you?' he said in a raspy voice that sounded like a loud whisper.

'Yes. I was hoping to see Deacon Brockenshire,' said Les.

'Deacon Brockenshire isn't here at the moment.'

'He's not?'

The man shook his head. 'All the ministers from Apollo Bay are arranging the funeral of a colleague in Portland. They won't be back until Friday at the earliest.'

'Oh,' replied Les, figuring out why nobody had answered when he knocked on the other doors. 'So are you the caretaker, mate?' Les asked.

'Yes. I'm Deacon Brockenshire's nephew. Uriah.'

'Nice to meet you, Uriah. My name's Les. Les Norton.' Uriah nodded, but he didn't reply or accept Norton's attempted handshake. In his God-fearing eyes, Norton looked like a philistine at the gate. 'All right, Uriah,' said Les. 'I'll tell you why I'm here.'

Les gave Uriah the usual spiel, adding a bit more about the sentimental value the paintings meant to his family and how the family had sent him a long way at great trouble and expense. He ended by offering a one-hundred-dollar donation to the church if he could take a peek in the storage shed. Uriah listened intently and Les thought for a moment he detected a brief sign of sympathy in Uriah's God-fearing eyes.

'I understand your position, Mr Norton,' Uriah said. 'But under no circumstances could I let you look through the storage shed without the deacon being here.'

'The deacon has to be here,' said Les.

'Absolutely.'

'And you couldn't just open the door and let me have a quick look around?'

Uriah shook his head slowly and adamantly. 'Not without my uncle's permission, and my uncle being here.'

From the look in Uriah's eye and the way he stood behind the stepladder, Les figured Uriah would lay down his life before he'd let him in the storage shed. And with God on his side, Uriah would probably fight like ten men if he had to protect the church's property.

'Right,' nodded Les.

'If you come back when my uncle returns from Portland, possibly he could arrange something. But definitely not until then. I'm sorry, Mr Norton.'

Les turned to the shed for a second. For some reason he had a feeling about this one. But he'd identified himself. So even if he did fight Uriah to get in, he'd be up for assault, as well as break and enter. And he couldn't sneak back and break in, either. Les found himself snookered behind the black. Unless he wanted to take the odds to spending time in a cold hard Victorian prison for the dud rap of assaulting a church worker and breaking into church property.

'All right, Uriah,' said Les. 'Thanks for your help. I'll come back later.'

'Do that, Mr Norton.'

Uriah picked up the stepladder and walked over to the house. Les returned to the car and got inside as the rain temporarily eased into drizzle.

Well, wouldn't that root you, scowled Les, looking back at the church. A quiet wet day. No one around. I could have knocked over those storage sheds like piggy banks. But between that copper pulling me over, and Uriah on the scene, I've been well and truly fucked. And maybe it's just the old forbidden fruit thing. But I got a feeling about this one. Les glanced at his watch and felt the cold seeping into his damp clothes. Fuck it, he cursed silently. And fuck heading straight back to Lorne. I'll have a cup of hot coffee and a sandwich in Apollo Bay first. Les started the car and headed into town.

He found a parking spot right outside a neat little coffee shop next to a camping store, and got out of the car with his overnight bag. A sign above the footpath with a girl's face wearing a sailor's hat said SAILOR GIRLS, CONSCIOUS CUISINE. There were sheltered fold-up chairs out the front and several Tibetan prayer flags hung above a wide doorway; on one wall inside were several racks of books, on the others murals and Eastern bric-a-brac. Les scanned the blackboard menu and ordered a pina colada muffin and a mug of flat white from a dark-haired man in black, then sat at a table next to three girl backpackers talking in Scandinavian. He took his notebook out of his overnight bag and started sourly doodling.

Les didn't have to doodle much to tell himself he'd struck out again; badly. Yesterday was just a waste of time. But today he'd been completely rooted. Mainly by bad timing. If he'd have left five minutes later or five minutes earlier, the cop might not have pulled him over. And if Uriah had of been somewhere else, the paintings could possibly be sitting in the boot of the car. Les looked up and gave the proprietor a thin smile as his order arrived, then drank his coffee and ate his muffin while his mood increasingly matched the weather.

So what now, Norton asked himself. The answer: nothing. It was all over Red Rover. Unless he wanted to stick around till the priests came back from Portland. And with the weather well and truly set in, that would be a real fun time. Even Thursday night with Claire had lost its allure. And she'd probably change her mind by then. No. The best idea would be to cut his losses, go home and come back another time. Catch an early flight to Melbourne, hire a car, check the churches out in Apollo Bay and fly home. You'd do it in a day. Les finished his coffee and ordered another one. By the time it arrived another thought occurred to him. The ministers in Apollo Bay obviously stuck together. Now that he'd been down there asking about the paintings, what was to stop the ministers from looking for them? And if they found them, keep them? A few phone calls and they'd soon find out Les wasn't Rosa-Marie's son. He could get stuffed and the paintings would be considered a gift from the Lord. Along with a nice little earner for the local ministers.

Les now wished Father Shipley had either burnt the paintings, sold them, or shoved them in his arse, and also wished he'd never got the letter in the first place. He was also looking for someone to blame for what had turned out to be a complete waste of time and effort. Warren? No. Father Shipley? It was all his fault for getting involved with Rosa-Marie in the first place. The dope. Les finished his coffee, paid the bill and sourly headed for Lorne.

The drive back was no joy either. The rain came down heavier than ever at Wongarra and Les finished up stuck behind a council truck just past Cape Patton. The radio reception was bad the entire trip and all he got was scratchy parts of songs he'd never heard, like Leonard Cohen's 'There Is A War On' and The Infernos' 'Cry Cry Cry'. And Les was in too lousy a mood to even change the station. Just outside of Lorne, the council truck finally decided to pull over and let everyone past.

After a slow, punishing drive squashed behind a seat belt, the two mugs of coffee had gone right through Les and when he made it to the old hotel opposite the jetty, he was absolutely bursting for a leak. But Norton's mood had overtaken him. He drove straight past the resort and down the main street, crossed the bridge, then veered left and started climbing towards the golf links. A left turn here and a right turn there and soon Les found what he was looking for. Lorne cemetery.

He stopped the car in front of the gates, got out and strode through the small one.

Left of the gate was a sheltered table with a list of all the graves and the names of the people buried in the cemetery engraved on it in alphabetical order. Les quickly scanned the names and found Father Bernard Shipley. Row 11, Plot 28. With the cemetery to himself, Les started off in the rain down through the graves.

There were elaborate ones and plain ones, recent ones and some going back to 1850. There was even a Ruby Blanche Norton buried there. Father Shipley's was almost at the end of the row going towards the tree line. It was just a simple plot edged in moss-stained stone with a faded stone cross. There were no dates. But inscribed beneath the cross was FATHER BERNARD SHIPLEY. LOVED BY ALL. ESPECIALLY THE PEOPLE AT THE CABLE STATION. Underneath that it said, SO HE BRINGETH THEM UNTO THE HAVEN WHERE THEY WOULD BE.

'Well, good on you, Bernie boy,' said Les, undoing his fly. 'Now I'm going to bringeth you something for causing me all this trouble. And for getting caught with your hand up Rosa-Marie's dress. You Bible-bashing hypocrite.'

Les closed his eyes with joyous relief and pissed all over Father Shipley's grave, giving it a good going over before squirting and shaking the last drops on the epitaph. When he'd finished, Les tucked Mr Wobbly back into his jox and tied up his tracksuit pants. Although he felt wonderfully relieved after emptying his bladder, suddenly Les didn't feel all that thrilled.

He watched some of the steaming froth get washed off the grave by a gust of wind-blown rain and actually felt quite disgusted with himself.

'Now why did I have to go and do that?' Les turned to the leaden sky and nodded sagely as the rain hit him in the face. 'You're right, boss. That was a bit out of order. Sorry.'

There was a bottle-brush tree at the edge of the cemetery. Les walked over and picked four yellow sprigs off the tree then walked back to the grave and placed them below the epitaph.

'My apologies, Father Shipley,' Les said quietly. 'I dunno what brought the nark out in me. Maybe it's the weather? Have a good sleep.' Les made a quick sign of the cross and walked back to the car.

So what now, Les asked himself as he stared out the windscreen once again. Have a hot shower, grab a bite to eat and get ready for another exciting night watching TV. And pack my gear ready to piss off early. To be honest, I'll be glad to get home. Shit! And won't Archie Goodwin give me a nice bagging when I get back. Warren'll feed off this for ages. Clover, too. The worst part is, I can't tell them I was going down to Melbourne anyway. Bloody hell! I've certainly put my head in a moose with Woz and his girl this time. Hang on a minute, talking about girls. What about Stepha? Didn't Stepha say something about a woman in a bookshop? Mrs Totten? She knows everything about down here? I can't see how she can help me. But what have I got to lose by calling in for five minutes and just saying 'g'day'? Les started the car and drove back into Lorne. He angle-parked across from the shops then locked the car and jogged across the road.

Les had noticed the bookshop before. It was a tiny wooden house, painted olive, set back off the main road in a laneway near the paper shop. A large window faced the street on the right and a set of steps ran up to a small landing in front of a doorway on the left. In the middle was a chimney stack with a sign on it saying OCEAN ROAD BOOK EXCHANGE. Thick vines grew alongside the wall in the laneway and amongst the groundcover out front stood a couple of small trees. Les jogged up the stairs and opened the door and a small bell tinkled overhead as he stepped through.

Inside, tables and Balinese wicker shelves stacked with books were spread over a polished wooden floor or standing against the walls. A couple of bird mobiles hung from the ceiling and sitting along a cornice were several abstract paintings without frames. The books were all listed in order: humour, history, action, romance, etc, and the little shop had a lovely, dusty ambience about it that made you want to spend hours just browsing. In a corner on the left a counter stood in front of a doorway leading out the back and seated in front of an old-style till, a little old lady was writing something down in a notebook. Les approached her slowly and smiled.

'Hello,' he said.

The little old lady looked up. She was in her eighties at least, short and stooped with signs of arthritis in her hands. Her face was lined with just a tiny bit of blue mascara round her eyes and her hair was grey and short and brushed down either side of her face. A pink cardigan hung across her shoulders over a blue top and a pair of blue woollen slacks, and asleep in her lap was an old tortoiseshell cat. The little old lady might have been getting on in years, but when she looked up, Les noticed her hazel eyes were as bright as buttons.

'Hello,' she said, returning Norton's smile.

'Are you Mrs Totten?'

'Yes. That's me.'

'My name's Les, Mrs Totten. Les Norton. Stepha sent me to see you. Dark-haired girl, works as a waitress. She said she gets her books here.'

'Yes. I know Stepha,' said Mrs Totten. 'She's a lovely girl. Likes lots of thrillers. John Grisham and Robert Ludlum.'

'They're a bit heavy for me,' said Les.

'Oh? And what sort of books do you like, Les?'

'Well,' shrugged Les. 'At the moment I'm reading *Hell's Angel*, the story of Sonny Barger.'

'I only just finished reading it,' said Mrs Totten. 'What a good book. He was a bit of a villain, that Sonny.'

Les gave Mrs Totten a double blink. 'You read that?'

'I read all sorts of things,' smiled Mrs Totten.

'I suppose you would,' replied Les, taking a quick look around the bookshop. 'Anyway, Mrs Totten,' he said. 'I didn't really come here to talk to you about books. I came to see you about something else.'

'Oh? And what was that?' asked Mrs Totten.

'I'm from Sydney, Mrs Totten,' answered Les. 'But Stepha said you know quite a bit about the area around here.'

'Yes. My late husband was the postmaster here for many years. And I've always maintained an interest in Lorne and parts of the coast. I got a little book together a few years ago.'

'All right. Well, I'll tell you what's going on, Mrs Totten.'

Without going into too many details, Les told the bookshop owner where he was staying and how he met Stepha, then gave her the usual spiel about the paintings. He told her about calling into the local churches and how he couldn't get into the storage sheds belonging to the churches in Apollo Bay because the ministers were all down at Portland. Mrs Totten listened intently, but something in the way she looked at him with those bright hazel eyes gave Les the impression she only half believed him.

'So that's what's going on, Mrs Totten,' concluded Les. 'I don't know if you can help me. But Stepha suggested I call in and see you anyway.'

Mrs Totten didn't say anything at first. The cat woke up, yawned and stretched then jumped off Mrs Totten's lap and went out the back. Mrs Totten watched it disappear through the doorway then looked up at Les.

'Well, you've been to all the churches there are, Les,' she said. 'So I can't help you there. But I did know Father Shipley.'

'You did?' said Les.

'Yes,' nodded Mrs Totten. 'A very nice man. Always doing things for people. Though he could be a bit of a devil at times if he wanted to,' she added with a knowing smile. 'He's been dead for years now.'

'Yes. I actually visited his grave,' said Les.

'That was nice of you.' Mrs Totten flicked a piece of cat fur from her lap. 'But apart from knowing Father Shipley when I was younger, I don't see how I can help you.'

'That's all right, Mrs Totten,' said Les. 'I didn't really expect you to.'

'However, I think I know someone who can.'

'You do?'

'Yes. Tania Settree,' said Mrs Totten. 'She runs an orphanage not far from where you're staying.'

'Oh?'

'She might not be able to help you actually find the paintings, but I'm sure she can get you into the church storage sheds in Apollo Bay.'

'She can?' said Les. 'Hey, that'd be unreal.'

Mrs Totten smiled up at Les. 'But it's going to cost you.'

'Sure,' said Les, reaching for his pocket. 'How much?'

Mrs Totten shook her head. 'You'll have to give Tania a small donation towards the orphanage.'

'Sweet as a nut,' said Les. 'It'd be a pleasure.'

'And you have to take me to the pictures.'

'The pictures?' said Les.

'Yes,' said Mrs Totten. 'We've got a lovely old theatre here in town. But I have trouble getting up the stairs.'

'Hey, no problems, Mrs Totten. I can do that. When did you want to go, and what do you want to see?'

'Tonight. And I want to see *The Two Towers*. The sequel to *The Fellowship of the Ring*.'

Les felt like he'd just been hit in the face with a huge, frozen tuna. '*The ... Two Towers?*' he said quietly.

'Yes. I absolutely loved the first one,' beamed Mrs Totten. 'And I can't wait to see the sequel. And going with a lovely young man like you makes it even better.'

'All right, Mrs Totten,' said Les. 'What time does it start?'

'The film starts at seven-thirty. If you can call back here at seven-fifteen, that would be lovely. In the meantime, I'll make some phone calls.'

'Okay, Mrs Totten. Sounds good.' Les gave the bookshop owner a thin smile. 'I'll see you here at quarter past seven.'

'Wonderful,' said Mrs Totten. 'I'll see you then.'

Les turned and left the bookshop, then drifted across the road in the rain back to the car. He opened the door and slumped over the steering wheel.

Les had seen *The Fellowship of the Ring* with Warren and Clover. Clover had free tickets. It was after seeing the movie, Les realised there was something wrong with him and he possibly needed some sort of counselling. It was one of the biggest-grossing movies of all time. The books sold in millions and the producers spent millions making a spectacular film with fantastic special effects. Yet Les hated it. He actually put it down as the worst movie he'd ever seen. Three tedious hours of stupifyingly boring waffle and an annoying, cock-eyed dwarf who needed a good bath.

Go here, go there. The river of blood. The castle of doom. The pub with no beer. Your life shall be forfeit. Oh great wizard of Middle Shitville. Where does our quest lead? Your journey will be long and fraught with many dangers. Blah, blah, blah.

The clunker seemed to go on forever. When it finished, Clover said it was okay. But she wouldn't like to sit through it again. Les told the others exactly what he thought of it. Warren didn't like it. But said he did just to nark Les. Now Les had to sit through another three punishing hours of the sequel. He stared out the window up to the sky.

'Why, boss? Why?' he pleaded. 'What did I do? Did I not return and put flowers on the priest's grave? Has not my quest down here been fraught with disappointment and misery enough?' With a heavy heart, Les started the engine and drove back to the resort.

The first thing Les did was have a shave and a shower. He watched the news then changed into his Levis, one of the shirts he bought in Melbourne with blue and brown diagonal stripes, and his black leather jacket. Even if he was in for a night of misery, he figured he may as well look half all right for Mrs Totten's sake. She *was* a bit of an old sweetheart. By then it was time to eat. Les thought he might have a change from room service and sample the cuisine at the local over a couple of cool ones. He locked up and caught the lift down to the lobby.

The hotel was directly across the road. A set of steps led from the footpath up to the beer garden and a bar facing the stools and tables. There was a dining room inside on the left and the kitchen and servery were along a corridor to the right. It had stopped raining, but it still looked a little wet to eat outside. Les walked into the servery to see what was on offer.

Behind the counter was a blackboard menu as well as the normal one. Les gave them both a quick peruse and ordered a dozen oysters kilpatrick and chicken schnitzel with chips and salad from a blonde girl in white, got his number and walked round to the bar. The hotel had Stella Artois on tap, Les got a pot and stepped round to the dining room, straight into a couple with a baby in a pram that was putting on a horrendous screaming and crying fit. Although the noise was louder than a brick saw and drowned out any other sound in the dining room, the baby's parents seemed completely oblivious to it. Les turned around and found a table outside that was sheltered and dry enough and sat down with his beer.

The beer was beautiful and a pot lasted barely a minute. Les got another one and downed the last of that just as the girl brought the oysters out. They were delicious, so was the schnitzel and by the time he'd finished eating, Les had sunk four beers. He ordered a double Jack Daniels with a beer chaser and drank it standing on the balcony staring out over the beach, then placed the empty glasses on a table and looked at his watch. Okay, he told himself, a boozy glow coursing through his body. I think I'm ready now to handle another three hours of *Conan the Barbarian* meets *Camelot*. Les zipped up his jacket and strolled down to the bookshop.

The light was on inside but the door was locked. Les gave a knock and Mrs Totten appeared from out the back. She'd brushed her grey hair to one side, added a tiny touch of mascara and looked very lady-like in a pair of grey woollen slacks, a black polo neck sweater and a green silk scarf with a horse design on it round her shoulders. In one hand was a small handbag, in the other an umbrella.

'I don't think you'll need the umbrella, Mrs Totten,' said Les when she opened the door. 'It looks like the rain's stopped.'

'Oh, you never know,' replied Mrs Totten, stepping out onto the landing and locking the door behind her. 'It might start again.'

'Do you live here?' asked Les.

'Yes. I have a flat out the back. Luke and myself,' she replied.

'Luke?'

'My cat.'

'Right.' Les smiled and gave Mrs Totten a quick once up and down. 'I'll tell you what,' he said. 'You've brushed up pretty good for a young country girl. I hope I don't have to fight too many blokes off tonight.'

'And might I say, Les, you look very handsome yourself,' smiled Mrs Totten. 'That's a lovely jacket.'

'Thank you, Mrs Totten,' said Les. 'So how did you go?' he asked. 'Did you make those phone calls?'

'I certainly did,' replied Mrs Totten. 'I'll tell you about it later.'

'Okey doke,' said Les. He offered Mrs Totten his arm. 'Well, just latch onto this, good-looking. And let's show the locals what style's all about.'

'Yes. Why don't we.'

Mrs Totten took Norton's arm and they proceeded to the picture theatre. Although it was like a trip to the gallows for Les, he still felt good helping the old lady down the road, and while she hobbled a bit from age, Mrs Totten was stepping out as she hung off Norton's huge arm, enjoying the occasion. They got to the theatre and Les helped Mrs Totten up the steps, through the wide glass doors, then up an equally wide flight of stairs to the ticket office where they joined the queue. Mrs Totten opened her bag to get her purse.

'Mrs Totten, please,' said Les. 'What will people think? I don't mind being your toy boy. But I refuse to be your gigolo.'

Mrs Totten gave Les a friendly slap on the arm. 'Oh you're a cheeky devil,' she said, closing her bag. 'I knew that the minute I saw you.'

Les pointed a finger at her. 'And no kissing on the first date, either.'

Les got the tickets and, knowing the marathon in front of him, stocked up on popcorn, mineral water and choc-tops for both of them, then helped Mrs Totten upstairs to their seats.

The picture theatre was big and grand and done out in lots of light brown with soft lighting. The carpet in the aisles was thick, the seats were comfortable and the old theatre would have been something else in its day. Even now it still maintained an air of old-time class. For a Tuesday night, there was a reasonable crowd, and Les and Mrs Totten sat down two seats back from the balcony. Mrs Totten took a pair of glasses from her bag then put them on and watched the screen advertising intently while she got into her choc-top. The ads finished, the lights dimmed then the curtain drew back to the crashing sound of flutes and harps. Les sunk back in his seat with his popcorn, and prepared for the worst.

Difficult as it was for Les to believe, the sequel was even worse. Go here, go there, cross that, climb those, ford this. There was absolutely no plot. Just three separate bunches of dorks with long hair and funny feet dressed like park winos, looking for who knew what? Only this time, one bunch of dorks had a thing tagging along with them that looked like a cross between a gecko on steroids and Marilyn Manson. And right in the middle of all the sword-rattling, shield-banging crap was the cock-eyed dwarf; and he still hadn't had a bath.

Mrs Totten, however, loved the movie. She oohed and aahhed and punched Les on the arm or slapped him on the leg with excitement. And when the trees got up and started walking around, Mrs Totten sighed and clutched her breast in rapture. Despite his misery, Les did get some satisfaction from the movie watching Mrs Totten having a good time. It was a buzz seeing the old lady enjoying herself to the hilt. Finally, after what seemed like a year, the film mercifully ended with one of the dork bunch and the gecko pitching up to the camera for another sequel. Then the curtain closed, the lights came on and Les straightened up in his seat bursting to go to the toilet.

'Well, what did you think of that, Les?' asked Mrs Totten.

'Yeah, just great,' replied Les, flicking popcorn from the front of his jacket. 'Almost as good as the first.'

'I thought it was better.'

'Maybe.'

Les helped Mrs Totten to her feet and they walked up the aisle then down the stairs to the landing. Les excused himself and made a dash for the gents. After hosing out the steaming remains of the Stella Artois and two bottles of mineral water, he rejoined Mrs Totten.

'Okay good-looking,' he said, happy now that his ordeal was over. 'Let's get you home before your parents start to worry about you.'

'And I'll make you a nice cup of tea,' said Mrs Totten.

'That I would like,' said Les.

With Mrs Totten's umbrella in one hand and her on his other arm, Les walked the old lady back to the bookshop and followed her through the front door. They went round the tables of books then through another door into a small kitchen with slate floor tiles, a shiny stainless-steel sink and a dishwasher set into a black granite top. A window opened onto the laneway, several small paintings hung round the walls, and beneath the kitchen table in front of the fridge Mrs Totten's cat was curled up on a rubber mat. It blinked a couple of times when she turned on the light then stretched and went back to sleep. Mrs Totten put the kettle on and turned to Les. 'I'll just change into a pair of slippers,' she said. 'Make yourself comfortable.'

'Okay,' said Les.

Les sat down at the kitchen table, careful not to kick the sleeping cat, then Mrs Totten came back and started fussing around getting the tea together.

'What about those talking trees,' she said, placing a cup in front of Les.

'Yes,' replied Les. 'I nearly fell out of my seat when they walked out of the forest.'

'They saved the day too, when the river burst,' said Mrs Totten.

'They sure did,' agreed Les. 'Now Middle Earth is once again safe from the forces of evil.'

Before too long Mrs Totten had a pot of tea with a crocheted doily on it sitting on the table along with a plate piled with slices of lemon and coconut sponge cake. She poured Les a cup of tea and told him to help himself to the cake. The tea hit the spot and the cake was sensational. It made Norton a little homesick for his mother's house in Dirranbandi. Les complimented Mrs Totten on her cake, they chit-chatted some more about the movie, then Mrs Totten slid a piece of paper across the table to Les.

'That's the woman's name and mobile phone number and the address,' said Mrs Totten. 'The orphanage is not far from where you're staying. She's expecting you round ten-thirty tomorrow. All you have to do is drive her to Apollo Bay and back.'

'Good as gold,' said Les. 'Thanks very much, Mrs Totten.'

Mrs Totten smiled at Les over her cup of tea. 'No worries,' she said, taking a delicate sip. 'She's a lovely person, Tania. Even though she's had a terrible lot of misfortune in her life.'

'She has?' inquired Les.

'Yes. I'll tell you a little about her.'

'Okay. If you'd care to.'

'Tania was an orphan herself,' said Mrs Totten. 'There used to be an orphanage in Apollo Bay. Before it burnt down.'

'None of the kids were burned, were they?' said Les.

'No. Everybody was saved, except the head nun, Sister Manuella. She never got burned though. A beam fell on her and broke her neck.'

Les shook his head. 'That's no good.'

'There were only a dozen or so children in the orphanage,' continued Mrs Totten. 'And when it burnt down they all managed to get adopted. Tania went with a local family. The Walmsleys. He was the town butcher.'

'I used to work in meatworks,' smiled Les.

Mrs Totten nodded over her tea. 'Tania eventually married a man named Grant Currie. He was a surveyor. And they had two children. A son, Grant Junior. And a daughter, Angie.'

Les looked at the piece of paper. 'I thought her name was Settree?'

'That was her second husband, Frank. He was an electrician,' said Mrs Totten. 'Her first husband died in Melbourne. He took Angie to visit his mother, and he fell under a train at Flinders Street Station.'

'Crikey!' said Les.

'Then not long after that, her son Grant Junior and Angie were out fishing, and young Grant fell out of the boat and drowned.'

'Poor bloody woman,' sympathised Les. 'So what happened to husband number two? The electrician.'

'He was electrocuted,' said Mrs Totten.

'Yeah. Well, that's an occupational hazard in that game,' said Les.

'Yes. But Frank was taking a bath. And a hair dryer accidentally fell in the water.'

'Cripes! I'd certainly call that misfortune,' said Les.

'Tania never remarried,' said Mrs Totten. 'She lives alone with her daughter and runs the orphanage.'

'What a sad sort of life,' said Les.

'Yes. But she's happy now. Even if running the orphanage is a constant battle. Although Angie's a little strange.'

'Her daughter?' said Les.

'Yes. She's nineteen. But keeps very much to herself. I don't think she's … you know. But she doesn't seem to like boys or men very much. Actually it's funny you're after your mother's paintings. Because Angie likes to paint.'

Les looked directly at Mrs Totten. 'Not devils or witches? Or anything like that?'

'No. Nothing like that,' laughed Mrs Totten. 'I've seen her paintings. It's all abstract dribble. She's never sold any and I wouldn't hang them in the shop. But don't tell Tania or her daughter I said that.'

'My lips are glued,' replied Les.

They both finished a second cup of tea at the same time just as Les polished off a third piece of cake. Mrs Totten smiled at him.

'Les, I hate to be an ungrateful host after all you've done for me tonight, but I'm awfully tired now.'

'Hey. No worries, Mrs Totten,' said Les. 'I understand. In fact I'm quite tired myself, after all that sword-fighting and dodging blazing arrows and axes and things.'

She placed a hand on his. 'I'll walk you to the door.'

Les stood up, sneakily leaving a fifty-dollar bill under his saucer. 'When I get back from Apollo Bay tomorrow,' he said. 'I'll call in and tell you how I went. We might have another cup of tea. And,' Les wiggled his eyebrows, 'maybe just another slice or two of your lemon sponge cake.'

'That would be lovely,' beamed Mrs Totten.

Mrs Totten walked Les to the front door and opened it. She looked up at Les then put her arms around him and hugged him. Resting on his chest, her head didn't even come up to the big Queenslander's chin.

'Les, I had a wonderful time tonight,' she said. 'You're a true gentleman. Thank you ever so much.'

Les went all funny inside. 'Hey,' he said, gently rubbing the old lady's bony back. 'Don't you think I had a good time. How often do I get to take a good sort out and see a grouse movie?'

Mrs Totten looked up again and waved a finger at Les. 'You're only saying that because it's true.'

'You're on to me, sweetheart,' smiled Les. He placed his hands on Mrs Totten's shoulders and gave the bookshop owner a kiss on the forehead. 'I'll see you tomorrow, Mrs Totten, and thanks very much for your help.'

'It was a pleasure.'

Mrs Totten closed the door, Les put his hands in the pockets of his jacket and walked towards the resort. When he rounded the corner he looked up and behind a bank of clouds a sprinkling of stars twinkled against the deep indigo of the night sky. Look at that, smiled Les. The rain's cleared up. Truly it is an omen from the great wizard of ... wherever that old fart with the silly hat comes from.

Once inside, Les changed into his tracksuit and cleaned his teeth, then had a cold glass of water in the kitchen. Bloody hell, he yawned, as he rinsed the glass. I don't know about Mrs Totten being tired. But I'm absolutely rooted. Christ! Why not? That movie'd be enough to root anybody. Still. The night wasn't a complete disaster. As well as being a real old sweetheart, Mrs Totten was a big help. And what about that lemon sponge cake. I should have snookered a couple of pieces when I was leaving.

Les switched off the lights in the hallway, then the ones in his room and climbed under the douvet. Well, I wonder how I'll go tomorrow, he thought as he shoved his head into the pillows. I'll more than likely strike out again, I suppose. And I wonder what Widow Settree'll be like? You couldn't bet enough money she'll whinge and whine about her miserable life all the way to Apollo Bay and back. Fair dinkum. If my quest hasn't been long and fraught with shit, I'm a cocky-eyed dwarf with a hygiene problem. Les yawned again then pulled the douvet up round his ears and in minutes he was snoring his head off.

Les slept in the next morning. When he finally got up and looked out over the balcony, the rain had stopped and patches of blue were appearing between the clouds, however the wind was gusting onshore and it was still cold. He raised an arm and sniffed his tracksuit. After sleeping in it since he'd arrived in Lorne, it was starting to get rather minty. Nothing anyone would notice in the restaurant, however. Les cleaned himself up, put his gym boots on, then caught the lift to the lobby and strolled down to have breakfast. The girl on the counter knew him by now and smiled a nice hello when Les gave her his room number. He found a table facing the beach then ripped into the usual, washed down with ample amounts of fruit juice and coffee.

Norton was in a fairly good mood as he ate, even though today was just a case of hope for the best and expect the worst. He had a good feeling about the last church in Apollo Bay. And if it turned out another no-result, at least he was going home and it was all over. He got a chuckle when he remembered how Mrs Totten punched and prodded him when she got excited during the movie, and got even more of a chuckle when he felt the slightest, tiniest bruise on his thigh. Les finished breakfast and went back to his unit, whistling.

Although his faithful, blue tracksuit needed a drink, Les felt it was no good wearing anything clean if he was going to be crawling around dusty storage sheds. And it wasn't as if he was taking the lady from the orphanage to Doyle's for a seafood dinner. He left it on, gave himself a few good squirts of deodorant then, making sure he had everything he needed in his overnight bag, caught the lift down to the parking area.

The Mitsubishi purred into life. Les gave it a few moments to warm up while he checked his map of Lorne, then switched the radio on and drove out of the car park. As he took a right at the roundabout, a barbershop quartet began harmonising beautifully through the speakers.

'Her vaginnnna. Her vaginnnna.

Just a quick reminder, take a peek in her vagina, if she's hur-a-ur-ting.

Brother you can betcha, gonorrhoea is gonna get you, without war-a-ar-ning.'

'What the fuck?' exclaimed Les. 'Has this radio station gone mad? Bloody hell! That's all I need playing when I pull up at the orphanage.' Les shook his head, switched the radio off and drove on up the hill.

The way to the orphanage was behind the white church where he met Vicar Rathbone. Les drove along a tree-lined street, then turned left and pulled up amongst some trees, just back from a driveway in a steep, deadend near some nice homes. The orphanage was on a long, wide sloping block of land facing the ocean. It was a rambling old two-storey building with a tiled roof supported by columns set along wide verandahs that commanded a million-dollar view of the ocean. Huge bay windows were spaced along the verandahs, the grounds were enclosed by stone walls, and there was a yard at the rear full of trees surrounded by a low green wooden fence. In the middle of the yard was a white wooden building with a flat roof, windows along the side and a door at the front. The driveway led up to a wide green gate that opened into a circular courtyard with a flowerbed in the middle. Les guessed the building to be heritage listed and possibly a hundred years old. It had seen better days and needed maintenance here and there. But it was still nothing short of magnificent.

Les got out of the car and walked over to the gate. As he did, he noticed a curtain draw back in the wooden building behind the orphanage and someone watching him all the way. Les opened a door in the gate and stepped into the courtyard. There was a laundry and a shed behind the orphanage and parked to one side of the courtyard was a plain, battered, black kombi-wagon. Les couldn't see a back door and he wanted to check out the view. So he walked quietly around the top verandah, past windows hung with thick blue curtains. Behind one of the curtains Les glimpsed a lounge room filled with furniture and a TV; the rest were bedrooms. When he got to the front of the orphanage Les stopped and reminded himself to bring his camera with him when he brought the woman who ran the orphanage back from Apollo Bay. The view had to be seen to be believed.

He followed the verandah past more blue-curtained windows around to the other side of the old home, stopping at a wide screendoor in front of a kitchen. All the while Les was expecting to hear children playing or making a noise of some description. But apart from a few magpies and kookaburras making their presence known, and the sound of the breeze stirring the surrounding blue gums, there was silence. Les rapped on the kitchen door and took a peek through the flyscreen.

The kitchen was quite big and although there was no light on, Les could make out an open range gas stove, a stainless steel fridge, and a wooden floor with a long wooden table sitting in the middle. Pots and pans and other cooking utensils hung over the stove, and around the walls long shelves of crockery sat above wooden cabinets with glass fronts. The sort of kitchen you would expect to find in a restaurant or place that catered for a number of people. From a corridor behind the kitchen a slender woman appeared on the left, wearing a white shirt and a grey cardigan over a long, grey, tartan skirt. She was holding a mobile phone in one hand and a pair of round-rimmed glasses in the other and opened the door as soon as she saw Les.

'Come in,' the woman said quietly. 'I won't be a moment.'

'Okay, thanks,' replied Les.

Les stepped inside and while the woman leant against one end of the table talking into the mobile, discreetly checked her out. She was about average height, wore no make-up and had a thin, plain face with worry lines radiating from a pair of soft hazel eyes. Her short black hair was clean and shiny and tucked behind her ears with two small combs and although Les couldn't see much grey amongst the black, guessed her age as approaching a hard-working fifty. Two thin hands poked out from under her cardigan and a glimpse of skinny white ankle poked out from below her long woollen skirt. The woman blinked constantly as she spoke on the phone and after she put her glasses on once she'd finished talking, looked very Miss Prissy. She walked nervously over to Les and kept her head slightly bowed when she spoke, giving Norton the impression of a woman who felt ill at ease around men; even a little frightened.

'You must be Mr Norton?' she blinked.

'That's right,' Les smiled softly. 'Les Norton. Are you Mrs Settree? The lady that runs the orphanage?'

'Yes. That's right.'

Les offered her his hand. 'Pleased to meet you, Mrs Settree.'

The woman gave Norton's hand a gentle shake. 'Thank you, Mr Norton.'

Les shook his head. 'I should be thanking you.'

Mrs Settree blinked and looked at Les for a moment. 'I'm sorry if it's a little dark in here,' she apologised. 'But we keep the lights off to try and save on electricity.'

'Good idea, Mrs Settree,' commended Les. He ran his eyes from the kitchen to the corridor running behind. 'It's very quiet,' said Les. 'I was expecting to see kids running everywhere.'

'All the girls have gone camping at Lake Colac while there's a break in the weather,' said Mrs Settree. 'They'll be back tomorrow afternoon.'

'How many girls are there?' asked Les.

'At the moment, twenty.'

'Are they very old?'

'Ten to fifteen,' replied Mrs Settree.

'Right,' said Les. He ran his eyes around the kitchen. 'Gee, it's a beautiful old house, Mrs Settree.'

'Yes. Would you like to have a look around?' she asked.

'I would,' said Les. 'But how about when we get back from Apollo Bay?'

'Very well,' said Mrs Settree. 'Can I get you something? A cup of tea? A glass of water …?'

'No. That's all right, thanks,' said Les. He smiled at Mrs Settree. 'So Mrs Totten told you what's going on?'

'Yes. You're looking for some paintings.'

'That's right. My mother did them a long time ago. The family thinks they still might be down here.'

'Well, I certainly hope you find them,' said Mrs Settree.

'Yes. I've come a long way,' said Les.

Mrs Settree blinked at Les a couple of times from behind her glasses. 'I'll get my handbag and scarf and we'll get going.'

'When you're ready, Mrs Settree,' said Les. 'There's no mad hurry.'

Mrs Settree turned and walked off to the right down the corridor at the back of the kitchen. She returned a minute or two later with a grey tartan scarf round her neck and holding a small black leather handbag.

'I'm ready,' she said.

'Okay,' replied Les. 'Let's go.' He held the kitchen door open, Mrs Setttree stepped through and they followed the verandah round to the back of the orphanage.

'Aren't you going to lock the door?' asked Les.

'My daughter Angie's here,' replied Mrs Settree. 'She'll look after things.'

'Okey doke.'

Les followed Mrs Settree across the courtyard then through the door in the gate and up to Norton's car. Les opened the door for her, she thanked him then got inside and did up her seatbelt and Les did the same. Les started the motor and absently switched the radio back on as he did a U-turn to go back up the hill. Through the four-speaker system the barbershop quartet started harmonising melodically again.

'*It's beginning to look — a — lot — like — syphillis.*'

'What the ...?'

Les stabbed at the dash and switched the radio off, then turned to Mrs Settree apologetically. However, everything appeared to have gone over her head and she just sat there like Miss Prissy, buckled up, clutching her handbag and staring out the windscreen. Les came back down behind the church to get onto the main road and drove for a while before speaking.

'So how long have you known Mrs Totten?' he asked.

'Oh, many years now,' replied Mrs Settree.

'She's a bit of a sweetheart,' said Les.

'Yes she certainly is. God bless her,' agreed Mrs Settree.

'She's not bad on her feet either,' chuckled Les. 'Do you know what she did to me?'

'No.'

Les told Mrs Settree how Mrs Totten cajoled him into taking her to the movies. But it had been fun watching her have a good time and she made him a nice cup of tea later. Her sponge cake was good too.

'*The Two Towers*?' said Mrs Settree.

'Yeah,' replied Les. 'Have you seen it?' Mrs Settree shook her head. 'Did you see the first one?' Mrs Settree shook her head again and Les was going to tell her she'd hadn't missed much.

'To take even ten girls to the pictures would cost a fortune,' said Mrs Settree. 'And I couldn't just go on my own.'

'Yes. I hadn't thought of that,' said Les. 'Anyway, Mrs Totten also threatened me if I didn't give a donation to the orphanage.'

'You're not obliged to, Mr Norton,' said Mrs Settree. 'But it would be greatly appreciated if you did.'

'That's okay,' said Les. He put his foot down a little as they began to leave Lorne behind them. 'So how long have you been running the orphanage, Mrs Settree?'

'Quite a few years now,' replied Mrs Settree. 'And you can call me Tania if you like, Mr Norton.'

'Okay. So how do you get on, Tania?'

'Get on? We simply get on as best we can,' replied Tania.

'Fair enough,' said Les. 'So who owns the building? It's in a beautiful spot.'

'The Church of the Holy Blood.'

'Is that the white one near the hotel?'

'Yes. Vicar Rathbone.'

'I met him,' said Les. 'He seemed like a nice man. Do they charge you much rent?'

'Not really,' replied Mrs Settree. 'I took over the home at the end of a one-hundred-year lease.'

'How long have you got to go on the lease?' asked Les.

'Five years,' said Mrs Settree.

'Five years,' said Les. 'What happens then?'

'Vicar Rathbone intends to sell the building.'

Les half smiled. 'They always do. So what'll happen to you and the kids?'

'I'm not sure,' replied Mrs Settree. 'But we're hoping something will turn up.'

'How much will they sell the building for?'

'The vicar's been offered over a million dollars.'

'I can see why,' said Les.

'Yes,' nodded Mrs Settree. 'It's in a prime position, as they say.'

The lady from the orphanage still kept looking straight ahead at the road, never making eye contact with Les when she spoke, and Les couldn't remember meeting a woman so mousy. But there was something about Mrs Settree he liked, so he thought he'd try and get her out of her shell.

'Mrs Totten said you were in an orphanage yourself,' said Les.

'Yes,' replied Mrs Settree. 'And I can't say they were the best years of my life either.'

'They weren't?'

Tania shook her head grimly. 'No. Not at all.'

Les thought for a moment. 'And might I hazard a guess, Tania,' he said, 'and suggest you took over the orphanage to see the girls there got a better go than you did.'

Tania slowly turned to Les. 'That's exactly right, Mr Norton,' she said.

'Well good for you, Tania. Well done. You're a deadset gem.'

Tania blinked at Les. 'It's funny,' she said. 'But I don't mind talking to you, Mr Norton. You have a polite honesty about you.'

'Well thank you, Mrs Settree,' smiled Les. 'That's quite a compliment. And I like talking to you also.'

'Oh? Why's that Mr Norton?'

'You're a person who gives of themselves, Tania. You don't see much of that where I come from. And I can tell you're honest, too.'

Tania went back to staring out the windscreen. 'There was another reason I took over the orphanage,' she said.

'Oh? Why was that?' asked Les.

'To get away from my husband.'

'Your husband?'

'Yes. He … he used to beat me.'

Les screwed his face up. 'Beat you? Christ! There's not much to beat.'

'Grant didn't seem to think so,' said Tania.

Les thought he might get Mrs Settree's version of what Mrs Totten had told him about her. 'So what happened to your husband?' he asked.

'He fell under a train,' answered Tania.

'Serves him bloody right,' said Les.

'In front of our daughter, too,' said Tania.

'Shit! That would have been traumatic for her,' said Les.

'Actually, Angie handled it quite well.'

'Right.' Les put his foot down to head off another council truck before it could pull out from the side of the road and slow him down. 'Did you ever remarry, Mrs Settree?'

'Yes. And Frank was almost as bad as my first husband. He even hit Angie.'

'He did? And what happened to him?' asked Les.

'Frank got electrocuted.'

'Well. I suppose it serves him right, too,' said Les.

'Possibly,' said Tania. 'But it's not a very nice thing to say.'

'It's not very nice to hit women, either,' said Les. 'Except in self-defence of course,' he added with a smile. 'In fact I thought I was going to have to give Mrs Totten a rabbit-killer last night. She got a bit excited during the movie and kept belting into me. I even had a bruise on my arm this morning,' Les sniffed.

'Bless her,' smiled Tania.

'Yes, the old darling.' Les slowed the car right down for a hairpin bend. 'She said you had a son who died. Is that right?'

'Yes. Grant Junior. He was out fishing with Angie and drowned.'

'Gee. That's bad luck,' said Les.

'He was a strange boy, though, young Grant,' said Tania. 'A lot like his father in many ways.'

'How do you mean?' asked Les.

'He was violent. My son Grant actually hit me on several occasions. And he used to hit Angie too.'

'Crikey! You've sure had it tough, Tania,' said Les.

'It was bad at times,' nodded Tania.

Les slowed down for a small white bus full of backpackers. 'So I imagine you and your daughter would be very close now?' said Les.

'Very close,' answered Tania. 'In fact I often think of Angie as my little guardian angel.'

'That's nice.'

Les now understood why Tania was nervous around men, and being stuck in a car next to a gorilla like him wouldn't have been a day at the beach for her. Conversely, it was a pleasant surprise to know she liked him. Les felt at this point it might be an idea to change the subject.

'So how come you can get into these church storage sheds in Apollo Bay, Tania?' he asked.

'The ministers let me have a key in case I need something for the orphans. Blankets, toys. Different little things.'

'That's decent of them,' said Les.

'Except for The Church of the Holy Order. But the caretaker's there. And he'll let me in.'

'Is that Uriah?' said Les.

Tania turned to Les. 'Yes. You met Uriah?'

'Yeah, yesterday,' said Les. 'Only for a few minutes.'

'How did you find him?'

'Find him? Polite,' said Les. 'A little wild-eyed. But polite.'

'Yes. That's one way to describe Uriah,' agreed Tania. She stared out the windscreen as Les manoeuvred the Mitsubishi around two hairpin bends then turned to Les. 'So tell me a little about yourself, Mr Norton.'

'Me? Okay,' smiled Norton. 'And you can call me Les if you want to.'

Les told Tania mostly the truth. He came from Queensland, worked at the Cross in Sydney and had a house in Bondi. By the time he got to Warren and Clover and different things, Les was driving into Apollo Bay.

'You lead quite an interesting life, Les,' said Tania.

'It has its moments,' agreed Les.

Traffic was light. But because the weather had improved there were more people around than the day before and the council was working on the road.

'We may as well go to the big brick church first,' suggested Les, driving past a lollipop-man in an orange vest.

'The Church of Our Blessed Lady,' said Tania. 'I know it well.'

'Daht's de one, 'oman,' said Les.

'I beg your pardon, Mr Norton?' said Tania.

'Nothing, Tania,' smiled Les. 'I was just trying out my Jamaican. I'll tell you about that on the way home.'

Les took a left at the war memorial, then pulled up on the grass at the rear of the church opposite the golf course. He took the torch from his overnight bag and followed Tania around to the storage shed. She took a key from her bag, turned it in the lock and the door creaked open. Having been there before, Mrs Settree quickly found the light switch near the door.

The shed lit up and apart from the usual junk, it was mostly gardening essentials stacked neatly on tables or resting against walls. In the middle of the shed was an old grey Morris Minor convertible up on blocks.

'Hey, look at that,' said Les. 'It's not in bad nick, either.'

'Rupert's been going to get that on the road for years,' said Tania. 'One of the parishioners gave it to him.'

'He should,' said Les, shining his torch along the dash. 'It's a classic.'

'Yes,' agreed Tania. 'Can I help you at all, Mr Norton … Les?'

'No. I'll be okay thanks,' replied Les.

Les started rummaging through what there was. Boxes of books, LPs, old clothes, suitcases, etc. There was everything from the old car to old Victa lawn mowers. But nothing remotely resembling a bundle of old paintings.

'No sign of any paintings, Mr Norton?' asked Tania.

Les shook his head. 'No. Fried egg, I'm afraid.' Norton turned the torch off and wiped his hands on the sides of his tracksuit. 'We go and have a look at the one up the road, past the war memorial?'

'Saint Quillan's.'

'Yeah. That's it.'

Tania locked the door and they walked back to the car. Les opened the door for her first, then got in and they drove the short distance to the white-panelled church with the low brick wall out the front. They got out of the car and Les followed Tania across to the storage shed. She found another key, turned it in the lock and the rickety wooden door almost fell off its hinges when it swung open.

There was no light inside; Les switched his torch on to find the shed was crammed mostly with old building materials. Bits of wood, sheets of corrugated iron going rusty, saws, sledgehammers, post-hole diggers. All placed on a dirty concrete floor spread with tins of paint, oil, weed killer and boxes of nails and screws or whatever. Again Tania offered to help. Les said it was okay, and started walking and crawling around with his torch. All he got for his trouble was a couple of skinned knuckles and more dirt on his tracksuit.

'Nothing again, Mr Norton?' said Tania.

Les let go a couple of robust sneezes. 'No,' he said. 'But there's plenty of dust and cobwebs.'

Les took out his handkerchief to blow his nose and wipe where he'd skinned his knuckles, then flashed the torch up around the ceiling. There was nothing there except some old rope, several blackened hurricane lamps and a rusty double-handed rip-saw. Les switched off the torch and turned to Mrs Settree.

'Well. One to go.'

'The Church of the Holy Order,' said Tania.

'Yeah. Let's call in and see Uriah.'

'Uriah's a nice boy,' said Tania as they stepped out of the shed. 'But I think he needs to get out more often.'

'Yes,' agreed Les. 'All work and no play makes Jack a dull boy. Or whoever the case may be.'

Tania locked the door to the storage shed and they walked back to the car. Although he'd struck out again with the last two churches, Les didn't feel so disappointed having the woman from the orphanage for company, and he still had a good feeling about the last church. They got in the car and proceeded on to Sandstock Road.

The yellow church looked a lot brighter in the sunshine and so did the flowers along the pathway. Les stopped the car in front of the gate, then he and Tania got out and took the slab path past the vestry and round to the residence. The sound of someone tapping metal was coming from the garage. They walked across and Tania knocked on the side door. A few seconds later Uriah appeared at the door in his khaki overalls. As soon as his God-fearing eyes fell on Mrs Settree, a slick formed on Uriah's forehead and he started to hyperventilate. He stared at her, then came out of the garage with one eyebrow twitching and his top lip curling like Benny Hill when he used to play the fat perv in the round glasses and beret on TV, ogling the bikini girls.

'Good morning Uriah,' smiled Mrs Settree. 'How are you today?'

Uriah's eyes bored into Tania as if he had Superman's X-ray vision, and if Les wasn't mistaken, the deacon's nephew had a roaring boner poking against his overalls.

'I'm good, Mrs Settree,' Uriah replied, in a rasping growl. 'Real good. How are you this truly wonderful day?'

'Fine thank you, Uriah.' Tania indicated to Les. 'You met Mr Norton?'

Uriah hadn't noticed Les standing beside her. 'Oh yes,' he panted. 'Mr Norton. Good day, sir. How are you?' Uriah glanced at Les before quickly riveting his gaze back on Tania.

'I'm all right thanks,' said Les cheerfully. 'And is that a Bible in your overalls, Uriah? Or are you just happy to see Mrs Settree?'

Uriah turned back to Les. 'What was that?' he rasped.

'I said, you've got your overalls on again, Uriah,' smiled Les. 'And you're a man of the Bible, who's happy when he's working. Which is good to see.'

'Yes, yes. I do. I mean, I am, yes,' drooled Uriah, his God-fearing eyes immediately clicking back onto Tania.

'Good for you mate,' said Les. Yeah. And if I wasn't around, you'd be all over poor Mrs Settree like ants at a picnic. You happy-clapping ratbag.

'Mr Norton's here to look in your storage shed for some paintings, Uriah,' said Tania. 'Is that all right?'

'Yes. I got your message earlier, Mrs Settree,' wheezed Uriah. 'That's quite all right. And Mr Norton explained things to me yesterday.'

'That's right,' said Les. 'And I appreciate what you're doing for me too, Uriah. Don't you worry about that.'

'I'll get the key,' said Uriah.

Uriah ogled Tania again, like the crazy little weasel in the Bugs Bunny cartoons always trying to steal the chickens off Foghorn Leghorn, then hobbled off to the residence on three legs. Les turned to Tania and smiled.

'Nice young man,' said Les.

'Yes,' said Tania. 'But if ever I'm here with Uriah, I always feel a little uncomfortable. I don't know why. Maybe it's just my imagination.'

'Maybe,' said Les. 'But I think you're right when you said he should get out a bit more.'

'You think so?' blinked Tania.

'I'm sure so,' Les nodded. 'Right out. Like Mars or Pluto.'

Uriah returned holding a key. He'd managed to tuck his roaring boner up under his overalls and was walking straighter. However, the lust in his God-fearing eyes for Tania hadn't receded one bit. If anything, it burnt brighter as he ogled her again.

'Here's the key,' he panted.

'Thank you, Uriah,' said Tania.

'Good on you mate,' said Les.

Uriah opened the door to the storage shed then switched on the light and they followed him inside. Les had a quick look around and gave a double, triple blink. There was lots of junk stacked neatly around the shed. But sitting on a wide bench taking up one wall was a small army of garden gnomes. They weren't ordinary garden gnomes. They'd all been repainted in bright colours, and their little gnome faces had been changed. There was an Alice Cooper gnome, a Marilyn Manson gnome, a Keith Richards gnome. Adolf Hitler, Joseph Stalin, Saddam Hussein, Whoopi Goldberg. There was a Boy George gnome and four gnomes painted like KISS, right down to Gene Simmons with his monster tongue hanging out. There was even a gnome amongst the others that looked suspiciously like Mrs Settree.

Les turned to Uriah. 'All ... your own work, Uriah?' he asked.

'Yes,' nodded Uriah. 'Do you like them?'

'Yeah,' nodded Les. 'They're great.'

'They're my little friends,' said Uriah.

'Uriah's very talented,' blinked Tania.

'I can certainly see that,' said Les. 'Why don't you put them outside in the sun, Uriah?' he asked.

'Uncle Lorimer doesn't like me to,' replied Uriah. 'He thinks they're evil. But I sneak them out sometimes. I'm just waiting for the paint to dry on Dame Edna. And I'm going to put them all out this afternoon. And we'll have a little tea party.'

'Just like Alice in Wonderland,' smiled Les.

'Yes,' Uriah smiled back. 'Just like Alice in Wonderland.'

'I'll start looking for the paintings.'

Les began searching around the storage shed, watching Uriah out the corner of his eye edging up to Tania, while she nervously shuffled away from him before he could start humping her leg.

If the paintings had been there they would have been easy to find because Uriah had the storage shed as clean as a whistle and everything was packed and sorted away neatly. Amongst the boxes of books, videos, records, golf bags, maps, mirrors, irons, coffee machines, crockpots, lamps, beer steins, old bottles and whatever, there wasn't a speck of dust or a cobweb. There was also no sign of any paintings or anything resembling a bundle of paintings. Norton's heart sank. This was it. The last blast. There was nowhere else now. He looked under the table full of gnomes, stood up and shook his head. And I had a feeling about this place. Les stared at a Johnny O'Keefe gnome in a leopardskin coat, red shoes and a string bow-tie. Some bloody feeling.

'Nothing again, Mr Norton?' asked Tania. She was standing not far from Les, keeping a small stack of school desks between her and a heaving Uriah.

'No. Nothing unfortunately,' said Les.

'Oh. I'm so sorry,' said Tania.

'Yeah,' nodded Les. He gave Tania a weary smile. 'So we may as well get going. Unless you want to stay here and talk to Uriah for a while. I can get a coffee and come back.'

'Yes, yes,' nodded Uriah. 'Mrs Settree could stay here with me.'

Tania latched onto Les's arm like she was going to tear it out of its socket. 'Mr Norton. Don't you dare ...' She let go of Norton's arm and composed herself. 'I mean. Don't you dare think I would stay here alone with Deacon Brockenshire's

233

nephew. My goodness! I'm old enough to be his mother. What would people say?'

'No, no,' whined Uriah. 'It's all right, Mrs Settree. You can stay.'

Les turned to Uriah. 'I'm afraid I have to agree with Mrs Settree, Uriah,' he said. 'A small town. People could get the wrong idea and construe that as some kind of subliminal incest.'

Uriah shook his head emphatically. 'No, no,' he said.

'Yes, yes,' nodded Tania just as emphatically.

Les stepped across and pushed the side door open. 'After you, Mrs Settree.'

'Thank you, Mr Norton,' breathed Tania.

Tania stepped outside and Uriah pushed in front of Les behind her. Les came out, closed the door and followed them down the slab path to the car.

Mrs Settree was walking fairly quickly with Uriah breathing down her neck. Les watched Uriah slip one hand inside his overalls then start stumbling along behind her, having a full-blown game of pocket billiards. They got to the gate and Uriah stopped as Tania opened it before she hurried across to the passenger side of the car. Les stepped past Uriah, closed the gate then turned around and smiled.

'Well, thanks for your help, Uriah,' said Les. 'Enjoy your tea party this afternoon.' Les squinted up as the sun appeared between the clouds. 'Looks like you've got a nice day for it.'

'Yes, thank you, Mr Norton,' wheezed Uriah as he kept furiously playing pocket billiards under his overalls. The veins started to bulge out round his temples, and he stared desperately over at Tania. 'Goodbye Mrs Settree,' he wailed.

Tania was holding onto the car door as if her life depended on it. 'Goodbye Uriah,' she called back. 'Be sure and say hello to your Uncle Lorimer for me.'

The second Les opened the car door for her, Tania got inside and quickly buckled up. With an eye still on Uriah, Les strolled round to the driver's side and opened the door just as Uriah's knees buckled and he gripped the gate with one hand for support. His blond hair flew back, then he let go a long, anguished groan of ecstasy and, seconds later, a huge wet patch started soaking through the front of Uriah's khaki overalls. Les climbed behind the wheel and turned to Tania, who was staring anxiously out the windscreen.

'Well, I guess that's that, Mrs Settree,' Les started to say.

Tania nodded to the keys in Norton's hands. 'Don't you think you should start the car, Mr Norton,' she suggested.

'Yeah, righto.' Les put the key in the starter and kicked the motor over. 'One thing, Tania,' said Les as he buckled up. 'At least the car doesn't suffer from premature ignition.'

Norton's mind was elsewhere as they drove back towards the main road. The Church of the Holy Order was the last roll of the dice and now Les realised it was all over. Still, he told himself. Nothing ventured, nothing gained. And at least he had a go. Les missed the turn-off he'd taken on the way out and was now driving along another road to the left, still deep in thought. Tania wasn't saying anything either.

Houses were thin and it was mostly sparse brown fields pushing up to the surrounding hills. Les pulled up at a crossroad and noticed on the left a large block of land with a weathered grey sliprail fence in front taking up the corner. A white metal sign in front of a tree next to a locked gate on a dirt driveway said BLUE DOLPHIN GALLERY. The driveway led to a glimpse of buildings obscured by tall green fir trees. Les turned to Tania and noticed she was staring at the dashboard and looked quite downcast.

'Are you all right, Tania?' he asked.

Tania turned to the driveway. 'That's where the orphanage used to be,' she answered.

'The one you were in?' said Les.

'Yes. Saint Benedicta's.'

'Looks like it's an art gallery now.'

'Yes.' Tania turned away and stared melancholically out the windscreen.

Les figured Mrs Settree had no desire to get out and reminisce about her childhood, and having figured out where he was, he turned right and eventually got back onto Sandstock Road.

'Mrs Settree,' asked Les as they drove along. 'What would you say to a nice cup of coffee right now?'

Tania brightened up. 'Yes. I'd like that very much,' she said.

'There's a nice little place in Apollo Bay sells good coffee and pina colada muffins. I was in there yesterday.'

'Sailor Girls,' said Tania.

'That's it,' answered Les. 'We'll hit there. And have a cuppa.'

'Lovely,' said Mrs Settree. They drove past some colourful wooden houses, then Tania turned and smiled at Les. 'Well, Mr Norton, I must say, you seem quite happy, despite your disappointment at not finding your mother's paintings.'

'Yeah, well, what can you do?' shrugged Les. 'You just got to cop it on the chin. It's not the end of the world.'

'No. But I imagine your family will be very disappointed as well. Having sent you all this way and everything.'

Les smiled at Tania. 'They'll just have to cop it on the chin too.'

It didn't take Les long to find his way back into town and there was a parking spot two down from Sailor Girls. He got out of the car, opened the door for Tania and they walked back to the coffee shop. There were a number of people seated out the front, but the same table Les had the day before was empty and Les pulled a chair out for Tania.

'Now. What can I get you, Mrs Settree?' he asked.

'A pina colada muffin and a mug of flat white, please,' she replied. 'Is that all right?'

Les gave Tania a wink. 'I'm going to have exactly the same thing myself.'

Les went to the counter and ordered then returned to the table. He sat down and smiled at Tania.

'Well, Tania. Despite not finding the paintings, you've been a great help, and I really appreciate you going to the trouble you have. I know how busy you must be, with the orphanage and all that.'

'That's all right, Mr Norton,' Tania replied. 'I enjoyed the drive down. And I enjoyed your company.'

'Thank you Mrs Settree,' said Les. 'And I'll make sure I leave a donation when we get back to the orphanage.'

'Whatever you can spare will do, Mr Norton,' said Tania, looking a little embarrassed.

'I can spare something, Tania,' Les assured her. 'And I'd like to take some photos when we get back too, if that's all right.'

'Of course, Mr Norton. It would be a pleasure.'

A tall curly-haired girl in black brought their order over. Les thanked her then he and Tania sugared their coffees and started in.

'So do you come down here much?' asked Les.

'Every now and again,' replied Tania, enjoying her muffin and coffee. 'Something gets donated I can use at the orphanage. And we bring the girls down to play netball or hockey.'

'Did you play sport when you were younger?' asked Les.

'I was quite a good runner,' replied Tania. 'I actually represented my school in the state titles. But I hurt my ankle bushwalking, and it was never the same.'

'Yeah. I got a crook knee from football,' said Les. 'It's okay now. But they're never a hundred per cent.'

'I used to like running too,' said Tania. 'Especially on a cold, crisp day.'

'Yeah,' nodded Les. He took a sip of coffee and looked at Mrs Settree. 'Did you ever know Father Shipley, from the Church of the Blessed Madonna, Tania?' he asked her.

'Yes,' replied Tania. 'But I never really got on with him. Right up until his death.'

'Oh?' said Les. 'How do you mean?'

'I don't know,' shrugged Tania. 'He'd say hello and that. But he always seemed to avoid me, for some reason.'

'Avoid you?'

'Mmhh. Even when I was young. He had a small sailboat, and he'd often take the other girls out sailing. But he'd never take me.' Tania made a tiny gesture with one hand. 'I mean. It's not as if I was ever rude to him. Or anything like that.'

'Yeah. People can be funny at times,' said Les. 'Actually I visited his grave yesterday. I left some flowers on it.'

'That was thoughtful of you, Mr Norton,' said Tania.

'Well, I was in Lorne,' said Les, magnanimously. He looked at Mrs Settree over his mug for a moment. 'It said on his grave, "Loved by all. Especially the people at the cable station." And something about? "So he ... bringeth them unto the haven — where they would be." I'm kind of curious what all that's about.'

Tania looked back at Les. 'I'm not overly religious,' she said. 'But the piece about, "unto the haven" is a passage from the Bible. Father Shipley saved almost twenty men from drowning once.'

'Fair dinkum?'

'Yes. He was quite an avid sailor,' said Tania. 'And he often used to sail his small boat from Lorne to Apollo Bay. He sailed down here one morning, just as a big storm blew in from Bass Strait and a timber vessel overturned. Father Shipley saved all

239

the crew, except for one, and brought them into Apollo Bay. The government gave him a medal.'

'Go on,' said Les.

'And he was also involved with the old telegraph cable station. Before it became a museum.'

'I noticed it on the way in,' said Les. 'What did you say it was? A telegraph cable station? What's that?'

'Before satellite technology came in. The original telegraph cable across to Tasmania was laid from here,' said Tania. 'It was completed in the thirties. But the building's over a hundred years old.'

'Is that right?' said Les.

'You may not think so, Mr Norton. But at one time almost everything came into Apollo Bay by ship. The roads in those days were little more than bullock tracks.'

'Really?' said Les.

'Oh yes. There was no Great Ocean Road then,' said Tania. 'And when the telegraph cable finally became obsolete, Father Shipley made sure the government would never sell the old building. So it would preserve the area's heritage. Then after he died it became a museum.'

Les stopped eating his muffin and looked directly at Mrs Settree. 'Did you say a museum, Tania?'

Tania smiled at Les. 'I feel I know what you're thinking, Mr Norton. But believe me, I've been in there on many an occasion with the children. And there's no paintings. Lots of old photos. But no paintings.'

Les watched Mrs Settree sip her coffee. 'Tania, did Father Shipley have any other connection with the old telegraph station? Apart from getting it preserved as a museum?'

'Oh yes,' replied Mrs Settree. 'He helped with the maintenance. Baptised the workers' babies. Took care of any widows whose husbands died on the job. Considering his parish was in Lorne, he spent a lot of time in Apollo Bay.' A coy smile formed on Mrs Settree's face. 'It was rumoured he was having an affair with one of the widows. And that she had a son to him, who became a well-known detective in Melbourne.'

Les kept his eyes on Mrs Settree. 'Does the museum have a storage shed?' he asked her.

'Yes. An old building out the back,' she replied. 'No one ever bothers much about it.'

'You wouldn't have a key to the storage shed, Tania?' asked Les.

Tania shook her head. 'No. But my friend Mrs Sheridan has. She's one of the museum's volunteer caretakers.'

'Any chance of getting the key off her?' asked Les.

'I don't see why not. She runs a gift shop with her daughter just a few doors up the road. I'll go and ask her.' Mrs Settree picked up her handbag and rose from the table.

'Do you want me to come with you?' asked Les.

'No. Stay here, Mr Norton, I'll only be a few minutes.'

'Okay.'

Les watched Mrs Settree walk off to the left and drummed his fingers on the table. Dear Father Shipley. Acting the good samaritan at the telegraph station while he was porking a lonely widow on the side. Mrs Totten said he was a bit of a devil. He could have sailed down here with the paintings and stashed them somewhere to get them out of Lorne. Maybe there was another roll left in the dice yet. Mrs Settree returned and sat down looking rather pleased with herself. She opened her handbag and took out a solid brass key tied by a strip of leather to a piece of wood with MUSEUM printed on it.

'Here it is, Mr Norton,' she smiled.

'Hey. Well done, Mrs Settree,' said Les. 'Thanks for that.'

'Do you wish to go there now?' asked Mrs Settree.

'Yeah. Why not?' said Les. He got up to pay the bill and they walked out to the car.

It was only a short drive back up the main road to the Cable Station Museum. Les swung left up a driveway then reversed round into a gravel parking area with a fir tree in the corner. He turned off the engine and had a look through the windscreen.

The old single-storey red-brick building was quite big and set in a large fenced-off block of land overlooking the ocean. A yellow double-door stood at the front between four whited-over windows, and there was a side entrance down to the left. A wide patch of grass ran down the right side and scattered around the grass or against the fence and the side of the building, were old wooden signs with WARNING: TELEGRAPH CABLE on them along with piles of greying timber and lumps of rusting metal. Les stopped the engine, took his overnight bag from the back seat and they got out of the car.

'Where to?' Les asked Mrs Settree.

'This way, Mr Norton.'

Les followed Mrs Settree down the left side of the building past the side entrance, then past a garage and, further along, a large concrete water tank. Where the block of land ended back from the water tank, an old sandstone building with a tarred roof pushed into the hill behind the cable station. There were no windows, but at the front was a sturdy greying wooden door with a rusty keyhole in it.

'Crikey,' said Les. 'It's a solid, big old thing.'

'Yes,' agreed Mrs Settree. 'They built them to last in those days.'

'Did they ever,' muttered Les.

Mrs Settree took the key, put it in the keyhole and gave it a turn. She gave it another hard turn. Got her strength back and gave it another.

'Oh dear!' she said. 'It won't open.'

'Give me a go.'

Les gripped the key and gave it a good twist. It might have moved, except the hole was full of corrosion from the salty air. Les removed the key, opened his bag and took out a small can of WD40.

'I'm a good boy scout, Tania,' said Les. 'I'm always prepared.'

'Yes. You certainly are, Mr Norton,' smiled Mrs Settree.

Les gave the keyhole a good squirt, then squirted some over the key. After waiting a moment or two, he put the key in and tried again. A couple more turns plus a bit of gentle persuasion and the lock clicked. Les pushed the door with his foot and it creaked partially open. He handed Mrs Settree back the key, then picked up his overnight bag and took out his torch.

'After you, Mrs Settree,' he said.

'Thank you.' Mrs Settree put the key back in her bag and blinked at Les. 'I've never been in here before.'

Les gave her a wink. 'There's always a first time for everything, Tania.'

Les pushed the door open and followed Mrs Settree inside. He shone the torch around the wall next to the door and found an old brass light fitting. Mrs Settree switched it on and a bulb sputtered a few times from behind a metal grille in the ceiling before filling the room with just as many shadows as light.

'Shit a brick!' said Les. 'Where do you start?'

Piled around the room, or lying on the cobblestone floor, were age-old objects covered in dust and cobwebs. Mostly to do with seafaring. Next to a wooden rudder in the middle, were halliards, capstans, brass portholes and enough parts stacked on top of each other to make a small sailing boat. In one corner was a sulky with its wheels removed and resting against it, along with a saddle. And in another corner was a ship's boiler with an anchor and a broken bowsprit sitting on top. There were huge springs, coils of rope, marlin spikes and block-and-tackles. And wooden and metal objects, with pieces of wood and metal screwed or bolted onto them that had Les completely mystified as to what they were ever used for. Lying on a padlocked metal trunk against one wall was a hard hat and diving suit, and stacked on a battered wooden set of drawers against another wall was a pile of lead ballast. On a wooden sea-chest against another wall was a ship's bell, a compass and a small anchor. Mrs Settree was examining something that resembled an extra-long handled machete.

'What's that?' asked Les.

'I think it's a flenser,' said Mrs Settree.

'A flenser?'

'Yes. For slicing up whales.'

'Ohh yuk!' said Les.

'Yes,' nodded Mrs Settree. 'The children and I are against whaling too.'

Les flashed his torch around the room and over the ceiling. 'Well, the sooner I start looking, the sooner we're out of here, I suppose.'

'Yes,' agreed Mrs Settree, wrapping her cardigan around her. 'It's not very warm in here.'

Les began going through all the old gear, flashing his torch in every nook and cranny. There was everything from big brass rings to little wooden plugs. Iron spikes to pieces of iron grate. He even uncovered an old wooden leg. But nothing even resembling a green canvas bundle of old paintings. Mrs Settree had been helping too and she couldn't find anything either.

'I'm afraid I can't see your paintings, Mr Norton,' she said, poking at a pile of old hemp rope.

'No,' said Les. 'It looks like I've struck out again.'

Norton walked over to the chest of drawers and pulled one out. It was full of copper nails. The rest were full of wooden dowels, small tools and other old junk. He pushed the last drawer in and turned to the wooden sea-chest. He looked at it, thought for a moment, then walked over and gave it a kick. The old wooden chest sounded a little empty inside.

'Hello?' said Les.

'You've found something, Mr Norton?' said Mrs Settree.

'I don't know. Maybe.'

The sea-chest wasn't locked. Les took the ship's bell and compass off and lay them on the floor. The lid had tightened up over the years. But Les was able to put his back into it and wrench the lid open. Inside was a stack of folded white canvas.

'Hello, hello, hello!' said Les.

Mrs Settree came over and watched Les pulling aside the canvas. He got halfway down and stencilled across one of the folds was MIZZEN LOWER SHROUDS. Les pulled a few more folds aside, then pushed them back in and dropped the lid.

'What was it?' asked Mrs Settree.

'Just an old sail,' replied Les.

'Oh dear,' sympathised Mrs Settree. 'What a shame.'

'Yeah.'

Les put the bell and compass back on the sea-chest and turned to the metal trunk. It was black and dented here and there with rust poking through the paint, around a metre and a half square and secured by a solid brass padlock on the front. Les walked over and gave it a kick. It didn't sound quite as empty inside as the wooden chest. Les looked at the lock then picked up a metre-long iron spike he had noticed lying on the cobblestones.

'Mrs Settree. What's that down there?' said Les, pointing behind the chest of drawers.

'Down here?' Mrs Settree walked over and peered behind the chest of drawers.

While Mrs Settree was looking the other way, Les jammed the iron spike in the lock, got a good grip and quickly wrenched it open. He placed the iron spike back on the cobblestones as Mrs Settree looked up from the old chest of drawers.

'I can't see anything, Mr Norton,' she said.

'Must've been my imagination,' said Les. 'Sorry.' He turned to the metal trunk. 'Hey, this old metal box isn't locked. I may as well have a look and see what's inside.'

'Yes. Why not?' agreed Mrs Settree.

Les lay the hard hat and diving suit on the floor then removed the broken lock and creaked open the old iron trunk. It, too, was filled with folded layers of white canvas. Across the top layer was stencilled MAIN ROYAL SAIL.

'It's another bloody sail,' said Les.

'Dear oh dear,' said Mrs Settree.

Les pulled a couple of layers out, then shoved his hand down one side of the metal trunk. He got down a fair way and felt tightened rope amongst the sails. Les got his hand under the rope and gave it a tug and found it was attachcd to something solid. He pulled several more layers of canvas sail out of the metal trunk and, sitting on the remaining layers of white canvas, was a bundle of green canvas a good metre square, bound with white rope. Les took hold of the rope with both hands and lifted the bundle out of the trunk. It was about a metre thick and, when Les lay it on the floor, he felt wooden frames along the sides.

'Holy bloody shit!' yelled Les. 'I think it's them.'

'The paintings?' said Mrs Settree.

'Yeah. Look. You can see where something's been painted over on the front. But maybe there might be something on the other side.' Les turned the canvas bundle over and, printed neatly on the back, was *From: Guichet Magazine, Bayswater Road, Kings Cross.*

'Yes,' howled Norton. 'It's bloody them all right. That's Talbot's place in the Cross, where Emile sent them from.'

Mrs Shipley looked mystified. 'I don't quite follow you, Mr Norton.'

'Don't worry, Tania,' said Les. 'This is them all right. You bloody little beaut.' Les stared at the bundle of paintings lying on the cobblestones and felt like breaking into a dance. 'I'm a genius,' he shouted. 'A bloody genius.' He grabbed Mrs Settree and planted a kiss on her cheek. 'Genius. Hah-hah. Hah-hah-hah!'

Mrs Settree blushed and put her hands to her face. 'And they're definitely your mother's paintings?' she said.

'My oath they are,' said Les. 'After all these bloody years.'

Mrs Settree clutched at her breast and looked a little faint. 'Oh my Lord!' she gasped. 'This is so exciting.'

'Is it what,' said Les.

'Nothing like this has ever happened to me before in my life,' said Mrs Settree. 'I do believe I feel quite dizzy.'

'I think I'm getting half a horn,' said Les. 'Anyway,' he said. 'We won't unwrap them here. We'll do it back at the orphanage. What do you reckon?'

'If you wish, Mr Norton.' Mrs Settree put her hand on Les's arm. 'Oh, I'm so happy for you, Mr Norton,' she smiled. 'This is marvellous.'

'Yeah. And I got you to thank, Tania.' Les gave Mrs Settree another kiss on the cheek. 'God bless you, sweetheart.'

'Mr Norton. Please,' blushed Mrs Settree. 'You're making me all embarrassed.'

'Good,' grinned Les. 'All right, Tania,' he said. 'Let's get out of here, and I'll put the paintings in the boot of the car.'

'Very well,' said Mrs Settree.

Les repacked the sails then closed the trunk and piled the old diving gear back on top. He picked up the paintings and carried the bundle through the door. Mrs Settree locked it behind them, then joined Les as he placed the paintings in the boot of the car.

'I'll have to take the key back to Mrs Sheridan, Mr Norton,' she said.

'Yeah, no worries,' said Les, closing the boot.

He opened the door for Mrs Settree then got behind the wheel and they headed back into Apollo Bay. Les was absolutely beside himself. Mrs Settree looked flustered and kept waving her hand in front of her face. She stopped for a moment and turned to Les.

'Mr Norton,' said Mrs Settree.

'Yes Tania,' replied Les brightly.

'Would you mind terribly if I was to have a little drink in town? I feel quite heady. There's a hotel not far from Mrs Sheridan's.'

'No. Not at all,' replied Les. 'In fact I might have a light myself. This calls for some sort of a celebration.'

'We could have a celebration back at the orphanage tonight, if you like. There'll only be Angie and myself there. I'll cook you dinner. I'm quite a good cook, too, people tell me.'

'Okay,' said Les. 'That's sounds good. I'll bring a bottle. Does your daughter drink?'

'Yes. Red wine.'

'Okay. Red wine it is.'

The Apollo Breeze Hotel was cream and brown with stairs running up to two entrances, and took up a corner of the main street next to a blue and white supermarket. Les did a U-turn and found a parking spot outside the supermarket. He got out of the car and walked with Mrs Settree as far as the hotel, then waited outside the stairs on the left. As he absently watched the people walking past Les couldn't believe his luck. He was right. Shipley must have brought the paintings down in his boat. The cable station was right across the road from the water and if anybody asked what the canvas bundle was, he would have said sails. And what a great spot to keep them. Locked in a trunk, in a place no one would ever enter, hidden amongst old sails no one would ever use. He removed his name just as a precaution and that's where they stayed. Rosa-Marie and Emile died without contacting him, and Father Shipley died taking his secret to the grave. And that's where the paintings would have stayed. Except for the world's greatest non-professional detective, Sherlock Holmes Norton, finding them. Les smiled across to the Mitsubishi. Now there was around half a million dollars worth of paintings sitting in the boot of a rental car. Hold on to them for a few years and they could be worth anything. Les had finally cracked the big one. The world was his oyster: mornayed, kilpatrick or on the half shell with pepper and a wedge of lemon. Any way you want it. Thanks mainly to a skinny old Miss Prissy who ran an orphanage. And what would be an appropriate remuneration for an old bag of bones running an orphanage, mused Les as he watched Mrs Settree walking back down the street towards him. I could pull fifty thousand out of that hole in my backyard without even missing it.

'Everything okay, Tania?' asked Les as Mrs Settree stopped in front of him.

'Yes,' replied Mrs Settree. 'I didn't say anything about the paintings. I said you were looking for an old map.'

'Good idea,' said Les. 'Okay. Let's go and throw a few double OP rums down our throats. Arhh, arhh, me heartys,' he growled.

'Oh, I don't know about that,' said Mrs Settree. 'But I'd like a nice gin.'

Les escorted Mrs Settree up the stairs and through the doors. There was a bar and food servery on the right, with model boats and ship's lanterns and wheels round the walls, that looked a little crowded. To the left was a smaller, quieter bar with a covered-over pool table, a fireplace in the corner and tables and chairs next to several windows offering a nice view of the street. Les sat Mrs Settree down at a table two back from the fireplace.

'What would you like, Tania?' he asked.

'A gin and tonic please,' she answered. 'Is that all right?'

'It sure is.'

Les walked over to a bar panelled with red cedar and ordered a pot of Carlton light and a double gin and tonic. He smiled at the other people round the bar while he waited, then took the drinks back to the table and sat down.

'Well cheers, Tania,' he said, clinking her glass.

'Yes. Cheers … Les,' she replied.

Les took a sip of beer and put his glass down. Mrs Settree had a swallow of gin and gave several blinks.

'Ooh, this is lovely,' she said, putting her glass down. 'Just what the doctor ordered.'

'Yeah. Me too,' said Les, taking another sip.

Mrs Settree had another mouthful of gin. 'What I can't understand, Mr Norton,' she said, 'is why Father Shipley erased his name from the front of the canvas. And why he hid the paintings?'

'Oh, probably for safekeeping or something,' said Les. 'Who knows? Things were different in those days.'

'And what did you say the address was on the back? A magazine?'

'Yes. My mother used to be an illustrator on it. She must have left the paintings there and … somehow they finished up down here.'

'Who was Emile?' asked Mrs Settree.

'A friend of Mum's,' answered Les. 'Another artist.'

'Oh.'

Les finished his beer and was surprised to see Mrs Settree finish her gin and tonic at the same time. 'Would you like another one?' he asked.

'Yes.' Mrs Settree took her handbag and went to stand up. 'I'll get them.'

'No. Let me,' said Les. 'After what you've done, the least I can do is shout you a couple of drinks.'

'Very well, Mr Norton. If you insist. Thank you.'

Les got two of the same and when he returned, noticed Mrs Settree's face was starting to get a bit of a glow up. He put the drinks on the table then sat down and clinked Mrs Settree's glass again.

'Well, at least you've got your paintings, Mr Norton,' said Mrs Settree. 'Your family will certainly be so proud of you.'

'Yes,' smiled Les. 'I can just see the look on one particular person's face when I walk in now.'

'What will you do with them? Just hang them?'

'Oh yeah. One for me. The rest for the others.'

'How many paintings are there?' asked Mrs Settree.

'Six,' replied Les. 'Three are Mum's. And three are by other artists.'

'And are you still going to unwrap them back at the orphanage first, Mr Norton?'

'Reckon,' said Les. 'After all your help, you deserve to be there for the unveiling.'

Knowing the nature of Rosa-Marie's paintings, especially ones they were going to burn, Les regretted having said that. But it was a bit late now. And if Mrs Settree got blown away by the contents, there wasn't much he could do. He only hoped it didn't affect a home-cooked meal that night.

'Angie would like to see them too,' said Mrs Settree.

'Yes. Your daughter's a painter, too, I believe,' said Les. 'What's she like?'

Mrs Settree smiled. 'I don't know a great deal about art, Mr Norton,' she replied. 'But she's different. Very ... colourful. And she has her own style.'

'That's good,' said Les.

'That's Angie's studio out the back. She lives in it and guards it like Fort Knox. She hardly ever lets anyone in there.'

Les raised his glass. 'Secretive creativity.'

'Yes. That's my Angie. God love her.'

'Your little guardian angel.'

'My little guardian angel,' nodded Mrs Settree. 'I don't know what I'd do without her.'

Les asked Mrs Settree one or two things about the orphanage before they finished their drinks, then Mrs Settree made a trip to the Ladies and they walked out to the car. Les was going to put the radio on, but he changed his mind.

Minutes later they were out of Apollo Bay and on their way back to Lorne.

Les was almost jumping out of his skin as he cruised along with the ocean on his right. But he drove slowly and kept himself alert, carefully steering the Mitsubishi around any hairpin bends. The last thing he wanted, after all the trouble he'd gone to, was an accident and the car bursting into flames with thousands of dollars' worth of paintings in the boot. Les didn't feel all that good inside, telling poor Mrs Settree a heap of lies. But when he sent her down a big fat cheque, Les felt that would make up for any minor indiscretions on his part. Les was whistling softly to himself as he pulled over to let a young bloke in an old hotted-up black Kingswood roar past, when he noticed Mrs Settree had suddenly gone very quiet. He glanced across and she was totally expressionless, just staring out the windscreen at the road ahead. Les manoeuvred his head around, had a good look and noticed tears were streaming down her cheeks. Ohh yeah, thought Les. Good old gin. The world's happiest drink.

'Are you all right, Mrs Settree?' he asked quietly.

Mrs Settree gave her head a tiny nod. 'Yes,' she whispered.

'You're crying, Tania.' Les found himself quite concerned. Mrs Settree didn't just have the sniffles. Tears were pouring out of her and in between sobs her thin shoulders would shudder under her cardigan.

'What's the matter, Tania. I didn't say anything to upset you, did I?'

'No. It's not your fault, Mr Norton,' cried Mrs Settree. 'It's just that driving past where the orphanage used to be. It brought back all the terrible memories.'

'Shit! I'm sorry, Tania,' said Les. 'I wasn't watching and I took a wrong turn.'

'Please don't blame yourself, Mr Norton. You're kind.' Next thing Mrs Settree turned to Les and completely broke up. Tears poured down her cheeks and sobs racked her poor skinny body. 'Oh, Mr Norton,' she wailed. 'They beat me there. They beat me so bad. They were so cruel to me. Oh, I'm sorry, Mr Norton,' howled Mrs Settree. 'But they were.'

'That's all right, Tania,' soothed Les. 'Let it all go.' He took his hanky out and handed it to Mrs Settree. 'Who beat you?'

Mrs Settree dabbed at her eyes with the hanky. 'The nuns. The nuns beat me.'

'The nuns?' said Les. 'The nuns beat you?' said Les. 'I …?'

'They beat me. They whipped me. They made me sleep in the toilets with all the smell.' More violent sobs racked Mrs Settree's body. 'They poured buckets of urine over me. They locked me in closets. I had to sleep out in the rain and cold. I slept in filth with the animals. They starved me. When it was hot they locked me in the toolshed without any water. And I was just a little girl,' cried Mrs Settree. 'A poor little girl.'

'Shit!' said Les. Mrs Settree's description of life at the orphanage was quite graphic and he found himself getting stirred up. 'The low rotten bastards,' he growled. 'That's bloody awful.'

'All the beatings they gave me,' sobbed Mrs Settree. 'When I got married and my husbands beat me, I didn't know any better. I thought it was the way life was. Until Angie told me I didn't have to take it.'

'Good for bloody Angie,' said Les.

'But Sister Manuella was the worst,' sobbed Mrs Settree. 'She beat me with a strap once and I couldn't sit down for almost a week. She broke coathangers on me. Rulers. Punched me. Dragged me down the stairs by my hair. I had so many bruises.'

'Sister Manuella?' said Les. 'Mrs Totten said she was the one who got her neck broken when the orphanage burnt down. Is that right?'

Mrs Settree turned to Les and for a brief moment a fierce gleam shone through the tears in her eyes. 'Yes. That was an unfortunate accident. Wasn't it.'

Norton's eyebrows rose. 'Yes. I imagine it was.' He slowed down for a hairpin bend, then put his foot down as the road rose above the ocean. 'So why did the nuns beat you all the time, Tania?'

'They said I was evil,' replied Mrs Settree. 'And I had the devil in me. They said my mother was a witch. And I was going to burn in hell.'

Norton turned slowly to Mrs Settree. 'What did you just say? The nuns said your mother was a witch?'

'Yes. All the time,' sobbed Mrs Settree. The tone in her voice now sounded like a little girl talking. 'Sister Manuella even made me wear a witch's hat and sit on a broomstick in front of all the other children. She wouldn't even let me go to the toilet. And when I'd wet myself she'd rub my face in it. Even the other children cried. Oh, it was so horrible.'

Les was trying to keep his eyes on the road and look at Mrs Settree at the same time. 'Tania,' he asked. 'How old are you?'

'I'm not sure,' sobbed Mrs Settree. 'The nuns kept it a secret from me. But I think I'm around fifty.'

'Fifty,' said Les.

'I think so,' sniffed Mrs Settree. 'I'm not really sure. But I do know one thing. I know what my real name is,' she said, a hint of triumph in her voice.

'Your real name?' said Les.

'Yes,' nodded Mrs Settree. 'I've always been called Tania. But when the Walmsleys adopted me, one of the nuns told my foster parents that when my mother left me at the orphanage, she gave them an envelope with some money in it. And a note that said, *Please look after Tanybryn.*'

'Tanybryn?' said Les.

'Yes. And Sister Manuella said it was an evil name. And changed it to Tania.'

'Did you ever find out who your mother was, Tania?' asked Les.

Mrs Settree shook her head and dabbed at her eyes with Norton's hanky. 'No. But I think she must have come from around Apollo Bay. Because Tanybryn's a little hamlet not far away. It's very pretty. I sometimes go out there and just sit.' Mrs Settree turned to Les. 'And often, it feels like my mother's there. Watching over me.'

Les drove on in silence till he found a space at the side of the road and pulled the car over. Mrs Settree looked up through her tears.

'What's the matter?' she asked.

Les stared at Mrs Settree for a moment trying to find the right words. 'Tania,' he said. 'I know this is a pretty lousy time to be telling you this. But I haven't been completely honest with you.'

'Oh?' Mrs Settree looked genuinely surprised. 'You haven't?'

Les shook his head. 'No. I haven't. And fair dinkum. I'm really sorry.'

'What ...?'

'Tania. You told me Father Shipley kept away from you. Is that right?'

'Yes,' nodded Mrs Settree. 'He used to avoid me, for some reason.'

Les reached over to the back seat and got his overnight bag. He sat it on his lap and took out the book on Rosa-Marie Norton. Inside the pages was a copy of the letter Warren had brought home from Bondi post office. He opened it up and handed it to Mrs Settree.

'Tania,' said Les. 'I want you to read that. Then I want you to have a look at this book. But read the letter first. Okay?'

'All right, Mr Norton,' said Mrs Settree, looking a little mystified behind her bloodshot eyes. 'If you insist.'

Mrs Settree dried her eyes, then adjusted her glasses and began reading. Les pulled out from where he'd parked and drove on in silence, staring impassively at the road ahead. His mind was working overtime, and if he was right, everything had suddenly turned pear-shape. Les drove on, and the further he went, the more numbed he felt. Mrs Settree finished the letter and, still holding it open in her hands, turned to Les.

'This letter, Mr Norton,' she said in a puzzled tone. 'It's … it's quite remarkable. But I don't quite understand what it's got to do with me.'

Les found himself searching for the right words again. 'Mrs Settree. Warren, the bloke I live with, brought it home from the post office. It had been lost in the dead letter office for years. But because my name's Norton, I finished up with it.'

Les told Mrs Settree the truth. How he got the letter, and borrowed the book from the local library and found out how much the paintings were worth. Then, without telling Mrs Settree about what happened in Melbourne, told her how he decided to come to Lorne to see if he could find the paintings. And after lying through his teeth to almost everybody he'd met, found them with her help.

'So Rosa-Marie Norton wasn't your mother?' said Mrs Settree.

'No, she wasn't,' confessed Les.

'Oh? I don't quite know what to say, Mr Norton.'

'But I do know whose mother she was,' said Les.

'Whose?' asked Mrs Settree.

Les looked directly at Mrs Settree. 'Yours.'

'Mine?' gasped Mrs Settree. 'Oh, don't be ridiculous.'

'Tania. Put the letter away,' said Les. 'And open up that book. To page six, I think.'

Mrs Settree neatly folded the letter then picked up the book on Rosa-Marie Norton. 'My goodness,' she said. 'Look at this cover.'

'Yes. She was one wild artist all right,' said Les.

Mrs Settree turned to page six and spread the book open. 'Dear me!' she said. 'If these are her paintings, she was more than wild.'

'Yeah. But have a look at the one with the baby and all the bunnies and things.'

Mrs Settree perused the pages from behind her glasses. 'Oh, this one is quite nice,' she said.

'Yes it is,' agreed Les. 'Now have a look what it's called.'

Mrs Settree squinted at the photo in the book then slowly turned to Les. '*Tanybryn*?'

'That's right,' said Les. 'That painting was Rosa-Marie Norton's secret tribute to you. The daughter she left behind.'

'Nooooo,' said Mrs Settree.

'Yes,' nodded Norton emphatically. 'She didn't come to Melbourne to have an abortion. She was too scared of getting blood poisoning again. She came down and put on an exhibition. Then she came to Apollo Bay to have you.'

'Me,' blinked Mrs Settree.

'Yes you,' said Les. 'Christ! It all adds up. The nuns knew who your mother was and took it out on you. Shipley must have known, too, and that's why he kept away from you. He might have even thought you were his daughter. Then there's the name. Tanybryn. Rosa-Marie grew up down here, and the place probably meant something to her. She would have known a local doctor who'd deliver her baby on the quiet. And she'd have known about the orphanage. So she left you there without knowing what a bunch of bastards the nuns were. Rosa-Marie and Emile had blackmailed Shipley at one time. And that's why Emile sent the paintings to him. Which is why Shipley hid them so well. He couldn't bring himself to destroy them. But he was terrified somebody would find them and connect them to him. Rosa-Marie died not long after that. So did Emile Decorice. And nobody would have known nothing. Only for that letter arriving at my place. And me, being the scheming low bastard that I am, always on the hunt for an easy dollar, I came down here looking for them. And ended up finding them.'

Mrs Settree stared at the photo of *Tanybryn*. 'Mr Norton. This is just unbelievable.'

'Unbelievable?' Les looked at Mrs Settree. 'It's more than that. It's horrible. Because even though it breaks my bloody heart to tell you this, Tania, those paintings in the boot belong to you.'

'Me?'

'Yeah.' Les laughed derisively. 'Wouldn't it give you the shits.'

Mrs Settree shook her head. 'This is all too much for me,' she said, and closed the book.

'Tell me about it,' said Les.

Mrs Settree stared at the book cover then turned to Les. 'Is there a photo of Rosa-Marie Norton in here?' she asked.

'Yeah. On the second page,' said Les.

Mrs Settree opened the book again and her bloodshot eyes almost bulged through her glasses. 'Oh my God!' she cried. 'Is that her?'

'That's her,' said Les. 'Rosa-Marie Norton. The Witch of Kings Cross.'

'Oh my God!' Mrs Settree closed the book and fell back against the seat. 'I think I'm going to faint.'

'There's a bottle of mineral water in my bag,' said Les. 'Have a drink.'

Mrs Settree's hands were shaking that bad as she got the bottle out, she could hardly get the cap off. She gulped some down and patted at her chest then cautiously opened the book again and took another look at the photo.

'And that's Rosa-Marie Norton?' said Mrs Settree softly.

'Yep. That's her, Tania,' said Les. 'Your dear sweet mother, Tania.'

'Oh my good God!' said Mrs Settree. 'Oh my God! This is all too much for me.'

'Yeah. Your mother was a bit out there,' agreed Les. They went round a bend and Les recognised a familiar part of the road. 'Anyway. We'll be back at the orphanage soon,' he said. 'And we'll unwrap the paintings and see what we've got.' Les gave Mrs Settree a sickly smile. 'What you've got.'

While Mrs Settree flicked gingerly through the book on Rosa-Marie Norton, Les drove on in silence, not knowing whether to laugh or cry. There was a fortune in paintings in the boot of the car, and it looked like he was going to have to give them to Mrs Settree. It was the only right thing to do. The money they'd bring would help her and the kids when they got booted out of the orphanage. But it would have looked a lot better in his bank account. What about poor, innocent Mrs Settree, though, thought Les. The last thing she would have been expecting was to find out who and what her mother was after all this time. It also looked like sneaky old Father Shipley might have been her father, too. Before Les knew it, he was approaching the pier and coming into Lorne. He hung a left near the church, drove up the hill and next thing he'd pulled up in the orphanage driveway.

'Well. Here we are,' said Les, switching off the motor.

Mrs Settree looked up from the book. 'Oh. We are too.' She closed the book and turned to Les. 'There's quite some interesting things in here,' she said. 'Do you mind if I show Angie?'

'No. Bring my bag with you,' said Les. 'I'll get the paintings.'

They got out of the car. Mrs Settree waited while Les got the paintings from the boot, then opened the door in the gate for him and they walked round to the kitchen. Mrs Settree opened the flyscreen.

'Round to the left, Mr Norton,' she said. 'Put them in the lounge room. I'm going to make a cup of tea. Would you like one?'

'How about a coffee?' said Les. 'Milk and two sugars.'

'If you want.'

Les followed a corridor with a tattered blue runner into a large cedar-panelled lounge room full of furniture that had seen better days. Three old grey Chesterfield lounges and a half-a-dozen lounge chairs of different shapes and patterns were sitting on several stained scatter-rugs. And about the same number of vinyl chairs sat round an old varnished table that had been cut down and turned into a long coffee table. A huge marble fireplace faced the blue-curtained windows looking out over the ocean from across the verandah, and to the side was a TV and a cheap stereo with a small CD stacker. Rock posters and a poster of the Sydney Swans were blue-tacked to the walls, church sale lamps sat in the corners and cheap light fittings hung from the ceiling, replacing what had probably once been chandeliers. Les placed the paintings on a lounge near one of the windows and turned on the lights at a switch near the door.

The green canvas bundle was tied securely. But the knots in the old white rope were thick and easy enough to get your fingers into, so there was no need for a knife. Les started pushing and pulling around and before long he'd loosened the knots. He was starting to undo them when Mrs Settree walked into the lounge room with his overnight bag over her shoulder, carrying a tray with two white mugs on it and a plate of mixed biscuits. She placed the tray on the coffee table and put the overnight bag next to it.

'Here you are, Mr Norton,' she said. 'Yours is the biggest mug.'

'That'd be me all right. Thanks.' Les turned and smiled at Mrs Settree. 'So how are you feeling now, Tania? You all right?'

'Yes. I'm a little better,' replied Mrs Settree. 'But my word, Mr Norton. This has certainly been a bolt out of the blue.'

'Yeah. I can understand that,' nodded Les. He picked up his coffee and took a sip. It was instant. But it was all right.

Mrs Settree sat down in one of the vinyl seats and sipped her coffee.

'Do you need a knife, Mr Norton?' she asked.

Les shook his head. 'No. I've just about got it undone already.'

'Oh good.' Mrs Settree looked up at Les. 'I must admit, Mr Norton, even though I'm absolutely flabbergasted, it's still very exciting.'

'Yeah,' muttered Les. He drank some more coffee, put the mug on the table and went back to the green canvas bundle. 'Anyway. Let's see what's in here. And see what all the fuss was about.'

Les dug at the knots and his strong fingers soon had them undone. He removed the rope and put it to one side, then carefully unfolded the canvas. Inside were six paintings, a metre square, three were in plain, wide, pinewood frames. Rosa-Marie's were in the middle with the others surrounding them, as Emile Decorice had described in the letter. Les placed the three other paintings on the floor, leaning against the lounge, then spread Rosa-Marie's across the lounge facing away from the window and stood back.

'Oh my God!' gasped Mrs Settree.

Les picked up his coffee and ran his eyes over the paintings. 'Yeah,' he nodded appreciatively. 'I think I know why they wanted to burn your mother's paintings years ago.'

On the right was a painting of a man, half eagle, half human, with an enormous erection, having sex with a woman, half tiger and half human, with massive breasts and nipples. The background was a whirlwind of amazing colours and strange, esoteric little figures with bulging eyes. On the left were two Medusa-type women with snakes for hair. Only the snakes were all soft penises. The women had huge bushes of pubic hair and growing out of the pubic hair were more snake-penises. Flying around in the background were sinister masturbating little cherubs with devil's horns poking out of their heads. The painting in the middle was a circle of stupid-looking fat pigs wearing policemen's hats and tunics, all sodomising each other. In the middle of the unbroken circle, one of the pigs was wearing a judge's wig and robes. Dancing around in the background on stumpy little legs with stumpy little genitals hanging down were moneybags with the old pounds and shillings signs on them and cunning, laughing faces. Although the subject matter in the paintings was open to discussion, the figures were wonderfully and skilfully composed and, as usual, the colours were fantastic.

'Are you absolutely positive this woman was my mother, Mr Norton?' said a shocked Mrs Settree.

'Absolutely positive, Tania,' answered Les. 'That's her all right.' Les pointed to the name. 'But, before you condemn anybody, Tania, just remember the old saying, never mind the quality, feel the width. Those paintings are worth a packet.'

'Dear me. I wouldn't like the children to see them.'

Les shrugged. 'I suppose so. But shit, the bloke I work for would love to hang that middle one in his office.'

'Yes. I noticed in one section of the book Rosa-Marie Norton didn't have a great deal of affection for the police.'

'Neither does this bloke.' Les put his mug of coffee down and turned to Mrs Settree. 'Well. They're your mother's paintings, Tania. What do you reckon?'

'I'm … I'm lost for words,' blinked Mrs Settree.

'Yeah. I see what you mean,' said Les. 'Anyway. Why don't we have a look at the others, and see what they're like?'

'Very well,' agreed Mrs Settree.

Les picked up the first one, had a look then placed it on a lounge chair. It was four people seated at a bar. Two men and two women. The colours were soft, yet eye-catching, and the people were all dressed in the style of the forties. The men wore hats and ill-fitting double-breasted suits; the women had print dresses and cheap hats. The four figures all had sad, almost comical faces. Poking out from under the frame was painted in fine, white lettering WILLIAM. The rest was obscured by the frame. Les stared at the painting and picked his chin.

'I've seen paintings by this bloke before,' he said. 'When I've been browsing through different books up at the library. Where's that letter?'

'It's a very nice painting,' said Mrs Settree.

'Yeah.' Les took the letter from his overnight bag, found what he was looking for and pointed excitedly. 'That's it. "Dobbo left a painting for you." That'd be a nickname. I'll bet that's a William Dobell. He was friends with Rosa-Marie from the Cross. She used to model for him. Shit!'

'I think I've heard of him,' said Mrs Settree.

'Yeah. He had a drama with the art establishment over the Archibald Prize.'

'Is it valuable?' asked Mrs Settree.

'Valuable?' said Les. 'Are you kidding? It's probably worth more than the others put together. Christ! What else is here?'

Les picked up the next painting. It was like a biblical scene of a half-a-dozen wide-hipped and buxom nude women seated out in the open on rugs, or standing holding parasols. Some were wearing hats or sandals. One of the women was holding a lion on a lead and in the background, two men in ancient Egyptian clothing were seated on horses. The colours were bright and the figures all had a casual haughtiness about them. At the bottom of the painting, just NORM was visible. The rest of the name was cut out by the wide frame.

'That one's a little risqué,' said Mrs Settree. 'It's quite nice, though.'

Les put the painting on another lounge chair and picked up the letter from where he'd placed it on the coffee table. 'There it is,' he said, stabbing his finger at the letter again. '"Normo". Another nickname. That's got to be a Norman Lindsay. Rosa-Marie used to model for him too. Holy shit!'

'I think I've heard of him,' said Mrs Settree. 'There was a movie?'

'Yeah. *Sirens.*'

'That's it,' said Mrs Settree. 'He was quite famous — I think.'

'Quite famous?' said Les. 'Just a bit. Bloody hell. This is worth a heap too.' Les put the letter back and picked up the last painting.

'Oh my God!' gasped Mrs Settree.

Les ignored her for the moment and placed the painting on another chair. It was just a mass of coloured lines and dots. As if the artist had squeezed the paint over the canvas like toothpaste. Nevertheless, in garish patterns of reds and blues and yellows and whites, the painting had a colourful intricateness about it that drew your attention. In the corner was written JACKSON. Like the others, the rest of the name was covered by the cheap frame. Les picked up the letter, looked at it, then dropped it back on the table.

'Oh no,' groaned Les. 'No. This isn't happening.' He turned to Mrs Settree who was staring at the painting. 'Mrs Settree,' said Les. 'In that letter Emile Decorice refers to a drunken bullshit artist called Jacques San. It was probably a false name he was getting around under. And in the book it says how he fell in love with Rosa-Marie, and she turfed him out. She called him Jacques the Dribbler. There was a movie about an artist with Ed Harris. Because of his style of painting, they used to call him Jack the Dripper. I was singing the lyrics the other night from the song by Alabama 3. "Reachin'": "Talking like Soprano,

Thinking like ..." oh shit!' Les turned to Mrs Settree, who was still staring at the squiggly painting. 'You'd have to pull the frame off to be sure. But I'll bet my life that's a bloody Jackson Pollock. And if it is, it's worth millions.' Les threw back his head and tore at his hair. 'Bloody millions.'

Mrs Settree continued to stare at the painting. 'This Jackson Pollock,' she said. 'Was he having an affair with my mother?'

'Yeah. Pretty heavy too,' said Les. 'He was in love with her.'

Mrs Settree turned to Les. 'Mr Norton, I'd like to see my daughter. And I want you to meet her too.'

Les stared morosely at the last painting. 'Yeah, righto. Why not.'

Mrs Settree stood up and Les followed her along the hallway and out through the kitchen. What have I done, he asked himself as they walked down the verandah to the courtyard. I've just turned this skinny old bat into a multimillionaire. And it should be me. Me. Shit! She's got to give me one fuckin painting.

A set of steps ran from the courtyard up to a gravel path crossing the land behind the orphanage, to a door at the front of the white building in the middle of the block. The door was painted bright red, with a brass knocker shaped like a monkey. A sign in Gothic print above the knocker read WELCOME TO ANGELA'S WORLD OF THE WEIRD AND WONDERFUL. Mrs Settree rapped on the door then pushed it ajar.

'Angela,' she said. 'Can I come in?'

'Yes. Come in, Mum,' replied a deep female voice from inside.

Mrs Settree opened the door, Les followed her through and she closed it behind them.

Inside was one big room made into an art studio, with a partitioned-off kitchen and bedroom at the rear. There were dark curtained windows on either side and a single fluorescent bulb in the ceiling, next to several mobiles of bats and spiders, partially filled the room with milky white light. A lounge, a small stereo and a TV sat along the left-hand side of the room and on the other side were shelves of gothic bric-a-brac and a bookshelf stacked with magazines, novels and hardbacks. Several abstract paintings hung on the walls, along with some weird posters and painted masks, giving the place an atmosphere of sinister gloom. The floor was covered in cheap green carpet and spread across the carpet was a large paint-spattered canvas tarpaulin. A girl dressed in a black top and a maroon velvet miniskirt over black stockings and blue Doc Martens was standing to one side of the tarpaulin, holding a can of paint in one hand and a long, skinny paintbrush in the other. A black beret was shoved on her head and a white cigarette holder with a roll-your-own in it, poked out from one side of her mouth while she dripped yellow paint onto a piece of plywood sitting in the middle of the tarpaulin. The young girl was very attractive, with loose black hair, sensuous purple glossed lips and plucked eyebrows that arched up, giving her a sinister haughtiness. Two obsidian green eyes peered down at what she was doing and, despite the girl's youth, she was the spitting image of Rosa-Marie Norton. Les gave a double blink and realised why Mrs Settree had reacted the way she did when she saw the photo in the book. He then noticed the painting on the floor and the ones hanging on the walls were in the same drip style as the Jackson painting sitting in the lounge room.

'Angela,' said Mrs Settree. 'This is Mr Norton. Mr Norton, this is my daughter Angie.'

'Hello … Angela,' said Les.

The girl nodded impassively and the obsidian green eyes studied Norton intently. 'Hello Mr Norton,' she said. 'How are you?'

'I'm good thanks, Angela,' replied Norton, hiding his shock and an icy feeling the girl had sent up and down his spine. 'And you can call me Les, if you like.'

'Whatever,' answered the girl.

'Angie. Stop what you're doing,' said Mrs Settree. 'And come into the lounge room. I've something interesting to show you.'

'Interesting?' said Angela.

'Yes. Mr Norton and I uncovered some paintings in Apollo Bay. And they were done by my mother.'

'Your mother?' said Angela, screwing up her face.

'Yes. I've found out who my mother was,' said Mrs Settree. 'Your grandmother. I think I've also found out who my father was, too, Angie.' Mrs Settree turned to Les then pointed out the drip paintings around the walls and smiled. 'What do you think, Mr Norton?'

Les stared at the paintings and shook his head in amazement. 'Yeah. I think I know exactly what you mean, Tania.'

Angela looked curiously at her mother, then suspiciously at Les. 'Okay,' she said, putting down the paint and paintbrush and leaving her cigarette holder in an ashtray near the bookcase. 'Let's go inside.'

Mrs Settree opened the door and Les followed them outside then back down the path to the orphanage. As they walked through the courtyard and into the kitchen, Les felt a sinister sense of deja vu. A mother and daughter in a deserted bay near Cooktown that he'd never told anyone about. They stepped into the lounge room and Mrs Settree pointed to the paintings.

'Well, Angela,' she said. 'What do you think?'

Angela studied the paintings then pointed to the ones by Rosa-Marie Norton. 'Who did these?' she asked. 'They're so cool.'

'This woman.' Mrs Settree took the book from Norton's overnight bag and handed it to her daughter. 'Rosa-Marie Norton. My mother. And I want you to read this letter.' Mrs Settree handed Angela the copy of the letter, then turned to Les. 'Would you like another cup of coffee, Mr Norton?'

'Yeah, righto,' replied Les. 'That'd be nice.'

Mrs Settree took the two mugs out to the kitchen leaving Les alone with Angela. Angela looked at the book then began reading the letter. Les sat on a lounge chair feeling very uncomfortable and as he watched Angela out of the corner of his eye, his mind started racing again. Mrs Settree returned with another mug of coffee and placed it on the coffee table as Angela finished reading the letter.

'Well, Angela,' said Mrs Settree. 'What do you think? It appears she never came down to Melbourne to have an abortion at all. She came down for her exhibition. And to have me. Then she left me at Saint Benedicta's.'

Angela nodded slowly and folded up the letter. 'Quite amazing,' she said. 'Quite amazing.' She turned to her mother. 'So how did all this come about, Mum?'

'I'll explain it to you in detail later, Angie,' said Mrs Settree. 'But see the comparison between that painting and yours.'

'Yes, I do,' said Angela quietly. 'That's quite amazing.'

'Mr Norton said it's by an artist named Jackson Pollock. And it's worth millions. Not only that. It appears he was my father. Your grandfather.'

Angela studied the painting and looked at the name half-hidden on the bottom. 'What an amazing coincidence,' she said composedly.

'Yes. Isn't it,' said Mrs Settree.

Angela turned to Les. 'And you say these paintings are worth millions of dollars, Mr Norton?'

'I'm positive,' answered Les.

'Does anybody else know they're here?' asked Angela.

'No. Just the three of us, Angela,' said Les.

Mrs Settree smiled at her daughter. 'Anyway, Angie. Mr Norton's coming around for tea tonight and a few drinks. We can all talk about it then.'

Angela looked at her mother for a moment, then turned to Les with a half-smile on her face, and her snake-like green eyes glowed for a second in a shaft of light coming through the window. 'You're calling round tonight … Les,' she said easily.

'Yes. Your mother's going to cook something special for me,' said Les.

'And we're going to drink some wine,' said Mrs Settree. 'Have a little celebration.'

'You're going to have a few drinks, Les?' said Angela.

'Ohh yeah,' said Les. 'Why not?'

'Well, leave your car,' said Angela. 'I'll come round and get you. Where are you staying?'

'At the Otway Resort,' said Les. 'Room 202.'

'I know it,' said Angela. 'I won't call up to your room. I'll park in the driveway out the front. And you can come down.'

'Okay,' said Les.

Angela turned to her mother. 'What time, Mum?'

Mrs Settree turned to Les. 'What time suits you, Mr Norton?'

Les looked at his watch. 'Oh. About an hour. Is that okay?'

'That would be fine,' said Mrs Settree.

'Yes. Excellent,' said Angela.

Les got to his feet and rubbed his hands together. 'All right,' he said to Angela and Mrs Settree. 'Well look, I imagine this has been a big day for both of you, and you want to talk about things in private. I'll go home and get cleaned up.'

'Okay Les,' said Angela. 'I'll see you out the front of the resort in an hour.'

'No worries.' Les left them with the copy of the letter. But picked up the book on Rosa-Marie Norton and put it in his overnight bag. 'I'll bring this back with me,' he said. 'I just want to have a look at a couple of things.' He turned to Angela. 'Your mother said you like red wine, Angela?'

'Yes. Especially burgundy.'

'There's a bottleshop across the road from the resort,' said Les. 'I'll get something extra grouse.'

'Thank you Mr Norton,' smiled Angela.

'I'll walk you to the door,' offered Mrs Settree.

Les shook his head. 'No. That's all right,' he said, picking up his overnight bag. 'I know my way out.' Les pointed to the mug of coffee still sitting on the coffee table. 'Look at that. I didn't even drink my coffee.' Les gave the women a warm smile. 'See you in an hour.'

'See you then Les,' they chorused.

Les left them in the lounge room and walked up to the car. He got behind the wheel and stared down at the orphanage for a moment before starting the engine. Minutes later Les drove into the resort. He didn't bother going down to the car park. He left the car in the driveway out front then walked inside and straight up to the reception desk. The dark-haired man in the blue suit recognised him and smiled.

'Mr Norton,' he said. 'There's a message here for you.' The man got a piece of paper and placed it on the desk. 'It's from a Miss Sonia Rouvray in Geelong. She asked for a Mr Klinghoffer. But insisted it was your room.'

'That's okay,' said Les. 'I know what it's all about. Anyway. I just got a phone call from Sydney, and I have to go home. So I'll be checking out early.'

'Oh. All right Mr Norton. No problems,' said the man in the blue suit. 'When did you wish to check out?'

'In about thirty minutes. I'll get my bags. And I'll be right back.'

'Not a problem, Mr Norton.'

'Thanks.' Les turned and walked down to the lift. On the way he read the note. *Solomon. I can be there tonight. Call me. Sonia.* Les screwed the message into a ball and and dropped it in a bin next to the lift.

As soon as he was inside his unit, Les began hurriedly packing things into his suitcase and getting rid of what he didn't need. He kept what was left of the bourbon, but left the beer in the fridge. And he didn't bother to get changed. Yes, Les told himself as he gathered up his tapes and unhooked the ghetto blaster, a nice mother and daughter duo, that one. Mum's not so bad. But what about the daughter? Where do you start? How about daddy number one that used to hit Mummy and fell under a train. Angie handled the trauma okay. Why wouldn't she? She pushed him off the platform. And husband number two. The stepdaddy that also used to beat Mummy. An electrician, and he finished up with a hair dryer in his bath. Mummy's little 'guardian angel' to the rescue again. Then there was the brother. Grant Junior. He used to hit both Mummy and his sister. Till his sister took him fishing. Which brings us to

Sister Manuella. Who used to beat poor young Tanybryn. 'That was an unfortunate accident. Wasn't it.' Okay. I don't blame Tania for setting fire to the orphanage and breaking Sister Manuella's neck. I would have done the same thing. But that daughter? I don't know about witches or things, but I saw the devil in those pretty green eyes. Les shoved the last of his socks and underwear into his suitcase and zipped it up. 'Does anybody else know about the paintings, Mr Norton? You going to have a few drinks, Mr Norton? Leave your car at the resort, Mr Norton. Les. I'll come and get you.' Yeah, thought Les. It's getting dark now. No one would notice that old black kombi pull up out the front, and me getting into it. Bloody hell! If I went round to that orphanage tonight, after Angie's got into her mother's ear about those millions of dollars' worth of paintings, I'd either get poisoned, cop a knife in the back or get hit over the head from behind. Or they'd probably just push me off the balcony. 'Stand here, Mr Norton. Where we can take a better photo.' I know one thing. No one would ever see me again. There'd be places in that orphanage you could hide an elephant.

I suppose I could just run in and grab a couple of paintings and piss off. But all they'd have to do is ring the police and have me nicked. Mrs Settree can prove they're her paintings more than I can. No. Even though it breaks my poor Queensland heart. They can have the fuckin things. It's all going to a good cause. And all in all, Mrs Settree's okay. I'll leave things as they are. Les checked around the unit, then glanced at his watch. Look at that. I've got a good twenty minutes up my sleeve before Rosa-Marie's baby gets here. Or granddaughter. Or whatever she is. I really don't give a shit. Les picked up his bags and caught the lift down to the lobby. Ten minutes later he had checked out and was turning left at the roundabout down from the resort.

Halfway along Mountjoy Parade Les slowed down for a bus and one last feeling of deja vu crept over him. Almost the same thing happened to him at Yurriki near Murwillumbah, when he found the painting hidden in the farmhouse and he gave it to Perigrine. And it turned out to be a van Gogh worth millions. Then before Perigrine could send him a thank you note written on a huge cheque, Perigrine got blown up, along with the painting. And Les missed out on another fortune. Now it had happened again. Only worse. Les watched the lights over the Erskine River disappear in the rear-vision mirror and a tiny tear rolled down his cheek.

'Bugger deja vu,' sniffed Les. 'You can stick it in your arse. It's nothing but the same bloody thing, over and over again. AIEEE!'

THE END